THE LAST LULLABY

ROBERTA KAGAN

Storm
PUBLISHING

Ebook ISBN: 978-1-80508-718-2
Paperback ISBN: 978-1-80508-720-5

Cover design: Debbie Clement
Cover images: Shutterstock, Trevillion

Published by Storm Publishing.
For further information, visit:
www.stormpublishing.co

The Wrath Of Eden

The Wrath Of Eden

The Angel's Song

A Million Miracles

I'll Never Cry Again

Standalones

A Nazi On Trial In God's Court

The Heart Of A Gypsy

The Gypsy Witch

A Time Of Anarchy

One Last Hope

*I am an old woman now, but I can still remember everything,
Bubbie. Everything... the matzo ball soup, the kreplach, the
delicious mandel bread, but most of all, I remember the stories
and the lullabies.*

ONE

1922

Max Levin lay shivering with fever on his bed. The sounds of Provins, a quaint medieval town located about seventy miles southeast of Paris, echoed through the window as his wife Chloe and his seventeen-year-old daughter Lily sat quietly at his side. Lily glanced over at her mother, wide-eyed and terrified. But even though Chloe was frightened, she managed to pat her daughter's hand reassuringly.

His horrible illness had begun two days ago with a blinding headache, and now Max was lying in bed delirious, coughing and hacking up mucus. Neither his wife nor daughter dared to say what they were thinking, but Max felt certain that he had contracted a deadly flu. Since he was showing no signs of recovery and he felt weaker each day, Max knew that his chances of survival were grim. He gazed weakly at the delicate blossoms swaying on the cherry tree branch outside the window. *Life is so fragile.* Then his eyes met Chloe's, and in that moment, he was transported back to the first time he saw her.

· · · ·

Chloe was a beautiful woman and Max adored her. The first time Max saw his wife she was lost in a dance routine at the ballet studio; her graceful form caught his eye through the window. He found himself rooted to the spot, mesmerized by the stunning blonde woman as she moved with fluid precision, completely absorbed in her steps. When the music stopped, she glanced towards the window and their eyes met. Max's heart stuttered—surely, she was going to be angry that he was watching her... But she wasn't. Her lips curved in a gentle smile and she giggled. He smiled back and waited for a little over an hour outside the studio, his heart racing each time the door opened, hoping she would come out and he would have an opportunity to speak to her. Finally, he was about to give up and leave when the door swung open, and she walked out of the studio as gracefully as a butterfly. She walked down the stairs and stood beside him with a mischievous glint in her eye. "You've been watching me?" she asked.

At first, he couldn't tell if she was angry or not. "I was just impressed with how beautifully you dance," he replied.

Chloe smiled. "Oh, so you are an admirer of ballet?"

"Oh yes," he lied. He had never cared for ballet. At least not until now, not until he'd seen her dance. But how could he tell her that he was drawn to her beauty?

"May I take you out for lunch, or for a coffee?" he asked nervously.

They'd shared coffee afterward, and when he walked her home, his heart nearly stopped at the sight of the *mezuzah* on her doorframe. Before he could stumble through an explanation of his Jewish heritage, she'd challenged him with flashing eyes: "Yes, I'm Jewish. If you don't like Jews, you can be on your way."

"I was only staring at the *mezuzah* because I'm Jewish, too," he had managed to say, and Chloe's laughter had filled the street.

Max's memories blurred, shifting to their small wedding in Frankfurt, his mother beaming despite her initial reservations about his French bride. After the wedding they moved back to Paris because Chloe became pregnant and she longed for her child to be born close to her family. However, in 1913 Max's mother became ill and although she recovered, she was weak. Max begged Chloe to return to Germany with him so he could care for her. Then the war broke out and he marched away in a pristine uniform, leaving her and their daughter Lily with his parents.

"Water?" Lily's voice pulled him back to the present. She held a cup to his lips, so much a woman now at seventeen, though he still saw the little girl who'd nursed his parents through their final days while he was at war. He could see Chloe's determination in their daughter's eyes, though Lily had inherited his dark looks instead of her mother's fair beauty.

Another cough seized him. A war hero, reduced to this. He'd returned from the battlefield to a defeated Germany with medals pinned to his chest and shadows behind his eyes. Each morning, he'd joined the crowds of fellow veterans searching for work, their hollow faces reflecting his own despair. All standing in breadlines, their degrees and dignity crumbling around them like the economy.

Some nights, he'd found himself in taverns with other broken soldiers, drowning memories of the trenches in cheap wine. They'd talk about the glory they'd been promised and recall how they'd run through artillery fire without fearing death, only to find themselves afraid of facing their hungry children at home. But Max couldn't bear the drink—it reminded him too much of his father's weakness. Instead, he'd walked the streets until dawn, past the darkened universities where he'd once studied, past factories that wouldn't hire him.

Hope had always been Chloe's gift. Even in defeated Germany, she'd spoken of returning to France as if it would solve everything. But her parents' reply to Chloe's letter explaining her family's plan to come back to France never came. Instead, a letter arrived from her father's old friend, bearing news that turned her face ashen—both of her parents, gone. Yet in the same breath, he offered Max work at his factory in their little old town outside Paris. Night cleaning work, but work, nonetheless.

Max watched Chloe's fingers trace her mother's pin as she called them lucky. *Lucky.* The word scraped like broken glass in his throat. They moved back to that little town, and each night he emptied waste bins and scrubbed toilets, his engineering degree worthless. The salary barely bought bread—a whole day's wage for a single loaf sometimes. He'd stand in the bread-lines remembering lecture halls and differential equations, wondering if his professors had ever imagined this future for their promising students.

Then Chloe took a factory job, twelve hours of grinding labor that painted dark circles under her eyes but brought home a few extra francs. She still danced sometimes, when she thought no one was watching, but her movements held a new weariness.

"I could work, too," Lily had offered, her chin set in that stubborn angle she'd inherited from her mother. "The factory is always hiring—"

"You'll finish school," Chloe had snapped, her hand flying to her throat, to the pin. "Education is everything."

But lying here now, watching fever-shadows dance across the ceiling, Max wasn't so sure. His own education hadn't saved them from poverty. It hadn't stopped his wife from working herself to exhaustion or his daughter from offering to sacrifice her future. And now, as death crept closer with each labored breath, he couldn't even leave them enough for his burial.

adjusted his gold cufflinks, taking his time before responding. "Miss...?"

"Levin, sir."

"Miss Levin. Your attitude suggests you don't really need this position." He waved his hand dismissively. "Goodbye, Miss Levin."

Now, as she walked home, Lily wiped angry tears from her face. One week's work, gone. The panic rose in her stomach with each step. What would they do for money now?

She found her mother at their small table, mending a torn blouse by the window's fading light. One look at Lily's face and Chloe set down her needle.

"What happened?"

"I lost the job." Lily's voice cracked. "The owner's son was treating us so awfully... I couldn't stay quiet."

Chloe drew in a sharp breath, but her voice remained gentle. "Come here, *ma chérie*." She opened her arms, and Lily fell into them, breathing in her mother's familiar scent. "You have your father's heart. He could never bear to see anyone mistreated either."

"His heart didn't put food on our table." Lily pulled away, bitter words spilling out. "I'm supposed to be helping, not making things worse."

"We'll manage." But Lily saw the fear flickering in her mother's eyes, noticed how her hand strayed to the silver pin at her throat. "There will be other jobs."

"I'll start looking again tomorrow," Lily promised, the weight of their circumstances settling back on to her shoulders. She was seventeen—too old for tears, too young to fail her mother like this.

. . .

The following morning and every morning for weeks, Lily got up early and walked to every one of the factories, local bakeries and shops. She waited outside restaurants for the owners to show up, her body broken with exhaustion. When they did, she begged them for a job. "I will do anything. I will wash dishes. I will clean. Please just give me a chance."

Some of them felt sorry for her and offered her a cup of coffee or some food. But every one of them told her that they didn't have any vacancies. Finally, early one evening, she gathered her courage and walked south where she entered a tavern on the rough side of town. It was dark and smoky, filled with men, most of them already drunk. The rest of them were well on the way to inebriation. A strong odor of perspiration and alcohol made her gag.

Several of the men turned around as Lily entered the bar. Some of them let out catcalls. Others whistled. Lily was trembling, but she straightened her back and kept her chin high. She knew the only women who usually walked through the doors were prostitutes.

"Is the owner here?" Lily asked the bartender as she cleared her throat.

"That's me," he said, eyeing her suspiciously. "What do you want?"

"I'm looking for a job. I can wait tables. I can learn to bartend. I'm a hard worker. Give me a chance. You won't be sorry," she said, putting on her most confident voice.

The bartender laughed heartily. "I see," he said, "but this is a rough place, and you aren't cut out for it. I can tell by looking at you."

Lily felt tears welling up. But she refused to cry. "I am tougher than I look, sir. And I promise you, I can handle it," she said firmly. "Just give me a chance."

"I don't think so. Sorry."

Lily's shoulders slumped under the weight of another rejection. Her stomach growled, reminding her of the dwindling supply of bread at home. *We're going to starve.* The thought came unbidden, but she forced it away, once again straightening her spine and lifting her chin like her mother had taught her. "Stand tall," Chloe always said, "even when you feel small."

She was halfway to the door when movement caught her eye. A soldier rose from his seat by the window—tall, with an easy grace that spoke of strength. Honey-brown eyes with an intense gaze met hers. He smiled appraisingly, and something in his eyes made her pulse quicken. He wasn't like the other soldiers who lounged about Paris these days, all bluster and swagger. There was a quiet confidence in how he carried himself as he crossed the room toward her.

American, she realized, noting the cut of his uniform. She'd seen enough Allied soldiers to recognize the different nationalities now. But there was something else about him, something in the way he watched her that made her breath catch slightly.

"Can I buy you a drink?" he asked.

A drink? I don't drink. The only alcohol I've ever had was wine on the Jewish holidays. But I guess I'm going to drink today, Lily thought. "Sure," she answered with a smile, but she could feel the corners of her lips quivering.

"Well, why don't you sit down?" He indicated a seat at the table where he'd been drinking. She sat down holding her small handbag close to her. "I'm Joe. Joe Rosenberg." He spoke French very well, but she could tell that he was not a native. He had been born elsewhere. "What's your name?"

"I'm Lily Levin," she said. *He's either German or Jewish,* she reflected, noting his surname. "Are you German?" she asked.

"I'm American. My parents were German Jews. I fought in the Great War and I liked France so much that I decided to stay here. At least for a while." He smiled and Lily was mesmerized by his laughing eyes, his dimples and the cleft in his chin.

But even though Joe was friendly and welcoming, Lily was

nervous. She had never been in a tavern before, and she had very little experience with men.

"So, what would you like to drink?" he asked.

She shrugged. "I don't know."

He smiled at her and called out across the room to the bartender, "Two whiskeys."

"Coming right up."

"So"—Joe turned his attention back to Lily—"what are you doing in a tavern?"

Lily fought back tears as she spoke, "I've spent the entire day walking through town looking for a job. I can't find anything. My father recently passed away and my mother and I are... well... we need money. So, I need to find work."

"I see," he said sadly. "And so you came in here, to this place, looking for a job?" Joe asked, shocked by Lily's situation.

She nodded.

"This is a rough place, not really somewhere for a girl like you."

Lily straightened her back. "I can handle it."

"Of course you can," he replied hurriedly, his face flushing red. "But as you can see, the men get real drunk in here and, well... a lot of fights break out. You could get hurt. You're too delicate. Too pretty."

"Is that supposed to make me feel better? Am I supposed to be consoled just because you think I am pretty?" Lily felt a flicker of anger and frustration. "Don't get me wrong. I am flattered. But I must earn money. I need work. And I've been everywhere. I just don't know where else to go."

"Well, maybe I can help."

She looked into his eyes just as the bartender placed two glasses in front of them. "How can you help?"

"I'm good friends with the owner of the bakery across the street. He'll hire you if I ask him to."

"But I already went in there and he told me that he didn't need anyone."

"It doesn't matter. He owes me a favor. If I talk to him, he'll hire you."

"You're very confident," she said.

"I am." Joe winked at her and then downed his shot of whiskey in a single gulp.

Lily lifted her glass and took a sip. She could feel him watching her. The liquid was hot as it traveled down her throat, and she coughed a little. She frowned as she met his gaze. "This is very strong."

"It sure is. Let me get you something else to drink."

He got up and went to the bar. A few minutes later he returned with a glass filled with fizzy black liquid.

"Oh, it doesn't look very good."

"You have to trust me." He smiled. "But just to assure you that it's not poison, I'll take the first sip." He drank some of the sparkling black liquid and then handed her the glass. "Your turn."

"Do I have to?"

"Of course not. But I wish you would at least try it."

Lily lifted the glass to her lips and drank. It was cold and sweet and surprisingly delicious. The fizz tickled her nose and she giggled. He laughed, too.

"So? What do you think?"

"I like it. I like it a lot. What is it?"

"It's cola."

"Do you want some more?" she asked.

"Nope, it's all for you. Enjoy it."

She smiled at Joe. He returned her smile, and she felt her heart melt.

"Shall I talk to the baker for you?"

She felt vulnerable. He was confident and powerful. And she hated to be so desperately in need of his help. But the truth was that she had nowhere else to turn. "Yes, please. Will you speak to him?"

"Of course. Let's go over there right now," he said.

They walked out of the tavern and crossed the street to the bakery. "Herr Feinstein," Joe said, greeting a graying heavyset man who stood behind a counter piled high with freshly baked loaves, "how are you doing?"

"Come in, Joe. I'm fine. What can I get for you?"

"Two of those rolls over there, please."

The baker handed him a paper bag containing two warm rolls and Joe gave him an American quarter.

"No need to give me any money back. Just keep the change," Joe said, smiling.

Herr Feinstein nodded appreciatively; the value of the coin was greater than the price of the bread. "Thanks, Joe," he said sincerely.

"Listen, can I ask a favor? I need you to give this girl, Lily, a job." Joe turned to Lily and asked, "Can you speak German?"

"Yes, my mother speaks Yiddish, she taught me. So I can speak fluent German."

"Yiddish, that's even better." Joe laughed. "You're a Jew?"

Lily nodded.

"So are we," Joe said, looking at Herr Feinstein.

"Please give this little girl a chance. She needs a job. Help her out, Gunther," Joe said, using Feinstein's first name.

"I'd love to, Joe. But I don't have enough business to be able to pay her."

"Yeah, well, if you need financial help... I'll help you," Joe said, winking.

Lily looked at Joe skeptically. But she didn't say a word.

"Alright. You want me to help her? I'll help her," Gunther Feinstein said to Joe. He paused and then added, "Can you please come with me? I want to talk to you."

Lily watched Joe follow Gunther Feinstein into the back

room. She twisted her hands in her skirt, straining to hear their muffled voices, but could only make out the low rumble of their conversation. The sweet scent of fresh bread made her stomach growl—she hadn't eaten since the thin, watery soup they'd had for dinner last night.

Minutes stretched like hours. She studied the loaves arranged in the window, trying not to calculate how many days' wages each one would cost. Finally, the men emerged; Joe's face was unreadable, but Feinstein was nodding slowly.

"Alright," the baker said to Lily, wiping his floury hands on his apron, "you can start tomorrow morning, six o'clock sharp. But mind you, the work is hard, and the pay isn't much."

Lily's heart leapt, but she kept her voice steady. "Thank you, Herr Feinstein. I won't disappoint you."

Joe smiled, a quick flash of white teeth, but something in his expression made her wonder what had passed between the two men in that back room. Before she could thank him, he was already heading for the door, touching his cap in farewell.

FOUR

Lily started work the following day, arriving at the bakery at five in the morning. It was fortunate that she was a quick learner because Gunther Feinstein was an impatient teacher. He had a lot to do before the shop opened, and very little time to get it all done. But by the third day, Lily knew what was expected and to Herr Feinstein's surprise she needed very little direction. Together, they were ready almost an hour ahead of opening time.

Joe dropped by the bakery each morning to purchase a sweet roll and a cup of coffee, which he ate while standing at the counter talking to Lily. Sometimes he would bring her flowers or a small box of chocolates. She was busy keeping the bakery clean and, at first, she found his visits annoying. But as time passed and he continued to pop in with a bright smile and a quick compliment, Lily found herself looking forward to seeing Joe.

Lily had never had a serious relationship. She'd only been out with a handful of boys during her school days. She didn't know how to behave around a man like Joe, so she acted aloof and disinterested. When he asked her to dinner she was intimidated and always refused, coming up with one excuse or another.

One morning, Joe did not make his daily visit to the bakery. Lily found herself looking out the window every few minutes hoping to see him. But when he didn't arrive by the end of the workday, she was devastated. Gunther asked her why she was looking so sad.

"I'm alright," she replied, fixing a smile on her face.

"Is it because Joe didn't come in this morning?" he asked gently. Over the month that she had been working for Gunther Feinstein, they'd struck up a friendship.

Lily nodded. "I think I ruined things with him," she said.

"Why do you say that?" Gunther asked.

"He wants me to go out for dinner with him, but I always refuse."

"Why? Don't you like him?" Gunther asked her.

"I do like him. I just feel so self-conscious around him. I don't know..."

Gunther nodded. "I understand. But Joe is a wonderful fella. He is so kind and generous. You are a very good employee and I love having you here, but I couldn't afford to keep you if he were not paying your salary."

"What exactly do you mean?" Lily seemed stunned.

"Well, I probably should not tell you this, but Joe has been funding your salary. I don't believe Joe wanted you to feel strange about it."

Lily was speechless and shocked, but a small smile turned the corners of her mouth upward. *He must like me,* she thought.

· · ·

When a week passed and then another and Joe still hadn't returned, Lily began to really worry. Not only was she afraid that he had lost interest in her, but she was terrified that he would stop giving Gunther money to pay her salary. Then she would be out of a job again. Gunther was yet to mention that Joe had stopped providing money, but she was sure he was going to break this news to her any day now.

One Sunday morning as she was waiting on a customer, Lily looked up as she heard the shop doorbell tinkle, and she saw Joe enter the bakery. Her stomach jumped and her heart raced. There was something magnetic about him; when she caught his gaze, it was as if a flame ignited in her soul. She hurriedly bagged up the customer's bread rolls and ushered her out of the shop before smiling broadly at Joe. Lily was so nervous that she could hardly speak.

"Hello there, beautiful," he said. "How have you been?"

"Fine," she managed to stutter. It wasn't what she wanted to say; she wanted to ask Joe where he had been and why he had stopped coming to see her. But she found herself frozen, wiping the same spot on the counter over and over. "Can I get you something?" she asked.

"Sure. A coffee and a sweet roll."

Lily's hands were shaking when she brought him his order and she spilled coffee on the table. "Sorry," she said.

"No harm done. It's only coffee," he said, smiling.

Lily didn't know what to say. She wanted to tell Joe that she liked him, and she had only refused his offers to take her out for dinner because she was shy and intimidated. But she said nothing. And he left the bakery without asking her out.

Joe didn't return to the bakery for several days. Each morning, Lily found herself watching the door, remembering how Joe's kindness and generosity had secured her this job. He was so different to the other soldiers who swaggered through Paris. At night, she would lie awake listening to her mother's quiet weeping from the next room, thinking about how her parents' love story had begun with a chance encounter, a moment of courage.

Her father had always told Lily the story of watching her mother dance, how he had waited outside the studio for hours just to speak to Chloe. "Sometimes," he had said, "love requires a brave heart." Perhaps he had been too gentle for this harsh world, but he had been brave enough to seize his chance at happiness.

Life was fragile—her father's death had taught her that. And now, on this crisp autumn morning, as Lily watched Joe finally return to the bakery, his dark eyes warming when they met hers, she felt something of her mother's spirit rise in her. Chloe had never been afraid to fight for what she wanted, had she? Even when it meant challenging convention, even when it meant choosing love over security.

Lily delivered Joe's order with steady hands, then slipped into the back of the bakery. She took a deep breath, gathering her courage. She was her mother's daughter after all; it was time to be bold.

This was going to take all her courage, but she had to do it. She didn't want to lose him. Trembling and weak-kneed, Lily walked back out to the front and over to where Joe was sitting. "Joe," she said, trying to make her voice sound mature and deci-sive. "I have decided that I would like to have dinner with you if the invitation is still open." *There. I said it,* she thought.

He didn't answer right away, and her stomach twisted with anxiety. The silence stretched until she could hear her own heartbeat. *Stupid, stupid,* she thought. *Of course he wouldn't want to—*

A slow smile spread across his face. "I thought you'd never say yes."

Lily's breath caught in her chest.

"Every time I came in." His honey-brown eyes held hers. "Tomorrow night?"

"Tomorrow night is perfect," she managed, hoping he couldn't hear how her voice trembled.

FIVE

When Lily got home from work that evening, she told her mother about her upcoming date with Joe. Chloe was concerned. "He sounds nice, but he's probably going to return home to America eventually, Lily. What is it you're hoping for with this fellow?"

Lily shrugged. "I don't know. Nothing really. We're just having dinner. I owe him that, at least. After all, he did get me a job."

Chloe frowned. Lily could tell that her mother was trying her best to hide her feelings. "Be careful. If you get into trouble, and you know what I mean, he's a soldier and he'll probably disappear, leaving you to bear the brunt of it alone."

Lily felt her cheeks color. "I don't know what you mean. Trouble?"

"Lily, I have been around a little bit in my lifetime. I know what a man wants from a woman," her mother said gently. "And I also know what the consequences of an unwanted pregnancy are for the girl. I saw it happen to a girl from the dance studio I attended. If it happens to you, it will ruin your reputation and your life. There are men out there who can be sweet one moment and cruel the next."

Lily sucked in her breath. She knew her mother was right, but she didn't like to hear her talk that way. "I am smart enough to say no to him."

Her mother shook her head. "I hope so. Men can be very convincing when they want something."

As Lily fastened the buttons on her dress, she thought about her mother's words of caution. Chloe was not like the other Jewish women in their little town outside Paris who had married local boys and followed traditional paths. Her mother had been a stunning beauty, graceful as a butterfly, who had left home young to study ballet in Paris. There she had met Lily's father, Max, a university student without much money but full of dreams. Though Max had swept her mother off her feet, Chloe had not been ready to give up her ambitions. She had been the first choice for leading roles until that fateful rehearsal when a dropped lift shattered both her ankle and her dancing career.

Max had supported Chloe through her long recovery, trying to make her smile. When it became clear that she would never dance like she had before, he had offered her a different life in Germany. Despite her love for Paris, she had agreed, hoping for happiness with the man who promised to cherish her forever. But Germany had never felt like home to Lily's sophisticated French mother, and after the war they had eventually returned to Provins, the small town outside Paris.

Lily studied herself in the mirror, seeing so little of her mother's delicate grace in her own frame. She had spent hours poring over photos of her mother on stage, admiring her brilliant blonde hair that looked like spun gold beneath the theatre lights. While Lily was attractive enough, she had never possessed that ethereal quality that had made her mother so magnificent.

Lily squared her shoulders. She was no ballerina; she was simply herself, facing a world that had no patience for gentle dreamers. Whatever happened tomorrow night, she would keep her mother's warning close—and her own heart closer.

SIX

During their first evening together, Joe took Lily to a small bistro where candlelight softened the war-worn edges of the room. As they shared a bottle of wine, Lily found herself drawn not just to Joe's handsome face, but to the way his eyes lit up when he spoke of his family back in New York and his mother's delicious Shabbat meals.

"And you?" he asked, leaning forward. "Tell me about growing up here."

Lily told him about her parents, about their town outside Paris where cultures and languages had mixed in her childhood home. Joe listened intently, asking questions that showed genuine interest, not just politeness. When she mentioned her father's death, he reached across the table and touched her hand briefly, a gesture so gentle it made her throat tight.

After that first night, they began dating regularly, meeting twice a week for dinner and dancing. She found him exciting—not just because he was a soldier with stories of battles and far-off places, so different from the struggling schoolboys she knew.

There was something more: a warmth in how he looked at her, a way he had of making her feel both protected and free. That he had a pocket full of American dollars, worth far more than French francs at the time, seemed almost incidental to the growing connection between them.

Although Joe never came out and said his family had money, he appeared to be wealthy by the way he dressed, and even though she tried, Lily could not forget that Joe paid her salary at the bakery. He gambled without worrying about losing. And sometimes he bought Lily small gifts of candy, little trinkets, and occasionally even jewelry.

"You're really falling in love with this fellow," Chloe said to Lily one evening while they were eating dinner together. "I must admit, I'm a little worried for you. Like I told you before, the time will come when he'll go home. What are you going to do when he returns to America?"

"I don't know, Mama." Lily sighed. "But I can't stop seeing Joe just because I might get hurt. I care deeply for him, and I have to see this through. Do you understand?"

"Yes, actually, I do," Chloe replied softly, wrapping her hand gently over Lily's, her eyes filling with tears. "I understand better than you know. It's just difficult to stand by and watch my daughter in a situation that could potentially hurt her."

Lily placed her knife and fork on her plate. "I can't say goodbye to him," she whispered, her voice breaking.

"Oh, my darling. I know. And I will be here for you no matter what happens."

A month later, the afternoon light slanted through Joe's rented room, casting long shadows across the rumpled bed. Lily lay in the circle of his arms, her heart still racing, when she felt him tense.

"I have to tell you something," he said, his voice rough with emotion.

She knew before he spoke—she had felt it in the desperate way he had kissed her, in how tightly he held her now. Still, Joe's words cut deep.

"They're transferring me. Tomorrow."

Lily sat up, clutching the sheet to her chest, suddenly cold despite the warm afternoon. "Tomorrow? But you said—"

"I know." He reached for her, but she pulled away. "Lily, look at me. I'm coming back for you. I promise."

She did look at him then, memorizing his face—the sharp line of his jaw, those dark eyes that had first caught her attention in the bakery. "When?"

"As soon as I can. Here..." He got up, rifled through his uniform jacket, and pressed a piece of paper into her hand. "Write to me. I'll write back, tell you where I am, when I can return."

She nodded, throat too tight for words. He pulled her close again, and she breathed him in, trying to fix this moment in her memory.

Later, when she told her mother, Lily's lower lip trembled despite her efforts to stay strong. "He said he has to go, but he will return for me." She clutched the paper with his address. "I have to believe him. I'll write every week."

"You can write, and you can believe him. But Lily, remember what I told you," Chloe said gently as she pulled Lily into her arms.

"I know, Mama. My heart feels so heavy."

With Joe gone, Lily was worried about losing her job at the bakery. Gunther was struggling to keep her on. "Only a small percentage of customers prefer German bakeries. We are in France, after all, and the French are known for having the best baked goods."

"I've always wondered, but I never found the right time to ask you. Why did you ever open a bakery here?"

"My wife is French. She refused to leave here. I am a baker. It is all I know. So, I opened a German bakery hoping that the German-style pastries and breads would become popular. I was wrong. That's why the bakery is never very busy."

Gunther Feinstein was a kind man and a good boss. But if he didn't earn enough to pay Lily, then there was nothing either of them could do. Lily wondered if she should start looking for another job. When she asked Herr Feinstein, he told her that Joe had paid him enough to keep her on at the bakery for the next six months. After that, Joe had promised Herr Feinstein that he would return and give him additional money.

Lily was relieved. At least she had a job for now. But in her heart, she hoped more than anything in the world that Joe would return to her.

SEVEN

Lily did not menstruate that month. There was no blood on her panties, and no blood on the rags she used. She tried to hide her panic, washing her undergarments as usual, keeping to her routines. But she caught her mother watching her with concerned eyes over breakfast, noted how Chloe lingered in the doorway when Lily claimed fatigue and went to bed early. Another week passed, then two. Lily avoided her mother's gaze, terrified of the knowledge she might find there.

As the second month slipped by without blood, Lily noticed her mother growing quieter, more watchful. She saw how Chloe's hands would pause in her mending, her eyes distant with worry. One morning, as Lily pushed away her untouched breakfast, Chloe finally broke the heavy silence between them. "You're pregnant, aren't you?" she asked gently.

"I think so, Mama." Lily felt a wave of nausea wash over her.

"Oh, Lily. I hate to say that I told you so. But I did tell you. Oh, my sweet girl, this is going to be very hard for you. The neighbors are going to talk once you start to show," Chloe said, wringing her hands as she paced the kitchen floor.

"I don't care what people say," Lily replied defiantly.

"I know, but this could ruin your reputation and if Joe doesn't return, it's going to be difficult for you to find a boy who is willing to marry you and raise another man's child," Chloe said quietly, her gaze intense.

"I realize that, Mama. If Joe doesn't come back, I am on my own." Lily felt light-headed and her legs began to sway. Chloe gently pulled her down onto a chair.

"You are never on your own. You are my child, my one and only daughter, and I will stand by you no matter what," she whispered softly into Lily's hair.

Lily began to cry. "I love him, Mama. I don't know how I'm going to live without him."

"Have you written to Joe to tell him about the pregnancy?"

"I've been writing to him since he left. He hasn't answered any of my letters."

They fell into silence as Chloe stroked Lily's hair. "We'll manage."

Chloe had warned her to be careful. She'd made it clear that Lily should never allow a boy to touch her in that way unless they were married. But Joe had been so irresistible. He was warm and caring, and his eyes lit up when he looked at her. It had happened so fast the first time that she hardly realized what she was doing but it had felt so special. Then, after that, they made love every time they saw each other. After a while, making love to Joe seemed natural to Lily. "I'll write to him and tell him that I'm pregnant," Lily said. "I hope he'll answer me."

Chloe was wide awake. She had soothed her daughter to sleep just like she had done when Lily was a little girl. But now it was the early hours. She could hear the birdsong outside the window, but it did little to calm the anxiety that gripped her. She doubted that Lily would ever hear from Joe again. Years ago, when she was still single and living in Paris, she had watched girlfriends who had been jilted by men. They were often left pregnant and alone. Chloe had sworn that this would never happen to her. And it hadn't. She had been fortunate. Her love affair with her husband had turned into a life of mutual respect, care, and romance. Chloe had tried to warn her daughter, but Lily was smitten. She was already caught in the web of Joe's charm. And now he was gone, and a baby was on the way.

Chloe couldn't change things, but she loved her daughter fiercely. And she would not abandon her the way she had seen other parents do. No matter the shame, no matter the difficulty, Chloe would stand behind Lily and help her daughter to raise her child.

EIGHT

Lily was shaking. Tears ran down her face as she walked into her room and took out a piece of paper and a pen from her desk drawer. Her hands trembled as she wrote.

Dearest Joe,

I have written you several letters and I have not received any from you. I know you must be very busy at your new post. But there is something I must tell you. Something has happened... something you should know about.

Lily tore up the paper. Then she lay her head down on the desk and wept. For several minutes she cried heart-wrenching sobs before lifting her head, taking a deep breath and wiping the tears from her cheeks. *I won't cry. I won't feel sorry for myself. I made a choice to trust Joe and now I will face the consequences no matter what they are. It was a mistake. I know that now. But I don't need him. And I don't care what people say or do. It doesn't matter to me that no decent boy will marry me. I don't want to get married anyway. I'll have this baby and I will raise it with my mother by my side. The whole community can be damned.*

By her third month of pregnancy Lily began to show, with a tiny bump appearing in her lower belly. She wore loose clothing and did her best to hide her pregnancy. But by the fourth month there was no denying it anymore. The little bump had grown too large to hide.

Everyone in their little primarily Jewish town knew each other. There were nosy women who had witnessed every child's birth and wept at the funeral of each resident who died—whether of disease or old age. These women made it their business to know who got married and when, and they counted the months to make sure that the children who came from the union were legitimate. They all knew that Lily was unmarried and that for a while she had been seen all over town with an American soldier. Now he was gone, and her stomach was growing. This was the kind of gossip these women lived for and they had easily put two and two together.

It would have been bad enough that they knew Lily was pregnant and unmarried, but they made sure to tell everyone else they encountered. And soon people were staring at Lily when she walked down the street. Self-righteous women, who were stuck in bad marriages that they dare not leave, would whisper and shake their heads as Lily walked by. Many times, she overheard the word "*shanda*" whispered as she passed, and she knew it meant shame or embarrassment. The girls she'd grown up with, girls who she had once called friends, now shunned her. They were polite if she saw them on the street, saying a quick hello, but they didn't dare stop to speak to her. No one wanted to be associated with a girl who had gotten pregnant out of wedlock. But Lily was determined to keep her head held high, even though inside she was consumed with sadness.

She was afraid that Herr Feinstein was going to fire her. After all, his business could easily be hurt by gossip. But he kept her on and she was grateful that he didn't ask her any questions.

Driven by gratitude for Herr Feinstein's kindness, Lily threw herself into her work with renewed vigor, returning home each evening with aching muscles and flour-dusted clothes. But then the whispers began. Regular customers who had once greeted her warmly now avoided her gaze, their visits growing less frequent until the bakery stood nearly empty most days. Finally, one quiet afternoon, Herr Feinstein called her into the back room, his usually cheerful face etched with worry. Though he praised her dedication and skill, the words he said next fell heavily between them; he explained that the town gossips had turned his customers against the bakery, and his business was failing. With genuine sorrow in his voice, he had no choice but to let her go.

Without work to sustain her, Lily felt herself unraveling. Her advancing pregnancy seemed to mirror her mounting despair, each day bringing new burdens to bear alone. Joe's silence had stretched from weeks into months, and the thin thread of hope she'd clung to—that he would somehow find his way back to her—was finally snapping. *He must have returned to America by now*, she thought bitterly. *And forgotten all about the girl he left behind.*

For a week, Lily went out every morning and tried to find a job. But she was so visibly pregnant that no one would even consider hiring her.

Without the money Lily earned, she and her mother found it impossible to pay the rent and buy food. Chloe was still working but her small salary was their only source of income. Finally, they were forced to abandon their apartment for a tiny room in a crumbling building at the edge of the little town. Even there, hunger became their constant companion. Night after night, Chloe pushed her portion of their scarce meals toward her daughter.

"Mother, please eat something," Lily would plead, watching her mother's face grow hollower by the day. "You're withering away."

"I'm not hungry, truly," Chloe insisted, though her hands trembled as she folded them in her lap. "The baby needs nourishment more than I do. If you won't eat for yourself, do it for your child."

So, Lily ate, each mouthful heavy with guilt as she watched her mother waste away in the name of maternal sacrifice.

Even though they could hardly afford it, Chloe insisted on putting a little money away each week, her bony fingers trembling as she counted out the francs. "We will need this to pay a midwife when the time comes for the baby to be born," she said, slipping the precious coins into the kitchen drawer. Her once-snug dress now hung loose around her shoulders.

Too tired to protest, Lily nodded.

Lily had started to take in sewing for some of the wealthier women who lived in a neighboring town. When Lily was younger, one of her girlfriends had taught her to sew. The girl's mother had been a seamstress, and she had taught her daughter to sew on pearls and to alter garments. Lily would spend time with her friend and began helping her and learning, too. When the girl's mother was very busy, for instance beading an extremely ornate wedding dress, she had insisted that her daughter help her. There was always a lot of work, especially with an upcoming wedding, and Lily had often volunteered to help her friend.

A few years later, Lily's friend's mother got a job working in a shop in Paris, so her friend moved away. But the skill Lily learned stayed with her. And now she was grateful to have a way to earn some extra money while working from the privacy of her own home. Lily wasn't busy and she didn't have a lot of clients, but because she kept her prices low, she had enough income to help pay the bills. So, when there was a knock on the door of her apartment, she assumed it was a potential customer. Her back ached from carrying the extra weight of her baby as she stood up. Quickly she stretched and then opened the door.

There, standing in front of her with that same sparkle in his eyes, was Joe. Her Joe.

"Lily!" Joe cried. "I found you. When I got into town I went to your old apartment. Someone else was living there. I didn't know where you had gone so I went to the bakery and Herr Feinstein told me your new address. I came here as soon as I could." He was talking so fast and looking at her so intensely but as he paused, his eyes travelling down her body, he let out a gasp.

Then he looked into her eyes. "Lily," he said softly, "you're pregnant?"

Her hands were trembling and her face was tight. Joe had hurt her, and she'd worked hard to close her heart to him but seeing him again opened every wound. And as she looked into his deep, dark eyes, she knew she still loved him.

"Joe... why didn't you answer my letters?" she asked, looking away from him so he wouldn't see how much she cared.

"I never received any letters from you. I arrived at my new post and then I was transferred again immediately... Is it... is it...?" He could barely get his words out.

"Yes, of course it's yours. I was pregnant when you left. I just didn't know it yet."

They were still standing in the doorway.

"Can I please come in?" he asked nervously.

Lily laughed a little, feeling foolish for making him stand in the hallway. "Yes, of course, come in."

He stepped within the cramped room. "I'm so sorry. I

should have been here. At the very least, I should have been sending you money," he said. "I didn't know about the baby."

"How could you know?" she asked. "But why didn't you write and tell me that you had been transferred?"

"I did. I wrote and sent you my new address as soon as I was permitted to. At first, they wouldn't let us tell anyone where we were."

"I never received a single letter from you. Then, we moved."

"It was all a mess but I'm here now. I hope you can forgive me. I will take care of you. We'll get married. And then after the baby is born, we can go to America."

"But don't you have to stay in Europe? Aren't the troops going to continue to occupy Germany?"

"Actually, no. I have good news. Harding, the American president, has finally said that soldiers can return home. You're sure going to like it in New York! You'll see."

Lily smiled to match Joe's excitement. But deep down in her belly she felt a pit of uneasiness. *I don't want to leave Paris, my mama, and everything I know. I thought he was in Paris because he wanted to be here, because he loved this city and me,* she thought to herself.

NINE

When Chloe got home from work and saw that Joe had
returned, she was thrilled for Lily. Her daughter looked so
happy and although Joe's long absence had made it difficult for
Chloe to fully trust him, it warmed her heart to see Lily smile
again.

That night, Joe went to the local delicatessen and returned
with a feast: hot knishes filled with potato; pickled herring;
fresh challah from the bakery; and a roasted chicken. Chloe
couldn't help but notice Joe's poor table manners. He held his
fork and knife incorrectly. He never put his napkin on his lap,
and he talked with a mouth full. *He might have money, but I
can see that he doesn't come from a cultured or refined family,*
Chloe thought, but she said nothing.

As they were eating their dinner Joe proudly informed
Chloe that he intended to marry Lily, and then after the baby
was born, he planned to take her with him to the United States.
Chloe smiled and nodded. But inside her heart was breaking.
Her daughter and grandchild were going to live overseas and
that seemed like a million miles away. *I won't try to stop her,* she
thought. *When I was young, I went to Paris. My parents didn't*

want me to go. And even though it is not nearly as far as America, I had to pursue my dreams. And now it's Lily's turn. But what if I never see my daughter and my grandchild again? I pray that Joe will be good to my Lily, that he will love and cherish her the way she deserves to be loved.

"Here's my plan. Of course, it has to be alright with you," Joe said to Chloe earnestly, interrupting Chloe's thoughts as he took a piece of bread and wiped up the sauce from his plate. Then with his mouth full of the dripping bread, he continued, "I am thinking that Lily and me will get married and stay here with you until the baby is born. I don't think it's a good idea for Lily to travel on a ship when she is pregnant. It can be rocky, and it would be a safer passage if she was not in such a delicate state."

"Of course, you can both stay here with me for as long as you like," Chloe said.

"Can my mother come with us?" Lily asked.

"I wish I had enough money to pay for passage for all four of us: you, me, the new baby, and your mom. But my funds are running low. So, how does this sound?" he said, smiling, "Once we are back in the States, I'll get a job and send your mom money. Then she can take a boat and come over and live with us." He turned to Lily.

"Really?" Lily said, her eyes beginning to fill with tears.

"I promise," Joe replied, squeezing Lily's hand gently.

Chloe looked at her daughter and then at Joe, catching a dark glint in his eyes. In her gut, she sensed that he would not stay true to his word.

TEN

Lily Levin, wearing a simple blue dress, and Joseph Rosenberg, in his United States army uniform, were married in a quiet ceremony at the local synagogue, on a rainy summer morning. Although Lily had invited some of her old friends, they all refused her invitation. Not one of them attended the wedding. It wasn't that the girls no longer liked her, but their parents had forbidden them to associate with her. She understood. Where she had been raised to ask questions of her parents, most of her peers had not been given this same privilege. Their parents had taught them to fear and respect, rather than love them. In fact, love was never discussed. But Lily had known for as long as she remembered that her parents loved each other, and her, fiercely. Even though she knew that her old friends were only behaving in line with their parents' expectations, their behavior hurt her feelings anyway. Her mother, faithful as always, was by her side as she said her vows. And as she glanced over at her Chloe, who was smiling through her tears, Lily knew that when the time came to leave France with her new husband, she would miss her terribly.

When they emerged from the synagogue, the rain had

cleared, leaving a brilliant rainbow arched across the sky. "Look Lily, look Joe," Chloe said, beaming, "a rainbow—that's a good sign."

In the days that followed her wedding, Lily waited to feel transformed – to suddenly sense that she was ready for the responsibilities of being a wife and mother. But as her time grew near, she found herself increasingly haunted by doubts about her ability to care for a child. One evening, she finally voiced these fears to her mother.

Chloe listened quietly as Lily poured out her worries, then drew her daughter close with a gentle smile.

"No one feels ready with their first baby," she said softly. "When I was carrying you, I lay awake many nights, terrified. One night, your father, may his memory be a blessing, turned over and awakened to find me lying in bed beside him with my eyes wide open." Chloe laughed tenderly. "He asked me why I wasn't asleep. I told him. And he promised that everything would be alright. He told me that his mother always said that if we just listen, God will show us what he wants us to do."

"Oh, Mama," Lily said softly. "I love Joe, but I am so afraid to leave you and go to America. I wish you could come with us."

"Germany was my home through the war but my heart has always been in France." Chloe squeezed Lily's hand. "And right now, we barely have enough saved for your passage, let alone two. But don't worry, my darling. Before you leave, I'll teach you everything: how to bathe the baby just so, how to swaddle those tiny limbs, how to nurse when the time comes. You won't face any of it alone, not while I'm here. We still have these precious weeks together."

ELEVEN
FRANCE, JULY 1923

On a bright morning when the sky was crystal blue, and the clouds were like cotton candy hanging in the sunlit heavens, Lily labored in the small bedroom she shared with her husband. Chloe sat holding her daughter's hand and Joe stood on Lily's other side wiping the sweat from her brow. The pains were growing strong when the midwife arrived.

Lily's labor dragged through twelve harrowing hours, each contraction tearing through her until she felt as though her body would shatter. Wave after wave of pain left her gasping, convinced she wouldn't survive.

"I'm so sorry, Lily," Joe choked out, his face ashen. "I never meant for you to suffer like this. It's all my fault."

"It's alright, Joe," Lily whispered between ragged breaths. "It's alright,"

"I had no idea," he confessed, gripping her hand. "I've never seen a birth before. God, I feel so helpless watching you in such pain."

"I'm glad you're here," Lily managed, squeezing his fingers weakly.

Joe turned away but not before Chloe caught the glint of

tears in his eyes. "She'll be okay," Chloe reassured him softly. "The pain is terrible, yes, but the joy that follows..." She let the promise hang in the air.

The midwife's examination brought fresh urgency to the room. "Alright, Lily, the baby is crowning. The time has come for your little one to enter the world. Now, you must push when I tell you to push."

Lily could only nod, her strength nearly spent.

"Now... push!"

She bore down with what little energy remained, her breath coming in short, desperate gasps.

"That's good, you're doing just fine," the midwife coaxed. "Rest a moment. Then push harder next time."

Lily struggled to obey, sweat streaming down her face and soaking her shift. The afternoon sun blazed through the window, turning the room into an oven under the ice-blue sky. Her head fell back against the pillow. "I can't," she sobbed. "It's too hard."

"Yes, you can," Chloe said fiercely. "Now, listen to me. Look into my eyes and squeeze my hand, and the next time the midwife tells you to push—push with all your might."

Lily closed her eyes and whispered, "Mama, it hurts."

"I know. And I wish I could take your pain away. I would rather go through this than see you suffer. But I promise you that once your child is born you won't remember this pain. It will all be worth it."

"Lily, it's time to push again," the midwife said. "Get ready and... push."

"Hold my hand," Chloe said. "You're alright... You're doing just fine. Now, ready, push. Squeeze my hand."

"Push," the midwife repeated.

And then a tiny bald head emerged, followed by two small shoulders, and suddenly their child slid into the world in a rush of blood and fluid. The midwife lifted the infant, gave her bottom a gentle slap, and a strong, defiant cry filled the room.

"You have a daughter," the midwife announced, laying the newborn on Lily's chest.

"Oh, sweetheart, look at her," Joe whispered, his voice thick with wonder. He leaned close, studying their daughter's tiny, wrinkled face. "She's beautiful, just like her mama."

Lily cradled her baby against her heart, marveling at how something so small could fill her entire world. "She's perfect," she breathed.

The midwife gently took the baby to clean her. "I'll bring her back to you in just a moment."

"Joe," Lily said softly, "my bubbie always told me that in the Jewish religion we name for the dead, and the deceased would watch over the living relative. And by using the letter 'M' it would mean that my papa could watch over her. We could call her Mimi. What do you think?"

"Mimi Rosenberg." He tested the name and smiled. "It's beautiful, like her."

When the midwife returned with their cleaned and swaddled daughter, Lily traced a finger over the white-peach fuzz covering Mimi's head. The baby's eyes fluttered at her touch and Lily felt her heart expand with a love so fierce it took her breath away. Here was her daughter, her Mimi, finally in her arms.

TWELVE

After Chloe taught Lily and Joe how to bathe Mimi for the first time, she wrapped the precious baby in a soft towel and kissed her grandchild's head delicately. "Why don't you stay here in France until Mimi is older?" Chloe asked them, her heart already aching at the thought of being parted from them. "Traveling will be much easier if she is older," she continued. "There's no hurry for you to leave Europe. I know that money is tight here and my apartment is small, but the three of you could stay with me and we will manage."

"I would love to," Joe replied, "but my father passed away last year and now my mother is ill. She's all alone and she needs constant care. In fact, in her last letter she asked me to return to America as soon as I was able to," he finished quietly as he gently cradled Mimi.

"I understand," Chloe said sadly.

"It will be at least a month before we can find a ship going to America, though. So you will have a little time together," Joe said, trying to soften the blow. Then he handed the baby to Lily and left the room.

After Joe had gone, Lily looked at her mother and asked, "Mama, will you help me pack?"

"Of course I will."

"And will you come to America as soon as we can afford to send for you?" Lily said.

"I'll see." Chloe smiled at Lily, knowing deep down that she would not be comfortable in America.

"But what if I can't stay in America without you?" Lily asked. "Can I come home?"

"You can. You can always come home. But you are a grown woman now. You have a husband and a child of your own. This is your family now. You must stay with them."

"So, you're saying you won't come to America even once we have the money to send for you?"

"I'm saying that I can't promise. We'll see," Chloe said. "Now, let me help you get packed."

THIRTEEN

Joe arranged for passage by ship on the Hamburg–America line. The boat was to set sail from a port city located on the Elbe River, on the first day of September. This would give Lily and Chloe a couple of months together before Lily was to leave. Lily was jittery and nervous. She felt like her heart was literally being torn in two, one half still bound to her past and her love for her mother, and the other half hoping to start a new life with her husband and child. Chloe tried her best to reassure her daughter, even though she wished Lily and little Mimi could stay with her in France forever.

Time passed quickly. There was so much that had to be done to prepare for the departure. Mimi wasn't yet sleeping through the night and Lily was exhausted from packing, so Chloe got up in the dark hours and after she brought Mimi to Lily's bed where Lily fed her, Chloe took her granddaughter to the rocking chair in her room and rocked her back to sleep.

September arrived with crimson leaves and a bitter chill that seemed to mirror Chloe's breaking heart. Over these precious months, her granddaughter had become her world—those tiny hands reaching for her face, that milky smile, the soft weight of Mimi against her shoulder as she hummed old ballet melodies. Now at the station, steam billowing around them like morning fog off the Seine, Chloe fought to keep her composure as the train whistle pierced the air. This vehicle would carry her treasures first to Germany, then across the vast ocean, leaving her alone with nothing but memories and an empty apartment. She adjusted little Mimi in her arms, the baby's warm weight both a comfort and a reminder of all she was about to lose.

Chloe gripped Joe's shoulders, searching his face. "You'll take care of my girls, won't you?" Her voice wavered, betraying the storm of emotion she was trying to contain.

"Of course I will. I'll always put their needs first. I promise you." Joe said the right thing, his tone was sincere, but something in his eyes—or perhaps something missing from them—sent a chill through Chloe that was unrelated to the autumn air. She nodded, pushing aside the shadow of unease she couldn't quite name.

"Mama, I am going to miss you so much. You've been my strength for my whole life," Lily whispered into Chloe's ears as she clung to her. "What am I going to do without you?" she sobbed. "You've always been there for me. I've been leaning on you for as long as I can remember. And it's only because of you that I was strong enough to face losing Papa. I can't live without you, Mama. I can't do this. I'm not strong like you."

Chloe's whole world was in this embrace. Her tiny grandchild, her only daughter. She steeled herself. *I must be strong for all of us.* "Shhhaaa, don't cry, mine kind, my child. Be happy," Chloe said softly, gently wiping away her daughter's tears. "Your life is just beginning. No matter how great the distance between us, we'll never really be apart. We'll write to each other, you and me. You'll come to visit me here in France.

I'll go to America and visit you, too. Everything will be alright. You'll see." Chloe reached up and touched Lily's cheek. *It might be years before we see each other again*, she thought with anguish. She closed her eyes for a moment and tried to memorize her daughter's face.

"Joe?" Lily said. "I—"

He took his wife in his arms and held her close to him. "Your mother is right. We'll come and visit every few years. And as soon as I make enough money, we'll send for her. She'll either come to visit us or she'll come to stay. But either way, you will see her again."

The train's loud whistle broke through the silence of the morning. Mimi began to cry. "Shhh, it's alright. It's just a whistle," Chloe crooned as she rocked the baby in her arms.

"All aboard!"

"It's time," Joe whispered softly.

"Mama... I can't say goodbye. I can't go. I can't leave you."

"Darling, please. We have to board now," Joe said gently.

"Then don't say goodbye. Just say 'until we meet again'," Chloe whispered, her trembling hands lingering as she passed Mimi to Lily one last time.

"Yes, until we meet again," Lily said, tears covering her face. "And we will meet again very soon, Mama. We will, won't we?"

"Yes, of course, but until we do, you must take this." Chloe felt as if her heart were being ripped out of her chest as she slipped an envelope containing some American dollars, converted from francs, into her daughter's handbag.

"What are you doing, Mama?" Lily asked.

"Nothing."

"What's in the envelope?"

"A little bit of money. That's all. Just in case you should need it. Keep it for an emergency."

"No, no, I can't take your money! You hardly have enough to live on."

"Don't be silly. I'll be fine. I had this saved for you anyway. It's yours. Take it. You'll have it in case you need it."

"I love you, Mama."

Chloe felt a lump in her throat. She dared not speak. If she did, she was afraid she would not be able to let Lily and Mimi go. Her voice cracked as she began to sing softly in Yiddish, smiling through her tears. Lily began to sing along with her. "In this song, my child, lie many wonders. When you become rich, Mimi, remind yourself of this lullaby. 'Raisins and almonds, this will be your calling... *ai-lu-lu...*'"

Chloe put her arms around Lily and hugged her tightly, greedily sucking in the fragrance of her hair. She reached down and gently rubbed Mimi's head. Then she whispered in Lily's ear, "This pin is a family heirloom. It belonged to my mother. It's worth a lot of money. If you need the money, don't hesitate to sell it. You and Mimi are the most important things in the world to me." Chloe pressed an embroidered handkerchief with a large gold pin adorned with emeralds and diamonds wrapped inside into Lily's hand.

"I can't take this, Mama."

"You can, and you must. Now, go. I love you, Lily."

"Come on, we have to board," Joe said. In a gentle voice he added, "I know goodbyes are hard. And I'm sorry. But we must board the train, otherwise we will miss our boat."

Lily nodded. "Goodbye, Mama."

"Not goodbye. Just goodbye for now," Chloe choked out.

Chloe's lips trembled as she tried to smile. The people who meant the most to her in the entire world climbed onto the train. Lily held Mimi in her arms as she turned back to look at her mother. Her face was covered with tears. Chloe waved.

Joe smiled and waved. And then the three of them disappeared.

Until now, Chloe had managed to keep her composure. But once the train left the station and she knew Lily could no longer see her, she fell to her knees and began to weep. For a long time, she knelt on the cold concrete platform. Passersby stared but no one said a word to her. Finally, she had no tears left to cry. So, she stood up and started walking back to her apartment alone.

FOURTEEN

The train ride felt like forever. When Lily, Joe and Mimi finally got off in Hamburg, they were ready for the final stage of their adventure to begin. Joe had always given Lily the impression that he could afford the finer things and therefore, Lily had believed that he had enough money to purchase comfortable cabins on the ship. After all, they were traveling with an infant. However, on board the boat, Lily realized that he had bought the least expensive accommodation. They had small cots buried deep in the belly of the boat, alongside immigrants from other countries hoping to start a new life in America. The steerage where their beds were located was humid and dirty. It reeked of sweat mixed with pungent smells of garlic and onions. The odor of dirty diapers was accompanied by the sound of crying babies.

"I hate to complain, Joe, but this is really awful," Lily said as the ship lurched into motion. She clutched Mimi closer to her chest. Back home, her mother would know what to do, how to protect a baby in conditions like these. "People are coughing everywhere, some are vomiting. I'm terrified that Mimi will get sick down here."

"Don't be silly, they're just not used to traveling by boat. That's all it is."

"The smell is making me ill," Lily said, watching a woman retch into a bucket nearby. She could almost hear her mother's voice issuing warnings about disease and keeping the baby warm and clean.

"You'll get used to it," Joe said, pulling out a cigarette and lighting it with practiced ease.

"Since when did you start smoking?"

"Only now and then." He shrugged, exhaling a cloud that mingled with the already stale air.

"At least admit how dirty it is down here," Lily pressed, noting the grime on the walls, the unwashed bodies pressed together. Her mother's spotless apartment seemed like a dream now, impossibly far away.

"Yes, sweetheart, I know it is," he said in that honeyed voice that still made her heart flutter, even as doubt crept in. "I had to get home, doll, and, well… it sure is expensive to pay for passage for three to America. So, I did the best I could."

Their accommodation was filthy, there were undefinable stains on the mattress, and the entire steerage section of the boat was dark, dreary, and poorly lit. The beds were hard and lumpy, and the bathroom facilities were far from satisfactory. Lily wanted to cry because she missed her mother, and she already missed France. But as she looked into her husband's eyes, she knew all over again just how much in love with him she really was. There was something about Joe that she could not describe. Something in his eyes, in his lips, the way he said her name, meant that she could not control herself around him. And not only was she madly and desperately in love with him, for the first time she realized that the minute she boarded that ship, she was completely at his mercy. Her command of the English language was weak. She felt for the envelope in her bag and gripped it tightly. The money her mother had given her was all Lily had; she had no way of earning any more of her own in America. Lily began to cry and Joe put his arms around her.

"I'm sorry, my love," he said. "I love you and I'm doing my best. I promise I'll take better care of you once we get home to America. You've gotta trust me." He reached over and touched her cheek, gently wiping her tears away. "Will you just trust me, please? Will you give me a chance?"

Lily softened. "I'm sorry, too," she said. "I didn't mean to be so critical. It's just that I'm not used to this. And I am afraid Mimi has a fever—she might be coming down with something."

"I know she will be okay, she's a strong girl," he said. "I told you that I love you, Lily, and I meant what I said. You'll see, I'm going to be a good husband to you and a good father to Mimi. No matter what it takes, I'm going to take care of you two. You just gotta let me get home so I can get on my feet."

He leaned over and kissed her. The gentle motion of the boat as it left the harbor had rocked Mimi to sleep. Lily looked down at her daughter and her heart filled with love. She placed the baby in the open dresser drawer that had been made into a makeshift crib.

"Come here," Joe said.

"Shush, she's asleep. I don't want to wake her," Lily said anxiously.

"No, neither do I," Joe said as he reached for Lily. He took her into his arms and began to kiss her passionately.

"Joe, we can't," Lily whispered, acutely aware of the bodies surrounding them in the cramped space. "There are people everywhere. There's no privacy here."

"We're married now," he murmured into her ear, drawing the thin blanket over them. "And we're not the only ones. You think all these other couples go weeks without touching?" His fingers traced her collarbone, and despite her protests, she found herself falling into those dark eyes, the crowded ship dissolving around them.

Later, as they lay close beneath the blanket, he whispered, "How could I last weeks without you? It would drive me crazy."

"I know," she breathed, curling into his warmth. In that moment, even the grimy ship felt like the beginning of something wonderful—their life together in America, just as he'd promised.

FIFTEEN

As the days on the boat passed, Lily made friends with other young women. Most of them were excited because although they were leaving their homes, they were going to a country that promised them streets paved in gold. They came without much money, but what they lacked in finances they had in hope.

One night, the ship ran into a storm. It rocked mercilessly with the waves. Many of the passengers became seasick and the smell of vomit mixed with sweat permeated the steerage area. The humidity and heat were stifling, and Lily's dress clung to her body. She became ill and vomited, but she knew she could not lie down, Mimi needed her. Caring for a small child in these conditions was difficult. The crash of thunder frightened Mimi, and even though Lily was hot and sick to her stomach she could not put the baby down. She thought of her mother. It wasn't until their voyage to America had begun that she realized how much work it was to have a child; she missed Chloe terribly. She remembered how her mother had sung the Yiddish lullaby,

"*Rozhinkes Mit Mandlen*"— "Raisins and almonds"—to her at the train station. *Oh Mama, I miss you,* she thought, longing for Chloe's strong and comforting presence.

In her broken Yiddish Lily began to sing, "Raisins and Almonds... *Ai-lu-lu.*"

Joe seemed unaffected by the circumstances. He was his usual happy-go-lucky self. Always gentle with his wife and daughter, but not one to spend his time helping Lily care for the baby. He preferred to drink and play cards with the other men. Lily was anxious that he was gambling away his money. The money he was supposed to be saving to start their new lives in America. She had been so happy when he had returned to her in Paris and she still loved him deeply, but Joe was not behaving like a partner. It was more like having another child. Lily was finding it hard to constantly be the responsible one and care for their little girl. By the time they woke up one morning to see the Statue of Liberty standing proudly outside the small, dirty ship window, Lily had begun to resent her husband.

At the sight of Lady Liberty holding up her torch and the welcome realization that the voyage was over, everyone on the ship was suddenly filled with joy and excitement.

"We made it, baby!" Joe said. His eyes lit up as he pulled Lily into his arms. "We're home. Look, look out there. That's the Statue of Liberty. I'll bet you heard plenty about it when you lived in Europe. Everyone wants to go to America. Don't they?"

Lily didn't answer. It wasn't that she didn't want to go to America. But during the voyage, she realized that she did not know her husband as well as she had once thought she did. And the truth was, she missed her mother and France. Joe didn't seem to notice that Lily was not as enthusiastic as he was. He was shaking with excitement. Then he turned to Lily and said, "When I left home to go to war I didn't know if I'd ever see the city again. Hell, I didn't know if I was going to make it back alive. But here I am. And we are just outside of New York. I can't wait till you see it. Now I'm returning with a beautiful wife and an adorable child. Everything is going to be just fine. I can't wait for you to meet my mother. She is going to love you."

Lily managed to smile. "I hope so," she said softly, preoccupied with worries. *Was it just the voyage making Joe so restless and wild? Will he be a good husband and father like he promised now that we're here in America?*

It took hours for them to go through customs. Mimi screamed because she was hungry and her diaper needed to be changed. Lily looked around her, other women were breastfeeding their babies. She frantically searched for a place where she could sit down and feed her little girl in private, but there was nowhere. They were surrounded by people. Lily felt exhaustion deep in her bones as she gently rocked Mimi and tried to settle her while they moved slowly through the customs building.

Lily and Joe got through all the red tape faster than most of the other people who were in line because Joe was an American citizen. Finally, after several long hours, the wait was over. Lily, Joe, and Mimi had passed their inspection, and they were permitted to enter the United States of America. Stepping out of the stuffy building, Lily blinked in the sharp September sunlight. The air hit her lungs, crisp and strange—so different from the familiar streets and smells of France. All around her, the city roared and clattered: trolley bells, automobile horns, vendors shouting in a dozen languages. The towering buildings seemed to touch the clouds. Overwhelmed, she found a quiet bench and sank down, cradling Mimi close, trying to steady herself in this vast new world that was now her home.

She changed the baby's diaper, then she covered her breast and fed Mimi who sucked greedily until it was almost painful for Lily. And when she was finished, Mimi fell asleep. Lily looked down at her beautiful sleeping girl and brushed Mimi's hair back away from her eyes. Her forehead felt warm.

It took almost an hour to complete these tasks and when she was finally finished, Lily took a deep breath. Then she glanced over at Joe who was tapping his foot and staring at her impatiently.

"Come on already. What's taking so damn long?" he said. His voice was hard and cold. The way he was speaking to her made the hair on Lily's neck bristle. "I'm getting sick and tired of waiting for you to take care of that little brat."

Lily trembled at these words—so unlike Joe's usual gentle manner—but she knew she must try to make peace with him. If Joe got angry enough, she was afraid he might leave her there and where would she go? In a voice as calm as she could manage, Lily said, "I know you are tired. I'm tired, too. But I had to take care of the baby's needs. She was hungry and dirty. I hope you understand."

"I'm sorry to be so impatient, it's just that I'm ready to go home," Joe said, his voice softening.

"I know," Lily replied, hoping that they could work things out now that they were off the ship.

Joe ran a hand through his hair, exhaustion etched on his face. "I thought I was prepared—your mother showed us everything before we left Paris. But seeing Mimi struggle with the fever these past few days..." He trailed off, looking at their sleeping daughter. "I hate feeling so helpless."

"She'll get better." Lily touched his arm. "Babies get sick sometimes, but they're stronger than they look."

"Yeah." He covered her hand with his own. "I just... I want to be a good father, Lily. Better than I've been so far."

Lily had noticed that Joe's hot temper flared up quickly and then dissipated just as fast.

"Alright. We're all ready to go," Lily said as brightly as she could, carrying her sleeping daughter in her arms.

"Follow me," Joe said, lifting their cases with a grunt.

They trudged through streets teeming with life and grit. Her exhaustion was so complete that the city blurred into a kaleidoscope of noise and motion, each block bringing a new assault on her senses until she could barely distinguish one street from the next. The ground seemed to sway beneath Lily's feet, her sea legs not yet adjusted to being on land. She clutched Mimi tighter to her chest, afraid she might drop her. But then, finally, as the sun was beginning to set, they turned a corner where they entered an old neighborhood filled with tenement buildings. Young children with ragged clothes and dirty faces played in the streets. Women hung bedsheets and clothing out of the windows to dry. And then a male voice, from an apartment upstairs, called down, "Hey, Joe? Joe Rosenberg? Is that you?"

"Hey, buddy," Joe called out. "Come on down."

"Sure, I'll be right down. We'll have a beer."

"I could use one. And I want you to meet my wife and kid."

Lily's understanding of English was getting better, and she knew that the word kid, in reference to a child, was a slang term. She gave Joe an annoyed glance, but he didn't notice. He was too excited to see his old friend.

A moment later, a tall, lanky man in his twenties came out the back door carrying two bottles of beer, one in each hand. The way he climbed down the metal stairs of the fire escape reminded Lily of an acrobat. Once he reached street level, he smiled broadly at Joe.

The two men fell into rapid English, their voices rising and falling in a rhythm Lily couldn't follow. She caught Joe's easy laugh, so different from his subdued manner on the ship, and watched him drink deeply from his beer. Her own throat felt like sandpaper, but neither man offered her anything to drink.

She shifted Mimi in her arms, trying to ease the ache in her shoulders.

The conversation flowed around Lily like water, leaving her stranded. She caught a few words here and there—"war," "Mama," "Chicago"—but their meaning slipped away in the current of strange sounds. Joe seemed transformed, his gestures looser, his smile wider than she'd seen in weeks. She studied his face, searching for traces of the gentle man who had won her heart in France.

When Mimi woke crying, both men shot her irritated glances that needed no translation. Lily bounced the baby gently, feeling more alone than she had even on the crowded ship. She heard her name mentioned once and smiled automatically, but Joe didn't even turn to include her. The conversation continued and Lily found her thoughts drifting to her mother's kitchen, to the comfort of familiar words and understanding looks. Here, she was a ghost, present but unseen, except when Mimi's cries made her an inconvenience.

Eventually, the men's conversation ended. The tall man went back into his apartment building and Joe put his hand on the small of Lily's back and led her up the creaky back stairs. She held Mimi tightly as she climbed the unsteady staircase all the way to the third floor. "This is it," Joe said. Then he turned the doorknob. The door was unlocked. "My mother refuses to keep her door locked. I've spoken to her about it. But she won't listen," he said to Lily. "She never has."

They walked into a messy, cramped apartment.

"Ma," Joe called out. "It's me, Joey. I'm home."

A heavyset woman with short, wiry gray hair and tiny, keen eyes like a reptile, came out of the bedroom slowly. "Joe? Joe, is that you?" She clasped her hand over her heart as tears began to stream down her face. "Is it really you?"

"It's me, Ma. I'm home."

"Thank God," she said. "You made it."

"And I brought someone with me. This is my wife, Lily, and your granddaughter, Mimi."

The old woman's eyes narrowed as she looked Lily up and down. "Joey, how could you do this? You mean to tell me that you got married over there?"

"Yes, I did. Lily is a nice Jewish girl like you always wanted for me."

"Do you speak English, honey?" Joe's mother asked Lily skeptically.

Lily understood what Joe's mother asked and answered the best she could: "A little."

"Do you speak Yiddish at least?"

"Yes, I speak some Yiddish and some German as well," Lily said.

"Well, that's good," Joe's mother said. "We'll communicate in Yiddish."

Joe's mother proceeded to speak in Yiddish when she wanted Lily to understand her, and in English when she wanted to speak only to Joe. Lily could not understand everything that was being said and it made her uncomfortable. Besides that, she could see by Joe's mother's expression that she was not pleased to have a new daughter-in-law and a grandchild.

"Come on, Mama. Be happy. I'm home. And just take a look at our little girl—your granddaughter," Joe said, ushering his mother forward to look at the baby in Lily's arms.

Lily stood frozen as Joe's mother pulled back the blanket from Mimi's face. Though she couldn't understand the rapid English that followed, she caught the word "blonde" and saw the older woman's eyes dart between Joe's dark hair and her own, then back to Mimi's fair curls. Her mother-in-law's tone made her stomach clench.

Joe's response came sharp and loud, his face flushing red as he gestured toward Mimi. Lily caught "mother" and "blonde" again, recognizing enough to know that he was trying to explain Chloe's coloring. But his mother kept talking, her voice taking on a hard edge that needed no translation.

The tension in the room thickened. Joe's hands had balled into fists and though Lily couldn't follow his words, their anger was clear enough. His mother's face crumpled then, her tone shifting to pleading as she reached for his arm. Lily heard "sorry" repeated several times and saw tears in the older woman's eyes.

Joe finally turned to Lily, his jaw still tight. "Come," he said. "I'll show you our room." He put his arm around her, guiding her upstairs, but Lily felt Joe's mother's suspicious gaze trail them.

She followed him to a small room with a twin bed at the end of a short hallway. On the walls were pictures of baseball players. The blanket was made of thin gray wool with holes in it and the bedsheets and pillowcase were yellowed with age. *Joe comes from poverty and I never knew,* Lily thought, taking in the run-down room. *I certainly didn't think there would be so many poor people in America. I don't know what I was expecting, but not this.*

"We can make a crib for Mimi out of one of my dresser drawers. Like we did on the ship," Joe suggested.

She nodded, not knowing what to say. *When I dreamed about America, I saw Mimi as a little girl sleeping in a canopy bed with pink satin sheets. I thought Joe's mother would live in a large home with beautiful furniture. And I saw myself going into town with the new girlfriends that I made, all of us wearing the latest fashions. This is nothing like that.*

Lily wished she had not left France. But her love for Joe was a powerful force. And she finally accepted the truth—it was their love that she had become addicted to. He knew her body like a master pianist knows his piano, and when he loved her, she lost sight of everything else. She wanted to believe that her love for him would carry her through the hard times and the poverty she experienced back in Paris. And she wanted to believe that she was going to like it in America, that this was the land of opportunity, and that Joe was going to provide a more lavish life for her and Mimi, but as she looked around the dingy room, she was growing doubtful.

SIXTEEN

As the days passed, Lily learned that life was different in America than Paris, and that sometimes she would have to boil water if she wanted to take a warm bath. And, if she did, she had to boil water for her mother-in-law, who always expected to be waited on. Lily felt as if Joe's mother didn't like her and used her as a slave. Her mother-in-law, Phyllis, gave Lily the responsibility of keeping the house. It took hours for her to scrub the ground-in dirt off the floors. Then she washed down the walls and the windows. Lily was expected to go to the market, buy food, and then prepare evening meals for the family.

Lily stared at the strange bills in her hand, trying to make sense of the American money Joe had given her for shopping. Everything here was different—the sprawling streets with their endless brownstones, the rush of voices rapidly speaking English—even the smells from the market stalls were unfamiliar.

The first time that Lily had tried to buy food, she had nearly burst into tears. Back home, she had known every vendor in their little town market, could bargain in French, and spot the freshest produce at a glance. Here, she pointed and nodded, fumbling with foreign coins while other customers sighed impatiently behind her. The butcher's exaggerated gestures made her feel like a child, and she had come home with cuts of meat that she didn't know how to prepare.

Now, three weeks in, she had found small comforts. There was a Jewish grocer two blocks away who spoke a little Yiddish —different from what she knew, but close enough that she could make herself understood. She had discovered that if she arrived at the vegetable stand just before it closed, the Italian woman there would add extra tomatoes to her bag with a sympathetic smile. These small kindnesses made her throat tight with gratitude.

But cooking in Joe's mother's kitchen was another kind of trial. Every cabinet was strictly ordered, every pot had a designated place. When Lily prepared the wrong vegetables or used too much garlic, her mother-in-law's tight-lipped silence spoke volumes. Phyllis hovered while Lily cooked, adjusting the heat on the stove, reorganizing ingredients Lily had laid out. Even when Lily made her mother's chicken soup—the one thing she could cook with absolute confidence—Joe's mother would add more salt when she thought Lily wasn't looking.

Mimi at least thrived in the chaos, her blonde curls growing thicker, her laughter a bridge between the strained silences. But sometimes, stirring a pot while her mother-in-law muttered in English behind her, Lily would close her eyes and imagine she was back in her mother's sunny kitchen in France, the scent of fresh bread drifting in from the bakery down the street.

Each month, she had to take her mother-in-law on a bus into town to see her doctor. Surprisingly, the doctor was fluent in French, so the first time that he met Lily he explained Joe's mother's condition to her. "She has a weak heart. I'm afraid that she is a very sick lady. She needs to take it easy."

. . .

One hot summer evening Joe returned from playing cards with old army friends, and Lily was exhausted. The house was a mess, Mimi had been fractious all day and Lily hadn't had time to prepare dinner. Joe was angry. But Lily could feel the rage burning inside her. "I spent all day carrying a baby on a bus into town to take your mother to the doctor. I am overwhelmed with caring for an infant and your mother at the same time. It's too hard for me. I need help. You're not working right now. The least you could do is stay at home once in a while and help me."

"I'd love to, doll, but I'm a man. And I'm not out fooling around. I'm out looking for work. I just haven't found the right job yet, is all. Give me a chance and I promise you that I'll get you some help. A nurse for Mom. A nanny for the kid. Trust me, will you?"

Lily's whole world was falling apart. She knew that Joe was not actively looking for a job, because every time he went out, he returned smelling of alcohol. She had recently learned that it was not legal to drink in the United States, so if he was caught, she wasn't sure what would happen. But she had heard that there were very strict laws against drinking alcohol, and she begged him to stop. He denied drinking to excess. "I had a single drink, that's all," he would say. "You're making this into a big problem. It's not."

"But it's illegal, Joe. If you get arrested, what will happen to us?" Lily had asked him.

"I won't get arrested for having a single drink," he had replied before walking away from her.

Joe's behavior worried Lily. The idea that he might be arrested and forced to serve time in jail, leaving her alone to care for his mother and Mimi, terrified her. However, when she brought up his drinking again later that night when they were in bed, he refused to listen to her. "I don't want to talk about this anymore," he said irritably. "We drank wine in France all the time and you never seemed to mind."

"Joe, it was not illegal in France. We have to follow the laws of the land where we are living."

He got up and left the bedroom. She was too tired to follow him.

Lily found out that Joe had gambled away most of his army savings during their voyage to America. Now, with no money left, the family had to line up outside the local church for a free bowl of soup. This humiliation infuriated Lily. She still had the money her mother had pressed into her hands before she left France, sewn carefully into the lining of her coat—their emergency fund, meant to buy passage home if America proved too harsh. Each time she stood in the soup line, she felt the weight of those bills against her heart. But with Joe bringing home nothing, and no prospect of work for herself with her broken English, that money was their only safety net. If she spent it now, what would happen to Mimi if things got worse? Still, watching her baby daughter try to fill her belly with watery soup made her question her choice anew each day.

She dreamt of her old life in France and missed her mother terribly. Sometimes she wished she could return home to France, but she knew she had to make this new life work – for Mimi's sake, and because Chloe had sacrificed so much for Lily and Mimi. So, when she wrote to her mother, Lily told her things were fine in America and that she and Joe were getting along very well.

In truth, Lily found that she was losing her infatuation with Joe. His laziness had begun to disgust her. When he came to her bed at night after he had been out and tried to make love to her, he smelled of alcohol and perfume. She found lipstick stains on his shirts, and it broke her heart to know that she was not enough for him. At first, she lay in bed and allowed him to do what he wanted with her, trying to suppress her tears from running down her cheeks. But after a while she could no longer bear his touch and she pushed him away.

"What the heck is wrong with you?" he growled at her, the drink still slurring his words.

"You're drunk, Joe. And I know that you've been with other women," Lily said, turning away from him and pulling the blanket over her bare shoulders.

"Oh, I see. You know that for a fact, do you?" He sneered.

"When I get close to you, you smell like women's perfume. I've found lipstick and long hairs on your shirt and jacket. I know you aren't faithful to me," she replied bitterly.

"So, what are you going to do about it?" Joe's voice was filled with sarcasm. "Face it, baby, you have nowhere to go. You don't know anyone here. Heck, you can't even speak English, so you can't get a job."

"You speak perfect English and, so far, you don't have a job," Lily bit back. "We have to stand in line at the soup kitchen if we want to eat. I would never have come to America with you if I had known that you were going to act this way."

"Come on, Lily. You were a pregnant woman without a husband. You needed me. You had to come with me or your child would be a bastard."

How dare he! Lily turned around and with all her strength she slapped Joe across the face. He glared at her. Then he hit her so hard that she fell to the ground, blood dripping from her nose and lips.

"Don't you ever do that again," he spat, his eyes full of hatred as he stormed out of the room and left the apartment.

Lily lay in bed shaking, her heart pounding. She finally managed to get out of bed and quietly went to the bathroom to clean herself up. *What am I going to do?* Her mind wouldn't settle. The man she had fallen head over heels for was a monster. She had nowhere to go.

Hours later, she heard the key turn in the front door and anxiety began to beat hard in her chest as his heavy footsteps grew closer to the door. She held her breath as he entered the room. "Oh, baby, I am so sorry," he sobbed, gently stroking her hair. "You gotta forgive me. I didn't mean to hurt you. It's just that I have been so frustrated. I can't find work. Do you have any idea how hard it is for a man not to be able to support his family?"

She sat up slowly and saw the pathetic look in his eyes.

"I'm sorry, baby," he pleaded. "I promise you I'll stop. No more drinking for me. You'll see. I'll be a good husband."

"What about the other women, Joe?" Lily asked solemnly.

"They never meant anything to me. You are my only true love. It was part of my frustration. I've been feeling like such a failure. Please, Lily, give me another chance. I'll make it up to you."

She didn't answer, but when he reached for her hand, she didn't pull away. His touch was gentle now, so different from hours before. When he kissed her, she felt a flicker of the tenderness that had first drawn her to him in that Paris bakery—the Joe she'd fallen in love with, the one with the honey-brown eyes that made her heart skip a beat.

Maybe we can start over, she thought, letting herself lean into his embrace. Maybe we can forget this ever happened. But even as his lips found hers again, softer this time, a shadow of doubt crept in. She remembered her mother's warning about men who could be sweet one moment and cruel the next.

Still, she wanted so badly to believe in him again, to believe in them. When he pulled her closer, she closed her eyes, trying to forget everything but this gentle version of her husband. But the memory of his raised hand lingered, a darkness at the edges of her mind that no amount of tenderness could quite erase.

SEVENTEEN

For several days Joe was a wonderful, considerate husband. He didn't drink and he even bought Lily flowers. He was attentive to Mimi, helping to care for her. But then, about a week later, he began to slide back into his old behaviors.

Lily was sipping a cup of tea when Joe came stumbling in. "If you keep this up, I am going to write to my mother and—" Lily struggled to finish her words.

"And what? And she's going to send you money? If I recall correctly, she didn't have any money. Didn't have a pot to piss in." The sarcasm had returned to his voice.

Lily left the room. She went into her bedroom, where Mimi was sleeping, and locked the door. She lay down next to her beautiful baby girl, watching her chest rise and fall with gentle breaths, and wept.

The next night when he came home for dinner, Joe tried to apologize, but Lily would not speak to him. He tried to embrace her while they sat at the dinner table, but Lily recoiled. She didn't want him to touch her.

"Is this the way you're going to be?" he asked, his eyes darkened, his tone threatening.

Her heart began to race. *Breathe, Lily. Breathe.* She just shook her head.

"Answer me." His voice became louder.

"I have nothing to say to you, Joe, and be quiet otherwise you'll wake Mimi and your mother," Lily replied coolly, placing her napkin on the table.

After that, Joe stopped coming home every night. Sometimes he stayed away for an entire week. Joe's mother defended her son's actions, blaming Lily for not being a good wife to him. Lily was at her wits' end with her demanding mother-in-law, and she began to tell the older woman how she felt about her. This caused a rift between them and little Mimi cried constantly, alert to the tension in the apartment.

After six months of living in this volatile situation, Lily felt she had to write to her mother and tell her everything that was going on. She could not go on like this and knew that her mother would do whatever she could to find a way to get the money for her and Mimi's passage back to France. Lily put Mimi to bed before taking a bath and going to bed, too. She planned to write the letter first thing in the morning, but that very same night Joe returned home at four o'clock in the morning. He was slightly drunk but beaming with excitement when he woke Lily.

"Doll, I've got some wonderful news," he said.

Lily rubbed her eyes, roused from sleep by the smell of alcohol on Joe's breath. Her stomach dropped.

"Listen to me, baby, I got a job. A good job. The pay is excellent. I'm finally going to be able to come through with all the promises I've made to you. I won't be a failure anymore."

She sat up in bed. "A good job? Really, Joe?" Lily felt a

flicker of hope. She couldn't explain why after the way he had treated her, but she still loved him. And looking into his eyes, she saw a glow of promise. *Maybe, just maybe, this would be enough to set things right.*

"Yep. I start work on Monday," he said proudly.

"What kind of a job?" she asked.

"Driving a truck. I can do it. I drove a truck in the army. So, I don't need to learn how to drive or anything. I can step right in."

The idea that they might live a normal life, that Joe might be the loving and wonderful man he was before they left France, and that they might no longer need to line up at the soup kitchen made Lily almost giddy with hope for their future. She imagined the two of them wildly in love again. She could see herself in her mind's eye, going to the market to buy good wholesome food. Once there was enough money, she hoped to purchase a little bed for Mimi instead of the makeshift crib she was outgrowing. Lily was so happy that she threw her arms around him and kissed him.

It had been a while since they had made love and Joe's eagerness caused him to be rougher than normal. But Lily didn't want to discourage him by telling him that he was hurting her, so she closed her eyes and gritted her teeth until it was over.

For the next two days, Joe was attentive, more like the man Lily had fallen in love with back in France than the stranger he had become in America. He helped with Mimi in the mornings, cradling their daughter while Lily prepared breakfast, and his smile when he came home from work made her heart lift. Even his mother noticed the change, retreating to her room more often to give them space.

Maybe things can be different now, Lily thought, watching

Joe rock Mimi to sleep one evening. When he kissed her later, it was gentle and tender—like those first stolen moments in Paris. For a brief time, it seemed as though the darkness of recent months might fade like a bad dream.

Joe had received an advance of ten dollars. He gave her five of it and Lily went to the store, hope lightening her steps. She bought everything they needed—bread, coffee, even a small piece of chocolate that reminded her of home. Standing in the cramped kitchen later, putting away her purchases while Mimi napped, she allowed herself to imagine a future where they could be happy here.

On Monday morning while Joe was getting ready for his first day of work, Lily went into her mother-in law's room to bring her the toast and coffee that she'd prepared for her. But to her dismay the old woman didn't turn around to look at her when she entered the room. "*Bubbie* Rosenberg," she said softly, "are you awake?"

The old woman didn't move. Lily put the breakfast tray down on the dresser. Then she put her hand under her mother-in-law's nose and mouth. Lily felt a shiver run down her back. There was no trace of breath. Trembling, she took the old woman's hand and held her wrist, feeling for a pulse. There was none.

How am I going to tell Joe that his mother has died? she thought, panic rising in her chest. *Today is his first day at his new job. If I tell him, he'll be so upset that he won't go to work, and he'll lose this job. It took him forever to find work. I can't risk him losing it. Can I just not tell him? Can I hold back and tell him when he gets home tonight?*

Lily closed her eyes and said a prayer in Hebrew, a prayer for the dead, that she had learned as a child when her grandmother died. Then she gathered herself and walked down the hall to the kitchen where Joe was waiting for his breakfast.

"I'm going to be driving for the next few days. So I won't be home until the weekend," he said. "I gotta drive to another state and make a pick-up."

"Alright," Lily said, feeling sweat pooling in her neck and down her back. By the time he returned, his mother's body would have been collected and since there was no money to bury her, she would end up being buried in a pauper's grave. Lily considered telling Joe about his mother. It was the right thing to do. But she just couldn't do it.

I need him to work, Lily persuaded herself. *Mimi needs a father who provides for her. He hasn't made any money. I can't let him lose this job or we'll be back to where we were before. And there are so many people out of work right now. I can't risk him collapsing with grief and refusing to leave the apartment or starting to drink heavily again and see other women.*

Joe looked at her skeptically. "Is something wrong?" he asked.

"No, I'm just worried about you." Lily forced a smile. "Promise me that you'll drive carefully?"

"Of course, doll. I'll think of you all day, every single minute of every day. Right, I gotta get going," Joe said, standing up and planting a kiss on Lily's lips.

He looks so handsome, she thought. She remembered how she felt when she had first fallen in love with him. "Are Mimi and Ma still asleep? I mean, I'd like to say goodbye."

She felt a chill come over her. *I have to lie to him.* "Yes, they're both still sleeping."

"I won't wake them. Just tell them I said I love them. Will ya?"

"Of course," Lily replied, trying to put on her brightest smile.

"And I love you, too, doll," he said as he walked jauntily out of the front door, whistling.

Lily watched Joe from their apartment window as he walked down the street. She had made the decision and now she was going to have to live with her choice. By the time Joe returned home his mother would be buried.

A cry from Mimi brought Lily back to the present. She rushed into her bedroom and lifted the baby out of the drawer where she slept. "There, there, my princess, are you hungry? Let me change your diaper first, then I'll feed you."

It was late afternoon when Phyllis' body was taken to the morgue.

Lily was sick with guilt about lying to Joe. Things had been going so much better between them and she hated herself for having lied. However, as hard as she tried, she felt little emotion saying goodbye to the older woman. Ever since Lily had arrived in America, Joe's mother had placed overwhelming demands on her. She had often meddled in Lily's marriage to Joe, and she had always taken her son's side. Besides all of that, she took a lot of Lily's time away from Mimi. Even so, Lily would never have wished her dead. Wishing ill on others, regardless of how much trouble they caused you, was something Lily's mother would never have approved of. But, with her mother-in-law gone, and Joe out of town for a few days for work, Lily could enjoy her daughter's company without the demands of others. She spent her days reading to Mimi. Mimi would always point to her "The Real Mother Goose" book; it was her favorite, and even though Lily preferred reading to Mimi in French, reading in English helped Lily practice, so she happily obliged. She baked a cake for Joe's return while Mimi cooed in delight as she nestled on a blanket on the kitchen floor watching Lily with delight.

Lily took Mimi for long walks in the park, laughing as Mimi squealed with pleasure when she pushed her back and forth on the swings. The days felt carefree but as the time for Joe to return grew near, Lily began to worry about how Joe would cope with the loss of his mother. He had been overseas for several years and he had not spent a great deal of time with her since his return.

The night before Joe was to return, Lily was bathing Mimi, pushing her little toy duck around the water while Mimi made little "quack quack" noises. Lily was overwhelmed with a pang of sadness. She missed her mother so much. Joe's mother's sudden death was a reminder that Chloe was getting older, and the day would come when Lily could no longer be with her. The thought of losing her mother terrified Lily.

She had said many prayers asking God for Joe to earn enough money to enable Chloe to move to America and be with them. *If she doesn't want to come to live in America or even to visit, at least Mimi and I will be able to go back to France,* Lily thought. *I would love for Mimi to see Paris. And Mama would be surprised and delighted to see how much Mimi looks like her with her white-blonde hair and blue eyes. She's graceful like Mama, too.*

Lily closed her eyes and, in her mind, she saw her mother teaching Mimi to dance and to speak French, but Lily knew she was only dreaming. She suddenly felt a wave of sadness wash over her, knowing in her heart these dreams would remain just that—dreams. Joe was not the perfect husband she had hoped he would be. He was a gambler, a heavy drinker and a womanizer, frittering what little money they had on alcohol instead of food and the essentials they so desperately needed.

Lily was thankful that at least for now she was able to nurse Mimi, because if she hadn't had milk... She couldn't even bear to think about it. But she knew she couldn't go on breastfeeding for much longer. Sometimes Lily was tempted to find a babysitter for Mimi so she could search for a job. But they couldn't afford the help, and she was afraid to leave her daughter with a stranger who might not take care of her the same way that Lily would.

Joe did not return the following day or the one after that.

Has he abandoned us? Lily's mind was racing as she got Mimi ready for bed. She could survive without Joe emotionally but financially it would be very difficult. *Maybe I can see if anyone needs a seamstress?* But no one in their apartment block could afford such a luxury, and just as Lily was thinking of walking further afield to the more affluent neighborhoods, Joe returned. He came waltzing into the apartment singing and carrying a bag of groceries in one hand and a doll for Mimi in the other. He put the groceries down on the table and took out a beautifully wrapped box of chocolates which he placed in Lily's hands as he kissed her.

Lily looked up at Joe's smiling face and she was suddenly filled with dread. She wished she could avoid it, but she had no choice. She had to tell him about his mother.

"Open it," he said excitedly. "I know how you love chocolate."

She nodded, slowly removing the ribbon. Then in a whisper she said, "You're right. I do love it."

"And look at this doll, will ya? Mimi's gonna love her. She's got bright blonde hair just like Mimi's. See that?" Joe held the doll up so Lily could see it.

Lily forced a smile, her heart hammering in her chest.

"I got a magazine for my ma. She can't read a word. But she loves to look at the pictures." He laughed. "You know how she is."

Lily nodded again but she felt her stomach drop.

"And come into the kitchen and take a look at all the food I bought. I got us some chicken. Plenty of fresh vegetables, too: potatoes, carrots, cabbage. Come on, come into the kitchen and look in the bag," he said, his voice full of pride and excitement. But Lily was frozen to the spot. "What's the matter?" Joe asked her anxiously. "You look like you're about to cry. Aren't you glad to see me?"

"Yes, Joe, of course I am." *I have to tell him. I hate to do it. I hate to ruin this moment. But I must tell him. He has to know.*

"Where's Mimi? Is she alright?" He suddenly looked concerned.

"Yes, Mimi's fine. She's in the bedroom taking a nap," Lily said, almost choking on her words.

"So, what is it, doll?" he asked, sitting down next to Lily on the sofa and taking her hand. "Talk to me. What the heck is wrong? Everything is going so well for us right now. I like this job. I make plenty of dough. I bought presents for everyone. I don't know what's happening here."

"It's your mother."

"Was she hard on you when I was gone, honey? I'm sorry, I know she can be demanding. But she don't mean no harm. She's old and it's just her way—"

"Joe..." Lily said, looking away from him, "I'm so sorry... I'm so sorry."

A shadow fell across his face as he stood up, "What is it, Lil? Come on, just tell me."

"While you were gone, your mother... well, she... passed away."

Joe stumbled back in shock. He didn't say a word.

"No... No... it can't be true. What? How?" he finally managed to stutter as he began pacing up and down.

"She died peacefully. In her sleep. The morning you left; she was still asleep when I went in to bring her breakfast." Lily swallowed, she couldn't look him in the eyes, afraid he would catch her in the lie. She paused before continuing, "So, I assumed she was tired. But later that morning, when she was still in bed and she hadn't called for her breakfast, I went in to see if she needed anything. That's when I found her."

"Aww, shucks," he said, shaking his head. "My poor ma." He collapsed on the sofa beside Lily. She took his hand in hers and they sat in silence alongside one another. A few moments passed before he spoke, his voice breaking, "Well, she was never the same after Pa died. I guess she just wanted to go so she could be with him. At least she didn't suffer, huh?"

"Yes, I was glad that the doctor said she didn't have any pain."

"Where is she...?" He couldn't finish his words, but Lily knew what he was trying to ask.

"She was buried, in the cemetery just down the road. We can go visit whenever you like. I'll come with you."

He nodded. She didn't tell him that his mother was buried in a pauper's grave, but she was sure he would realize. After all, there was no money for a funeral.

"Do you want to sit *shiva*?" she asked.

"Nah, what's the point?"

"I can set things up for you if you would like. I can cover the mirrors and set up a box for you to sit on. We can gather your friends to say Kaddish for her."

"I'd rather not bother them. She's with Pa now. He'll take care of her," Joe said quietly as he got up and walked to the bathroom. "I'm gonna go and take a shower."

Lily went into the kitchen and put away the food that Joe had bought, except for some of the potatoes and a head of cabbage which she chopped up. She put it all into a large water-filled, white soup pot on the stove and added the meat. *We'll have a nice hearty soup for dinner tonight.*

When Joe came out of the shower, Lily saw that his eyes

were red and she knew he'd been crying. She went to comfort him, but he drew back from her.

"I'm gonna lie down until dinner. I'm awful tired. It's been a long week," he said softly.

"Of course, Joe. You go ahead and get some rest. I'll come and get you as soon as dinner is ready."

EIGHTEEN

Joe was home for three days before he received a call telling him that he had to report for another job. He would be gone for a week. Lily didn't complain. She was glad that he was working and that there would be money coming in to support them. Besides, Joe didn't mind. He seemed to enjoy his job, never uttering a single complaint. But when Lily asked him what he did, all he would tell her was that he drove a truck. When she asked what he transported, he only said, "Different things. I don't work for a single company. I drive for lots of different companies."

At first it was nice just to be able to pay the rent and buy food without pressure, and by the time Joe had been working for eight months, he was earning enough money for them to move to a better apartment. Lily was thrilled when he told her. When he took her to see the new apartment he'd chosen, she was delighted by the nice neighborhood with manicured front lawns. And when Joe suggested that she go to a department store in the city and purchase a real bed for Mimi, Lily was so happy that she threw her arms around his neck and kissed him.

"While you're shopping, why don't you get some new furniture for the place? Most of the stuff we have now was handed down from my ma's parents. The sofa is old and worn. Buy a new one."

"Can we really afford it?" Lily asked.

"Sure, doll. I promised you that I'd get on my feet. Didn't I?"

"You did, Joe. And you're keeping your promise. I'm so happy that things are going well for us now," she replied. *I'll give him a little time,* Lily thought, *and then I'll ask him to send for my mother like he promised.*

He smiled. "I've gotta go on a delivery. I'm leaving in the morning, so you'll have to take Mimi with you to the city when you go shopping."

Lily returned Joe's smile. She was afraid to upset Joe by asking about a budget, and she had no idea of how much money she could spend on furniture. If she spent too much, Joe might get angry. So, she would purchase furniture that was inexpensive but at least it would be new and clean. A fresh start.

NINETEEN
NEW YORK CITY, 1925

When Joe walked out of the house, he felt the power of freedom take hold of him. It was nice to have a wife and child at home. It gave him a sense of stability, of family. He could provide for them and enjoy driving the truck back and forth to Canada. He had even met a couple of girlfriends on his travels. And he loved knowing that they were far enough away from New York City not to cause him any trouble with his wife. He saw these girls if and when he wanted to, slept with them if it pleased him, and when he didn't want to see them, or he was too busy, he just didn't call. A smile ripped across his face as he climbed into the cab of the semi-truck that he was driving. His partner, Mike, was already sitting in the passenger's seat smoking a cigarette. Mike was a slender, quiet man, nowhere near as handsome as Joe, but he was very smart and he had taught Joe everything he needed to know about transporting illegal whiskey for the mob. Mike had been working for the mob for a while now and the boss trusted him. On their last run together, Mike had told Joe that the boss was pleased with his work. This made Joe beam, because when the boss was pleased it meant that a raise in salary might be in order. So far, there had been no mention of extra money and Joe knew better than to bring up the subject. It was best to wait until the boss suggested it.

As they drove along in silence, Mike looked out the window and then lit another cigarette.

"I'm hungry," Joe said.

"Here." Mike pulled a candy bar out of his pocket. "We have a deadline so we can't stop. The boss wants us to make it to Ontario before nightfall. We gotta meet the other fellas right after dark, then head straight back to New York. But after we get this load delivered, we'll stop and grab something to eat."

TWENTY

NEW YORK, 1928

The years flowed past like the letters that Lily exchanged with her mother—weekly at first, then monthly as their new life took root. Each milestone of Mimi's childhood was carefully recorded in Lily's cramped handwriting: first steps, first words (in French, though Joe insisted she learn English), first curls cut and preserved in tissue paper. Chloe wrote back about life in their little town, her work at the factory, and always sent a pressed flower or a ribbon for her granddaughter. Though Lily ended each letter pleading with her mother to join them in America, Chloe's replies grew more resolute. She could not leave the little town where she had danced, where she had loved Lily's father, where every street held memories of the life they'd shared. More than that, something in her bones told her to stay rooted in France, as if by keeping their home intact, she could anchor her Lily and Mimi to their heritage, their history, their true home.

By Mimi's fifth birthday, everything had changed. Joe's mysterious "transportation business" had bought them a handsome brownstone in Manhattan, far from the cramped rooms they'd shared with his mother in Brooklyn. Their neighbors were the families of Joe's associates—men with expensive suits and nervous eyes, women who wore silk stockings and pearls to the grocery store.

Their wives were polite to Lily, but their smiles never reached their eyes. They spoke slowly to her, as if her accented English made her simple, though she'd learned faster than any of Joe's immigrant cousins.

One evening, during a dinner party that filled their dining room with cigarette smoke and forced laughter, Mary Castellano pulled Lily aside. "You want to know what your Joe really does, hon?" She glanced around, lowering her voice. "He drives the whiskey trucks. That's why there's so much money."

Lily managed to keep her smile fixed, though her stomach clenched. *I never wanted to really know where he got the money from,* she thought. *If I didn't ask any questions, I could pretend he was doing some type of good deed for it.*

"Don't worry." Mary squeezed her arm. "These fellas know what they're doing. The cops are all paid up. Come get something to eat," she said when Lily remained silent. "You worry too much. Everything will be just fine."

Lily wasn't as certain of Joe's safety as Mary was. Perhaps Mary was right and Joe and his group were paying off the police. But she couldn't be sure that things wouldn't go sour and if they did, Joe could easily end up in jail. The other wives had family in America. They had people they could turn to if their husbands went to jail, but she had no one. And if Joe were arrested, she had no idea what she would do.

That evening when Mimi was asleep, Lily found Joe counting a thick stack of bills in the kitchen.

"Joe, we need to talk," she said, her hands twisting together nervously. "I'm worried about where this money's coming from."

Joe's shoulders stiffened. "What's that supposed to mean?" He shoved the money into his pocket.

"The mob work—it's dangerous. What if something happens to you? To us?"

"Nothing's gonna happen." His voice had an edge. "I provide good for this family, don't I? Nice apartment, food on the table, clothes for Mimi?"

"I just—"

"Just what? Want me to go back to breaking my back doing odd jobs for pennies?" Joe paced the kitchen. "This is the best thing that's ever happened to us. Don't ruin it."

Lily fell silent, knowing she couldn't argue. The money was good—better than they had ever had. But fear still gnawed at her.

Weeks later, when she missed her period and the familiar symptoms started, she knew she was pregnant again. Her stomach churned with morning sickness and worry as she told Joe.

His face lit up. "A baby? That's fantastic!" He swept Lily into a hug.

Lily tried to match his enthusiasm. *Babies are a blessing,* she reminded herself. But with Joe working ever longer hours for his "associates," she was already struggling to manage with Mimi. The thought of caring for two children mostly alone made her dizzy—or maybe that was just the pregnancy. Unlike her easy time carrying Mimi, this pregnancy was already taking a harsh toll on her body.

As Joe rattled on about names and buying a bigger place to live, Lily pressed a hand to her churning stomach and forced a smile. She had to be strong, for all of them. But she couldn't shake the feeling that their good fortune came with a price they might not want to pay.

. . .

When Mimi's sixth birthday came around, Lily was heavily pregnant and exhausted, but she was determined to throw a beautiful party for Mimi. The children and their parents who attended the party were the families of Joe's associates. It was a catered event with fancy finger food and sweet little pastries— though they were nothing like the delicate *pâtisseries* she recalled eating on one of her childhood birthdays in the Marais *arrondissement* of Paris. Every now and then Lily was hit with a sharp reminder of her old life in Europe.

Lily smiled and thanked everyone for their generosity as Mimi opened her presents. But after the gifts were all unwrapped and the birthday cake served, she slipped away into the kitchen to wash her face with cold water. She was feeling sick to her stomach and she thought she might vomit. Doris, one of the other mothers, came into the kitchen to get a glass of water for her son. Lily and Doris had children the same age and their husbands were friends, so they attended many of the same parties and luncheons.

"You look peaked," Doris said, frowning at Lily. "Are you feeling okay?"

"Yes, this has just been a difficult pregnancy," Lily said with a weary sigh. "I've been so tired."

"Well, it's no wonder. You have an active six-year-old to take care of. That's a lot for anyone. Have you thought about getting some help?"

"No, I haven't actually."

"You don't even have a maid to help you with the house-work, do you?"

"No, I never asked Joe for any help. And he never offered me the money to hire anyone."

"Oh, heck, come on, sweetie. Men never offer. You have to ask them. In fact, you have to demand it. When I wanted a nanny for Elizabeth, I told George that I needed help. I had to stamp my feet a little before he agreed. But I must admit, the nanny is my salvation." Doris laughed. "Just ask Joe. You'll be glad you did."

"Yes, you're right. I think I will."

"Why don't you sit down for a few minutes? Have a cup of coffee. You need the break. I'll keep an eye on the kids," Doris said warmly.

TWENTY-ONE

The following morning Joe left on another work trip. When he returned several days later, he brought a large rocking horse for Mimi. He was excited about the gift. "Look at this thing," he said proudly. "It's hand painted."

"It's very nice," Lily said, trying to brush aside her worries about where he had got it from. She asked him to sit down at the table with her.

"Your English is getting so much better," Joe said. "I think it's because you're palling around with all the wives. They're teaching you, huh?"

"I don't think they like me much. I've tried to befriend them but except for Doris, most of them are cold to me. I invited them over here for lunch when you were out of town and every one of them made up an excuse. I guess I'm just improving my English by shopping at the market."

"Well, I think you're doing just great and I'm proud of you, honey. You're really acclimating yourself here," he said.

"I miss France, Joe... I miss my mother. I wish I could go home and see her," Lily said.

"Yeah, well, maybe next year. Right now, I'm busy

securing my position at work. You know how these guys are—one wrong move and they drop you from the gig. I can't let you go. Besides, who is going to take care of the kid if you're gone?"

She flinched inside, hating it when he referred to their daughter as "the kid."

"I'll take Mimi with me."

"I don't think it's a good idea. Maybe next year," he replied dismissively.

Lily felt tears sting the back of her eyes.

"Aww, come on. Don't be sad." Joe pulled her gently toward him, but Lily stayed stiff, her stomach still queasy from morning sickness that lasted all day. "I just don't wanna be without you for a month."

"Joe, about Mimi's party..." Lily pulled away slightly, needing him to understand. "I saw how disappointed she was, watching the door. Waiting for you."

"I told you I had that meeting—"

"On your daughter's birthday." The words came out sharper than Lily intended. "You should have seen Mimi's face, Joe."

Joe's jaw tightened.

Lily stood up, one hand pressed to her churning stomach. "The gift you bought her is still wrapped on the hall table. Maybe you could give it to her tomorrow, if you're not too busy with another meeting?"

"Yeah, sure. Meanwhile, I got a gift for you waiting right here." He patted his manhood. "I sure missed you, doll. Let me show you how much."

She nodded in agreement and managed a weary smile. Lily almost fell asleep when she put her head on the pillow. She was hardly in the mood to make love to her husband, who smelled strongly of diesel fuel. At first, as he made love to her, he didn't seem to notice that she was unresponsive. Eventually, registering Lily's detachment, he asked, "What's wrong? Are you upset with me about something?"

This is the perfect opportunity to ask him about getting some help around here, Lily thought. "No, it's just that... well... my pregnancy is taking a toll on me. It's been rough this time. And I didn't want to tell you, because I didn't want to complain. But I've been feeling a little bit overwhelmed with caring for Mimi when I'm suffering with morning sickness." Lily cleared her throat before saying, "Please don't be angry, Joe. You see, I'm just hoping you can understand and, well, I was hoping that you might allow me to hire a nanny to help with Mimi." *There, I've said it.*

"A nanny?" he repeated. Lily could tell from his twinkling eyes that he wasn't angry. "I guess that would make us like the rest of our rich friends, wouldn't it? Everyone would have to respect a fella who has hired help."

She looked into his eyes, waiting for his answer. Lily knew that Joe aspired, more than anything, to be part of the upper class. She remembered how he had acted when she met him in France, as if he had come from a great deal of family money. He hated anything that reminded him of the poverty he had endured in his life before he'd started this job.

"Yeah, why not? I like the idea of you having some help with the kid. I mean, it would be good for you. And maybe this nanny could do some of the housework, too. Of course, I wouldn't want her to do any cooking. You know why?" Joe didn't wait for Lily to answer. "Because you're the best cook I know." He smiled.

She threw her arms around his neck and kissed him. Sometimes she loved him so deeply that it hurt. Other times... Well... other times...

TWENTY-TWO

Mimi screamed with delight when she got up the following morning and Joe showed her the rocking horse. The wooden horse's back was so high up that she had to be lifted onto it. As Mimi might fall if she was left alone, Joe held her while she rocked. He enjoyed playing with her during that first day after he returned from work, but by the following morning, Joe had had enough. He wanted to be left alone to relax after his week of working.

Mimi, however, was still excited about her rocking horse and she constantly begged her mother to put her on it, but Lily was nervous that frequently lifting Mimi could harm the unborn child. To distract her daughter from the appeal of the rocking horse, Lily took Mimi out for a walk to the park. It was becoming very hot outside and although Lily was feeling a little dizzy and nauseated, she agreed when Mimi begged to stop for ice cream on the way. Lily thought the cold ice cream might help with her queasy stomach. But it didn't. So, Lily threw her cone in the trash and waited while Mimi finished hers.

When they arrived at the park, Lily plopped down on the bench, glad to take the weight off her feet. She watched Mimi run on her short little legs all the way to the sandbox to play with a boy who looked like he was about seven or eight. He was building a sandcastle using a shovel and a pail. The little boy's mother, who was standing beside him showing him how to fill the bucket, appeared to be about Lily's age.

"Can I play, too?" Mimi asked earnestly.

"Of course you can, dear," the boy's mother replied, then she turned to her son. "Nick, let this nice little girl play with your shovel for a few minutes. Alright? I know that you want to be a gentleman like your daddy was, now, don't you?"

"Yes, Mama."

"Well, good. Then play nicely with this little girl. What's your name, dear?" the woman asked Mimi.

"Mimi."

"This is Nick and I'm Gloria," the boy's mother said, smiling warmly.

Mimi beamed back.

"Now, you two have fun, I'm going to go and sit down on the bench. No fighting. Alright?"

"Yes, Mother," Nick agreed.

Gloria sat down beside Lily, smiling. "Is the little girl yours?" she asked.

"Yes," Lily answered as she watched Nick hand the shovel to Mimi. "Your son is quite the little gentleman."

"He's a good boy. Things are hard for him. His father died last year in a factory accident. I'm all he has left." The woman smiled sadly.

"Gosh, how sad. I'm so sorry," Lily said. The woman had kind but tired eyes and Lily couldn't help but notice that her summer dress was threadbare.

"I don't mind doing everything on my own. But he doesn't have a man in his life who he can look up to. So, it's all up to me to teach him how to be a good man. Oh, I'm so sorry. Here's me telling you my life story and I haven't even introduced myself."

"Gloria, right? Well, it certainly looks like you're doing a good job. I'm Lily, it's lovely to meet you."

"Lovely to meet you, too. Your accent... French?" Gloria asked her.

"Yes. I'm from a little town just outside Paris."

"Wow, Paris." Gloria's eyes lit up. "I would love to visit there one day. It always sounds so chic. You must miss it terribly. My family is from Düsseldorf, but I have never been there."

Lily felt a crushing sense of homesickness wash over her—a deep longing for her mother and her country that she couldn't shift, even after all these years. "Yes..." she answered softly.

Gloria seemed to sense the weight of Lily's silence. She reached over and patted Lily's hand. "It's not easy being away from family, is it? Especially when you're expecting." She nodded toward Lily's rounded belly.

This simple gesture of understanding made Lily's eyes well up. The two women sat in comfortable silence for a while, watching their children play together. Nick was showing Mimi how to pack the sand just right so that the castle wouldn't crumble.

Finally, Gloria turned to Lily, her voice warm. "It sure would be great to do this again. What days do you come to the park?"

"We try to come every day for an hour or so," Lily said eagerly, grateful for the prospect of friendship. "But we can meet you whenever you're free. The children seem to get along so well." She hesitated, then added honestly, "And I must confess, it's nice to have another adult to talk to. My husband is so busy with work lately... well, sometimes the days feel very long."

"Oh, I know exactly what you mean," Gloria said, relief evident in her voice, too. "How about tomorrow, around four o'clock? I know it's later, but I'm at work in the morning."

"Four o'clock works perfectly," Lily replied, already looking forward to it. Despite having only just met Gloria, she felt she had found someone who understood the particular loneliness of being a young mother far from home.

As they gathered their children to leave, both women moved with the unhurried motions of people reluctant to end a promising encounter. Sometimes, Lily thought, the best friendships start with nothing more than two lonely people willing to make room for each other.

TWENTY-THREE

It had been a long time since Lily had a friend. She had Mimi to care for, and that kept her busy, but she had desperately missed having an adult woman to share her thoughts with. At the park, the two children would play, while the women would sit on the bench and chat. It was wonderful to see how well Nick and Mimi got along. At first Lily had been afraid that Nick might be too rough to play with Mimi because he was older. However, he was very gentle and remarkably protective if another child got a little boisterous around her.

As the two women watched the little ones, they both opened up about their past experiences. Lily told Gloria all about France—the food, the music, the culture—but most of all she spoke about her mother who she missed terribly. "If I could have one wish, it would be for my mother to see Mimi growing up. Mimi looks just like her."

Gloria smiled. "Your mother was blonde like Mimi?"

"Yes, I got my dark hair from my papa," Lily said, a fleeting memory of her father flashing in her mind.

"Mimi is such a lovely child. Beautiful, inside and out."

"She reminds me of my mother," Lily said softly. "Mama was a ballerina before her injury."

"That explains Mimi's natural grace."

"Yes, it's certainly not from me." Lily laughed. "I take after my father—he used to say he had two left feet."

Gloria smiled warmly. A comfortable silence settled between them before Lily asked, "What was it like growing up here—in America?"

"Well, let's just say that when they tell the Europeans that the streets are paved in gold, they're lying," Gloria said dryly.

Lily nodded. "When Joe and I first arrived, we lived in a tenement. Things only improved after he got his current position."

"I would never have guessed. Perhaps it's your French sophistication."

"Oh no." Lily shook her head. "Mother and I struggled in France, too."

Gloria hesitated, then confessed, "You know, I don't have many friends here. Once I had Nick... well, an unmarried mother isn't exactly welcomed in polite society."

"The wives of Joe's colleagues keep their distance from me," Lily admitted. "They smile, but I'm still the foreign woman who doesn't quite belong."

"Well," Gloria said, reaching across to squeeze Lily's hand, "we have each other now."

Lily squeezed back, grateful. "Yes, and I'm so thankful for that."

It was almost lunchtime so Lily took sandwiches and cookies from her basket. Turning to Gloria, she asked, "May I give Nick a sandwich and some cookies?"

"Yes, that would be very nice of you." Gloria's voice held a note of relief that Lily pretended not to notice. "But you didn't have to bring extra food."

"I wanted to," Lily said gently. "I brought some cheese, crackers, and fruit for us, too."

Gloria's eyes lingered on the food for a moment too long before she said, "You are so kind, Lily."

Lily got up and brought the snacks to the children, watching as Nick carefully helped Mimi unwrap her sandwich. *Such a sweet little boy.*

Back on the bench, she handed Gloria the package of crackers and cheese, noticing how the other woman took small, measured bites, as if making each morsel last. "This is delicious," Gloria said. "Thank you for sharing."

Lily knew that Mimi began to look forward to meeting Nick each day because she started trying to put on her clothes as soon as she got out of bed every morning.

On a bright, sunny Tuesday morning, Lily and Mimi arrived at the park. Gloria and Nick were usually early, but today they were not there. Mimi looked around anxiously. "Mama, where are they? Where's Nick?" she asked Lily, her face crestfallen.

"They'll be here soon, sweetheart. We're early. Come, sit down with me and we'll wait together."

Mimi sat beside her mother, swinging her legs impatiently and glancing around eagerly for Nick.

When Gloria finally appeared thirty minutes later, Lily's heart sank. Her friend's dress was soiled, her hair wild, and Nick's absence spoke volumes.

"Nick?" Mimi called out, looking around.

"I... I didn't just come to explain our absence," Gloria's voice trembled. "I need help, Lily. Nick is terribly ill."

"What's wrong with him? Where is he?"

"My neighbor's watching him. He was up all night, vomiting. His fever's so high..." Gloria's composure cracked. "I've never seen him this sick."

"Have you called a doctor?"

Gloria's eyes dropped to the ground. "I can't... I don't have..." She couldn't finish.

"Wait." Lily caught her friend's arm as she turned to leave. "Let me pay for the doctor."

"No, I couldn't possibly—"

"Please, Gloria. You came here hoping I would help, didn't you?" Lily said softly. "Don't let pride keep Nick from getting the care he needs."

Gloria's shoulders sagged, relief and shame warring on her face. "I came here hoping you might be able to help... I just didn't know how to ask. I'll never forget this kindness, Lily."

"Don't be silly. Let's hurry and get Nick to a doctor."

TWENTY-FOUR

Nick was so weak that he couldn't walk. Lily insisted that Gloria put him in Mimi's wagon. Mimi walked beside them, clutching Nick's hand as Gloria pushed him along the crowded street toward the neighborhood clinic.

When they arrived, the waiting room was packed with coughing patients. Lily approached the nurse at the desk, leaning in close. "Please, I have a very sick child with me. His fever's dangerously high. I can pay something extra to have him seen quickly."

The nurse, her gray hair pulled tight beneath her white cap, glanced at Nick's limp form in the wagon. "Two dollars now," she said quietly. "I'll see what I can do."

Lily pressed the bills into the nurse's hand and, true to her word, they were soon called into a small examining room that smelled sharply of carbolic acid. Dr. Weinstein, a thin man with wire-rimmed spectacles and graying temples, entered promptly. After examining Nick thoroughly, he spoke with concern. "The boy is showing signs of a severe parasitic infection. We'll need to run tests to be certain, but he needs immediate treatment." He turned to Gloria. "How long has he been ill?"

"Since last night. He couldn't keep anything down." Gloria's voice trembled.

The doctor nodded gravely. "I'll write you a prescription. The medicine isn't cheap, but—"

"I'll pay for it," Lily cut in. "Whatever he needs."

"He'll also need proper food to recover his strength," Dr. Weinstein added. "I suggest taking the little girl outside while we complete the examination and draw blood for testing."

"Gloria, let me stay with Nick," Lily said gently. "You look faint yourself. Why don't you go and sit down with Mimi?"

As if understanding the gravity of the moment, Mimi took Gloria's trembling hand and led her from the room, leaving Lily to watch over Nick as the doctor prepared his instruments.

An hour later, Lily emerged, pushing Nick in Mimi's wagon. Gloria and Mimi sat together, still hand in hand. Gloria jumped to her feet. "Is he alright?"

"Yes, he'll be fine. The doctor's given him some medicine, and with rest and good food, he'll recover."

"Oh, thank God." The tears that Gloria had been holding back now fell on to her cheeks. She leaned over the wagon and began to speak softly to Nick while Lily paid the bill.

"Let's take a taxi back to my house," Lily said, touching Gloria's shoulder. "We can all have some lunch and then Nick can get some rest."

Gloria nodded gratefully.

By the time they arrived at Lily's home, Nick was already showing signs of improvement, even though he was still weak.

"Please, come in and sit down," Lily said, ushering them inside. "I'll make us all something to eat."

"This is all so kind of you, Lily," Gloria said, her voice cracking. "I don't know how I'll ever repay you."

"You're my friend. You don't need to repay me. Friends

help each other. That's what they do," Lily said, squeezing Gloria's arm gently. Then she went into the kitchen and soon returned with a tray of sandwiches.

"Chicken salad! Yummy!" Nick said brightly, taking a big bite.

Lily saw Gloria's shoulders relax as she watched her son eat. "See," Lily said to Gloria, "the medication is kicking in already. His appetite is coming back strong."

After lunch, Nick was tired. Lily put him down in her bed to take a nap and Mimi, worried about her friend, lay beside him and fell asleep.

"They were both exhausted. It's been a hard morning for them," Lily said wearily.

"Thank you again... for everything," Gloria said quietly.

"I'm glad I could help."

There was a long silence before Gloria spoke again, "I try my best. But Nick spent all day yesterday with his babysitter and her tyrant son who acts like a little monster, I don't know if she gave him something to eat or if he got sick from the water." Gloria wrung her hands together in despair. "Living in a tenement is not easy. And trusting your child's welfare to a stranger is even harder. But what can I do? I need to work. We have no other family; it's all up to me. We must eat and have a place to live. I have to make do..."

"I understand, I really do," Lily said, remembering the hardships that she and her mother had endured after her papa had died. Her mind was ticking. She turned to Gloria and said, "I have an idea."

Gloria looked at Lily and waited.

Lily said, "As you can see, I'm in a family way."

Gloria nodded, glancing down at Lily's large extended belly.

"How would you feel about bringing Nick with you to work?"

"At the factory? They would never allow it," Gloria replied.

"No, not at the factory. I'm wondering if you might consider becoming a nanny for Mimi? I need help, especially now while I am pregnant. But I'm sure I'll need it even more once the baby is born. I own a home. You and Nick could move in with us. You would have your own room, which has a small powder room attached to it. I would pay you a good salary. All you would need to do is care for Mimi along with your own little boy." Lily hesitated. "What do you think?"

Gloria looked stunned. Her eyes brimmed with tears. "I think it sounds wonderful. I could care for my own child and earn a little money while we have place to live... all at the same time. Mimi is such a delight, too. I would love to take care of her."

"So, will you accept my job offer?"

"Of course I will," Gloria replied, throwing her arms around Lily. "Do you think you should discuss this with your husband?"

"He won't even notice. When can you start?" Lily asked.

"I can move in tomorrow."

"Will you need help to move your things? Is Nick well enough for the move?"

"What things?" Gloria gave a sad smile. "We have nothing but a few clothes and photographs—I can carry those by myself. And Nick is getting stronger by the hour—he will be okay."

"What time can you arrive?"

"Is ten in the morning too early?"

"Ten is fine. I'm so glad about this arrangement. It feels very right. Don't you think so?" Lily asked.

"I do. I've been praying for God to send something, or someone, that would help me and Nick to survive." Gloria ran her fingers over the tiny wooden cross she wore around her neck. "There have been nights when I've had to go to bed without eating so I could afford to feed my son. This offer is a blessing. And you, Lily, are an angel."

"I'm just a woman who remembers what it was like," Lily said softly. "When Joe and I first came to America, we were very poor, too. He was fortunate to find well-paid work, but I haven't forgotten how it feels to struggle."

"I'll never be able to repay your kindness. But I promise you, I'll care for Mimi as if she were my own."

"Thank you," Lily said, reaching for her handbag. She pulled out a pencil and paper, then hesitated. "I should give you my address, but I still can't write in English."

"Don't worry—once I've been somewhere, I can always find my way back," Gloria replied.

TWENTY-FIVE

By the time that Joe came home for dinner that evening, Gloria and Nick had gone home to pack. But Lily was so excited that as soon as Joe walked in the door, she told him the story of how she had met Gloria, and that she had hired her to help with Mimi and the housework.

"Good, I'm glad you found someone. I hope she turns out to be capable and reliable."

"I think she will. She's very nice, Joe."

He smiled. "It all sounds real good. Now, quiet down, because I have a surprise for you."

"A surprise?"

"Yep."

"Well, what is it?"

"Come with me and I'll show you," he said with a broad smile, his eyes twinkling with excitement. Lily followed Joe outside to find a shiny black automobile parked by the house. "It's mine," Joe said proudly.

"What? You bought a car?" Lily gasped.

"Yep. Now we never have to take another bus again. You and me can travel in style, doll."

"It's beautiful," Lily said.

"Well, get in. Don't you want to sit inside and see what it feels like?"

"Yes, but Mimi is napping and if she wakes up and I'm not there—"

"We'll only be out here for a few minutes. Come on, doll, just get in."

Joe opened the door and Lily slid inside the car, her breath catching at the luxurious interior. The leather seats were butter-soft and deep blue, matching the gleaming exterior. Everything sparkled—the polished dashboard, the chrome handles, even the steering wheel seemed to shine with promise. The rich scent of new leather mingled with something else—maybe cedar?—creating an aroma of wealth and possibility that made her think of the perfume counters in Manhattan's finest stores.

Lily ran her fingers over the smooth upholstery, remembering the wooden bench seats of the horse carts in her little town. She had come so far from those dusty roads outside Paris.

"I love it," Lily admitted, catching Joe's proud smile.

"I knew you would," he said. "Want to go for a ride?"

"Yes, of course I do, but I can't right now. I can't leave Mimi alone in the house. Can we just wait for Mimi to get up and then all three of us can go? Or maybe it would be better if we take a ride tomorrow when Gloria is here and she can look after Mimi?"

"You really trust this girl, don't you?"

"Yes, I do," Lily replied.

"So, we'll go for a ride tomorrow then. But you know what? I'd like to take Mimi with us for our first ride in the new automobile as a family. What do you say, shall we pack a couple of sandwiches and have a picnic?"

"I'd like that very much, and I'm sure Mimi would like it, too. Now, come inside, Joe, your dinner is getting cold."

. . .

Mimi wandered sleepily into the living room, giggling as soon as she saw her father. "Good evening, princess," Joe said as he lifted his daughter high in the air.

"Hi, Daddy," Mimi said, still giggling.

"I have a surprise for you. Tomorrow we're going to go for a ride in a car. And we're going to have a picnic."

"That sounds like fun," Mimi squealed.

"It will be fun." He winked at her settling her down at the table to eat.

"My best friend is Nick. Can he come with us?" Mimi asked earnestly. Her cheeks were still flushed pink from her nap.

"Is she talking about the maid's kid?" Joe turned and asked Lily.

"Yes." Lily twisted her napkin under the table, her heart racing. "His name is Nick, and..." She took a breath, steeling herself. "He and his mother, Gloria, will be living here with us."

Joe's fork clattered against his plate. "Living here?"

"That's wonderful!" Mimi bounced in her chair. "Nick can be like my brother!"

But Joe's face had darkened, his jaw tight as he turned to Lily. "Princess, why don't you go up and play with your toys?" he said to Mimi. "Mama will be up soon."

Once Mimi's footsteps had faded upstairs, Joe's voice came low and dangerous. "You want to explain what you're thinking, bringing these people into our home?"

"Gloria lost Nick's father, Joe. They've fallen on hard times—"

"I worked real hard to get us out of that lousy neighborhood," Joe said, cutting Lily off, "to give our kid a chance at a better life. And now you're bringing some low-class kid in here?" He leaned forward. "Wouldn't Mimi be better off with friends from families in our circle?"

Lily's hands shook as she gathered the dishes, remembering

how she had once been the outsider: the poor immigrant that the other wives looked down on. "They're good people, Joe. Nick and Mimi have become such good friends already. Mimi likes him and he is very kind to her—"

"A friend?" Joe's laugh held no warmth. "Is that what this is about? Our daughter needs better friends than some low-class charity case."

"And what are we?"

"Not low class. Not no more," Joe said firmly. Then he turned to see Mimi who was standing at the foot of the staircase, staring at him wide-eyed and listening to their conversation. "I don't think it's a good idea for your friend Nick to come with us on our picnic."

"But Daddy!" Mimi's eyes began to fill with tears.

"I said no. And that's all there is to it. No means no!" Joe's shout echoed through the house.

Lily's heart clenched as she heard Mimi's small feet pounding up the stairs, followed by the slam of her bedroom door. Her daughter's muffled sobs carried down the hallway and Lily instinctively moved toward the stairs. She couldn't bear to hear Mimi cry. But Joe's grip on her arm stopped her. "Listen, doll." His voice dropped low, dangerous. "We might have been stuck in a lower-class situation before I got this job, but now I'm making good money."

Lily stood torn between her husband's grip and her daughter's crying, each sob like a knife in her chest. *I should go to Mimi*, she thought. *I should comfort her, tell her everything will be alright.* But the pressure of Joe's fingers reminded her that sometimes a mother's comfort had to wait until a father's anger cooled.

Lily went into Mimi's bedroom where she found her daughter

laying on her bed and crying. "Daddy is so mean sometimes," she sobbed.

Lily sat down on the edge of Mimi's bed, her heart aching at the sight of her daughter's tear-stained face pressed into the pillow. She began to stroke Mimi's back in slow circles, the way her own mother used to comfort her. The familiar lavender scent of Mimi's freshly washed hair brought a lump to her throat—how many times had she sat like this, trying to smooth over the rough edges of Joe's temper?

"*Ma chérie,*" she whispered, slipping into French the way she always did in these tender moments. "My sweet girl."

Mimi turned over, her face blotchy from crying. "Why doesn't Papa want Nick to come? He's my only real friend."

Lily gathered her daughter close, pressing a kiss to her damp forehead. "Your papa..." She paused, searching for words that wouldn't deepen her daughter's hurt. "Sometimes he forgets what it's like to be young and lonely. To need a friend." She thought of her own first days in America, how desperately she'd longed for someone to talk to.

"But Nick and I already planned what sandwiches we'd share." Mimi's voice quivered.

"I know, *mon coeur.*" Lily rocked her gently. "Listen—when Papa goes on his trip next week, we'll have our own special picnic with Nick. Right here in the garden. We can make those little cakes your *Grandmère* Chloe taught me to bake. Would you like that?"

Mimi nodded against Lily's shoulder, her breathing slowly steadying. "Can we invite Gloria, too?"

"Of course." Lily managed a smile, though her own eyes stung. "Now, shall we go down and have some dinner? You need your strength if you're going to help me bake those cakes."

She held her daughter a moment longer, breathing in her innocent sweetness, wishing she could shield her from every harsh word, every disappointment. But for now, all she could do was hold her close and promise her better tomorrows.

Lily had been up since dawn, anxiety making her restless. She had already prepared coffee and set out fresh bread, straining to hear Joe's breathing upstairs while she worked. When the soft knock came, her heart jumped.

Gloria stood on the doorstep, one hand on Nick's shoulder, the other clutching a battered cardboard valise. Dark circles shadowed her eyes, and her coat—though carefully pressed—was threadbare at the cuffs. Nick's shoes were scuffed, his socks darned, but his dark curls were neatly combed.

"Come in, both of you," Lily whispered, glancing nervously at the ceiling. Joe's snores still rumbled faintly above. *He sleeps so late when he's not working,* she thought as she led them through to the warm kitchen, where morning light spilled across the table. "Please, have some breakfast."

"Oh no," Gloria started, though Lily saw how her eyes lingered on the fresh bread. "We ate already, didn't we, Nick?"

Nick looked up at his mother, then back at the bread. "I'm hungry," he admitted. "I'm very hungry."

Gloria flushed, but Lily was already pulling out chairs. "Don't be silly. I can see you're both hungry." She caught Gloria's eye, remembering her own first days in America, how pride had warred with necessity. "Please. Let me do this for you."

Gloria's shoulders slumped slightly. "Thank you," she said softly. "The truth is, we'd love something to eat."

Lily busied herself with plates and cups, giving Gloria a moment to compose herself. The valise sat lonely by the door— one small case to hold all that remained of their life before. She thought of her own journey across the ocean, how she'd carried her whole world in a single trunk, her heart full of hope and fear.

"There's plenty," she said, setting out butter, jam, and the last of yesterday's eggs. "Eat as much as you like." Under the table, she felt Nick's feet swinging, heard Gloria murmur a quiet grace.

"Let's put your suitcase into your room. Then we'll have breakfast. But we have to be quiet. Mimi and Joe are still sleeping."

"Mimi sleeps late," Nick observed, carefully spreading jam on his second slice of bread. "Once she starts school, she's going to have to get used to getting up a lot earlier."

Lily glanced toward the stairs, a familiar guilt tugging at her. Joe insisted that Mimi shouldn't be woken before she was ready —it was another way they were different from other families. "Yes," she admitted softly. "I worry about that, too." She caught Gloria's understanding look across the table. "Perhaps... perhaps you could help her adjust, Nick? It would be nice for her to have a friend who knows the routine."

Nick straightened, pride flickering across his face at being given such responsibility. "I can walk with her. I know all the shortcuts, and where to cross the streets safely."

"Don't you worry about it. I'll help you get her ready for school each morning. She'll be fine. She won't be late," Gloria said reassuringly.

"Mimi and I are going out for a ride this afternoon. So, you and Nick will be in the house alone. This should give you two a little time to unpack and adjust to your new surroundings."

"Sounds perfect," Gloria said.

"Good. I'm glad. Now, would you like to see your room?" Lily asked.

"We'd love to."

When Gloria saw the room where she and Nick were going

to sleep, she let out a little gasp. Then in a whisper she said, "It's truly lovely."

"I wish it were bigger for you."

The room was big enough to hold a bed for Gloria and a small cot for Nick that Lily had borrowed the night before from one of her friends who lived a few houses away. There was a little dresser in one corner and a small closet in the other.

"It's perfect," Gloria said, her eyes welling with tears. "I'm so happy that you have taken us into your home. I will be forever grateful to you."

"This is so kind of you, and very unnecessary," Gloria said.

"Don't be silly. Mimi and I have to eat, too. Now, please, both of you, sit down."

Nick ate so quickly and so much that he gagged and almost threw up. Gloria was angry with him and she told him as much. But Lily just shook her head. "It's alright. The poor little fella is hungry." Then she turned to Nick and put her hand on his shoulder. When he looked up at Lily she said, "From now on when you are hungry you come to me and just ask for some food. Alright?"

He gazed at her, astonished, and Lily could tell from his expression that he had gone to bed hungry plenty of nights. But he nodded.

Mimi padded into the kitchen barefoot in her nightdress, clutching the stuffed rabbit that Joe had brought back from one of his runs. She climbed onto Lily's lap, her small face serious.

"I'm glad Nick's staying," she whispered. "He will make the house feel less lonely when Daddy's away."

After breakfast Lily stroked her daughter's hair, watching Gloria and Nick as they set up their few belongings. Something in her chest eased at the sight of them—as if their little family was finally complete.

TWENTY-SIX

After breakfast Gloria took the two children to the park, so Lily could rest for a while before the picnic. As she was about to lie down, Joe appeared in the kitchen doorway. "Did your new nanny show up?"

"Yes, she's taken the children to the park."

"So, she did bring her kid with her?"

"Yes, he's a nice little boy, Joe. I wish you'd give him a chance. He's so good with Mimi."

Joe's face darkened. "Keep an eye on him. You can't trust little boys—they get curious about sex at an early age."

Lily felt her stomach tighten. "She's only six."

"How old is he?"

"Eight, almost nine."

"That's old enough to start being curious. Just watch them."

"Of course I will, Joe," Lily said, fighting to keep her voice steady.

He shook his head, looking annoyed. "You never take me seriously."

"I always take you seriously."

"I'm not happy about this whole situation, but I know it

makes you happy. Anyway, I'm leaving for work early tomorrow morning, so I'd like to cancel our picnic and get some rest today."

"Of course, whatever you need." Lily hesitated. "Though Mimi will be disappointed."

"She'll have to get used to it. I can't live my life to please a child." Joe turned away. "I'm worn out. I can't help it. I gotta get some rest."

"I'll talk to her," Lily said. She knew that Mimi would be more than happy to stay at home and play with Nick. "Don't worry about it."

"Good," Joe said and then cracked his knuckles as he sat down at the kitchen table. "Now, what's for breakfast?"

When Gloria returned with the children, their cheeks flushed from play, Lily wrung her hands as she explained that Joe had changed his mind about the picnic. "I'm sorry," she said to her daughter, watching Mimi's face fall. Turning to Gloria, she continued, "I hope it won't be difficult for you to get settled while watching them."

"It will be no trouble at all." Gloria smiled, resting her hands on the children's shoulders. "They play so nicely I don't ever have to intervene."

Lily pressed her fingers to her temples, where a headache was building. "Do you think you'll be able to keep the children quiet so that Joe and I can rest?"

"Of course," Gloria said brightly. But the children were so full of energy and Mimi was so excited to have another child to play with that their laughter woke Joe up from his nap. When he came out of his bedroom, he was furious. "What the hell is going on here? I told you to keep the little monsters quiet. Didn't I?" His face was crimson, and his fists were clenched as he glared at Lily.

Then Lily saw him glance over at Gloria who was kneeling on the floor playing with the children. The full skirt of her floral dress was spread around her knees. She looked young, vibrant, and beautiful. When Joe saw her the anger in his face disappeared and his eyes lit up. Lily watched him for a moment. She knew him well enough to tell that he was attracted to Gloria. Her heart sank. For the past couple weeks, things had been going so well between her and Joe. He had more kind than angry moments, and she had almost started to believe that Joe had changed. Lily watched Gloria as she tried to be inconspicuous, and to quiet the children. She pulled Mimi on to her lap and took Nick's hand, then in a quiet voice she hushed them and told them in a whisper to stay beside her and be very quiet. For a moment Lily was consumed with jealousy. Living with Joe and his constant problems had aged her. Her hair was sprinkled with gray and there were lines around her eyes.

The pregnancy had changed her body in ways that made her feel like a stranger to herself, and for a moment, watching Gloria's graceful movements, a flicker of insecurity made her consider letting her go to protect her marriage. But beyond her desperate need for help with the house and children, Lily had come to treasure their conversations over coffee and the way Gloria could make her laugh even on her darkest days. Gloria was the first real friend she had made in America, the only one who truly understood what it meant to struggle here. *No,* Lily thought firmly, *I won't let Joe's wandering eyes poison this friendship. I trust Gloria—she's shown me nothing but loyalty and kindness. I have to believe in her.*

But even though she wanted to trust Gloria, Lily couldn't help but worry. She remained cool towards him. But watching his behavior made Lily remember how attentive and romantic Joe had been when he was courting her. She knew how easy it was to be swept away by his advances. Yes, Joe was the kind of man who, when he wanted something, was hard to resist. And she could see that he was already setting his sights on Gloria. Even so, when Lily watched Nick playing with Mimi, she couldn't imagine sending that little boy back to a life of poverty.

Thankfully Joe was scheduled to leave the following morning. He was going to be gone for a little over a week. Lily prayed that the time away at work would cool his obvious interest in Gloria, give him a chance to remember his responsibilities as a husband and father. But even as she hoped this, she knew it was wishful thinking—Gloria would be here each day when he returned home, a constant temptation that she couldn't remove without losing both her friend and the help she desperately needed.

That night Joe had no interest in making love to Lily. He blamed his lack of desire on the fact that he had to get up early. But Lily knew better.

<h1 style="text-align:center">TWENTY-SEVEN</h1>

The following morning Joe got up and dressed quickly. He had to meet his partner, Mike, and get on the road as early as possible. When he went downstairs, he was hoping to see Gloria—he loved how vibrant she was, and her smile filled the room with joy—but she was not in the kitchen. Instead, Lily, still in her nightgown, was waiting for him with a simple breakfast of toast and coffee. Joe sat down at the table. He never liked to talk much when he had to get up early for work. So, he sat quietly and ate quickly. Then he planted a passionless kiss on Lily's lips and said, "I'll see you next week," as he walked out the front door.

When Joe was gone, Lily brought her fingers to her lips. *He seems so distracted lately. He has never kissed me like that. So emotionless, and he kept looking at Gloria's door. It was like he was hoping she would come out of her room before he left,* Lily thought to herself, a cold weight settling in her chest.

The automobile rumbled north toward Canada, both men silent in the gray morning light. Neither Joe nor Mike had much appetite for conversation as the miles rolled past. It wasn't until they pulled over for lunch, unwrapping the sandwiches that they had packed, that Joe finally broke the quiet. "Say, I never asked you, I know you have your side thing, but—are you married, Mike?"

"Nope. I was, but not no more. I got out of it last year. Got me a divorce. Cost a little bit of money for a lawyer, but it turned out to be the best thing I ever did," Mike said.

"I don't want a divorce. I love my kid. I gotta admit, I love my wife, too. But... Well, did you ever feel like you were bored with just having sex with one woman? Did you ever feel like you needed a little bit of variety?"

"Sure, all men need variety." Mike chuckled, winking at Joe.

"Not women, though. They're not like that," Joe said, unsure about the truth of this generalization.

"No, they're not like that at all. They can sleep with one man for the rest of their lives and never get tired of him. Sometimes they hold on so tight a fella can't breathe. They suck the life outta ya. You know what I mean? Anyway, it just ain't like that for a fella. Us fellas see a skirt twitching and we gotta find out what's under it." He laughed. "Right?"

Joe nodded. He trusted Mike and felt comfortable admitting to him that he couldn't be faithful for the rest of his life. Besides, he thought Mike probably knew a lot about women, so it made him feel good and secure to hear Mike say that. "My wife just hired this young nanny. She's a real looker. I mean, she's something, if you know what I'm saying? Anyway, here's this gorgeous broad living right under my roof. And when I saw her for the first time yesterday, I just... well, you know."

"So, you already did it?" Mike asked.

"No, but I want to," Joe replied.

"Sure you do. But you know the old saying, right?"

"Which saying? I know plenty of them." Joe laughed.

"Yeah? Well, I'm sure you've heard this one. It goes like this: 'you don't crap where you eat.' Find another girl who makes your pecker dance. Find her far away from your house, far away from your wife and kid," Mike said before taking another bite of his sandwich. "When we get back to New York after we deliver the booze, let's check into a hotel. Then we'll go to one of the speakeasies I know of and see what kind of girls we can find," Mike then suggested. "It'll be perfect because your wife won't even know you're back in town. Just take a few days for yourself. Heck, you deserve it. You work hard. And I'm sure she doesn't think twice about spending the money you make now, does she?"

"No, she sure doesn't. Just like all women, my wife sure can spend," Joe said, shaking his head.

"So, you owe it to yourself. When we get back you really oughta take some time for you. Do what you need to do."

Joe welcomed the idea of time away from his family, even as a flicker of guilt nagged at him. His memory drifted back to his days as a soldier—the jingle of coins in his pocket, the thrill of anonymous encounters in strange beds. He pushed away the image of Lily at home with Mimi; this could just be a bit of harmless fun if he was careful. No one needed to get hurt. As long as he played it smart and didn't get caught, he could keep his family intact while tasting freedom again.

TWENTY-EIGHT

Once Joe and Mike returned from Canada and dropped off the illegal whiskey at the hidden warehouse in New York, they were free of responsibilities until the next job. They left the company truck at the warehouse and got into Mike's car.

"I know where we can get a cheap room right here in town," Mike said. "We can grab a few hours of sleep before nightfall. Then we'll go out drinking. There should be plenty of loose women at the speakeasy. There always are." He smiled at Joe. "We'll give 'em fake names. That way after we leave them, the gals will never be able to find us again."

Joe knew he should feel guilty about his plans with Mike, but this wasn't the first time he had been unfaithful during his marriage. He'd had lots of quick indiscretions. He had a couple girlfriends from when he would visit Canada, but he had never gone out specifically looking for women: quick, uninvolved sexual encounters seemed safe to him. But this thing that Mike was proposing was even safer. The women he would meet and sleep with would never even know his real name. They would not have dangerous husbands who worked with Joe either. He felt certain that whatever he did over the next few days could never come back to haunt him.

Joe and Mike checked into the hotel that Mike had suggested. The room had two small beds where they both collapsed and took a long nap. They always had to stay awake for days when they were making a run and needed to catch up on sleep when a job had been completed.

It was nightfall when they both stirred awake. Still sleepy, they both went down the hall and showered. Joe had been so tired when they had arrived at the hotel that he had not noticed how dirty the room was. But now he saw the spiderwebs on the ceiling and the ground-in dirt on the floors. The sheets had undefinable stains that made him cringe.

Mike didn't seem bothered by any of it. "You hungry?" he asked Joe.

"Yeah. Very," Joe said.

"Good, me too."

They went downstairs to a small diner with sticky tablecloths that looked like they could use washing. Mike ordered eggs, bacon, and toast. Joe decided to do the same. But when the meal arrived, Joe was keenly aware that it was not nearly as good as the food Lily prepared for him. And even though he'd slept well, he knew that the bed in this hotel was lumpy and not as soft as his bed at home. But Joe longed to feel the wings of his freedom and so, instead of going home, he followed Mike to a speakeasy. It was in the basement of a pharmacy. Tables and chairs had been set up in a dark room that reeked of cigarette smoke. A small band was playing jazz music, and several couples danced on a small dance floor.

"Sit down, I'll get us both a whiskey," Mike said.

Joe found a table at the back of the room where he sat down and waited in the dark for Mike.

"Here you go. This right here is the fruit of our labor," Mike said proudly, placing two cut-glass tumblers on the table.

"You mean this place buys their alcohol from our boss?"

"Yep, most of these speakeasies do. They have to. Our boss demands it. When they try to refuse, we shake 'em down until they realize it's in their best interest to buy from us."

"What do you mean, 'shake 'em down'?"

"I know the boss likes to keep all aspects of his business separate. Something about control. And I know you haven't been on this side of the business yet, but you know what I mean. Anyway, I used to do that job. But then I got into some trouble with the law and the boss changed me from hit man to running the whiskey."

"I still don't know what you mean by shake down."

"Yeah, well, when we found a speakeasy who wasn't buying their stuff from us, I'd go in with a couple of other fellas and we'd ask the owner where he bought his alcohol. It didn't matter how he answered. If the owner wasn't buying from us, then he wasn't buying from the right place. So, me and the other fellas would just tell that owner that from now on he was going to buy from us. We were fair. We always gave them a decent price. And, for the most part, it was an easy job because usually they were too scared to argue. But the ones that told us that they were loyal to their current suppliers and had no intentions of switching to us, well, we'd knock some sense into them."

"What do you mean? You mean you beat them up?"

"Yeah, until they saw things our way. If you know what I mean."

Joe nodded. "Yeah, I know what you mean."

"That's why the boss is so rich, because everyone buys their stuff from him. They have to: they have no choice."

"Pretty smart business," Joe said, sipping his whiskey.

"Yeah, it is. The boss is a smart fella. For the most part,

anyway," Mike said, downing his glass of whiskey in a single gulp. "Ready for another?"

"Sure." Joe emptied his glass.

Mike motioned to a hard-looking woman wearing a low-cut dress that was overly adorned with fake pearls, "Honey, can you get us two whiskeys? Tell the bartender that it's for Mike and his buddy. There should be no charge."

"Sure," the woman said.

"They don't charge you?" Joe asked Mike, clearly impressed by his partner's status in the speakeasy.

"We're important men, you and me. We work for the Stilata family. Everyone bows down to the don of the Stilata family."

"I like that," Joe said.

Mike was scanning the room. "There's a couple of girls over there. I gotta admit, they're not gorgeous. We can either go to another speakeasy and check out the girls there or we can make this easy and take what we can get for the night. Look at those two broads and tell me what you want to do."

Joe glanced over to where Mike was pointing. He caught the gaze of two women wearing too much black makeup around their eyes and very red lipstick. They both smiled. Their dark hair was bobbed and their flashy dresses looked cheap.

"What do you say? Should we offer to buy them drinks? Or go to another place? Personally, I'd rather stay. Who knows what we'll find at the other places? Anyway, it doesn't cost us anything to send them drinks."

"Sure, let's stay here," Joe said, not wanting to disappoint Mike. But he wasn't attracted to either of the girls at that table. In fact, he wanted to go home. Joe was still tired and the food he had eaten at the cheap restaurant earlier that night had upset his stomach.

"Waitress," Mike called out. The waitress came to the table. "See them two girls over there? Tell them that me and my friend want to buy them drinks."

The waitress nodded. "Sure, Mikey. I'll do it right away," she said.

Joe watched the waitress as she walked over to the table where the girls were sitting. He couldn't hear what she was saying but he saw both girls glance at Mike and himself. They giggled and nodded their heads.

"Let's go to their table. They like us," Mike said, already half-rising from his seat with an eager grin.

Joe followed, noting how the prettier of the two women tracked his movement with dark, inviting eyes.

"Hello," Mike said, swaying slightly as he reached their table.

"Hello," one girl answered, while her friend's red-painted lips curved into a slow smile aimed directly at Joe.

"Mind if we join you ladies?" Mike's hand rested on an empty chair.

"Yeah, sure." The second girl shifted over to make room, her perfume heavy in the air between them.

Mike nodded to Joe and they both pulled chairs up to the table just as the waitress arrived with four glasses of whiskey.

"I'm Frank, and this is my buddy, Hank."

Frank and Hank? Joe almost laughed out loud. Mike's choice of rhyming names combined with the strong alcohol made him feel silly. *These girls can't be so stupid as to believe that these names are our real names, can they?* But if the girls doubted Mike's honesty, they never let on.

"I'm Sally, and this here is Betty."

"It's real nice to meet you both," Mike said, smiling.

"Likewise," Sally said. In the light of the single candle on the table, Joe could see that Sally was batting her overly mascaraed eyelashes.

Mike and the girls talked and made stupid jokes that soon started to annoy Joe. They drank what seemed like endless shots of whiskey until Joe's watch read two in the morning. He rubbed his eyes, feeling tired. Heavy smoke from cigars and cigarettes filled the small room; it made it hard to breathe and irritated his eyes. He wondered why he had gone out looking for women with Mike in the first place. This night on the town was supposed to make him feel young and free, but all it had done was make him yearn to be at home with Lily and Mimi. He couldn't leave now though. If he did, Mike would be angry with him, because if he left, the girls might decide to go, too. Joe couldn't bear another minute in this place. "Are you girls hungry?" he asked.

"Yes, actually, I am," Sally said. "I'm starving."

"Me too," Betty chipped in.

"Let's go get some food," Joe said. Mike nodded. He looked annoyed with Joe and Joe knew why. Mike didn't want to go and eat. He wanted to take Sally and Betty up to that dirty room. But Joe needed some coffee and some food to wake him up if he was going to go through with the rest of their plans.

He helped Sally with her coat and then the four of them walked across the street to an all-night diner. It was a sleazy neighborhood and the diner was no exception. They sat at a booth in the back and ordered fried eggs and toast. It had been a long day for Joe. Now, sitting across from Sally and Betty in the bright light of the restaurant, he noticed how lined the women's faces were and how hard their eyes looked. He realized that they were older than he had originally thought in the dark, forgiving light at the speakeasy.

After they had finished eating, Mike suggested they all go back to the room he and Joe had rented. "We have a bottle of whiskey up in our room and we can all have a quick drink before we call it a night," he told the girls. They agreed immediately. Mike winked at Joe. The four of them walked across the street into the lobby of the hotel and upstairs into the room.

Sally began to kiss Joe as soon as the door closed and the sour taste of old liquor on her breath made him sick to his stomach. *What a damn mistake,* Joe thought, watching Mike's hands roam over Betty's grimy slip. *I let myself get talked into this, hoping it would kill this thing I'm feeling for Gloria.* He shifted uncomfortably on the bed, the sour smell of Sally's sweat mixing with her cheap perfume making his stomach turn. Mike had an excuse—he was single, free to chase whatever pleasure he could find in places like this. But Joe had Lily at home, beautiful and loyal, and here he was in this filthy room with a woman who repulsed him.

His heart clenched with a moment of clarity—he did love Lily. But that old restlessness was eating at him again. Yet lying here with Sally, his body refused to respond to her practiced touches. This sad encounter was nothing like the forbidden scenarios he had been imagining with Gloria.

"I'm sorry," he muttered, turning away from Sally's disappointed face. "Long day. I can't... not tonight. Maybe some other time." Even as he said it, he knew he wouldn't be back.

"It isn't my fault. I did everything I could do to get you hard. You're the one who can't go through with it, so I still expect to get paid for tonight," Sally said.

"Sure, of course."

They lay side by side in bed, barely touching, while waiting for Mike and Betty to finish.

Joe listened to Mike grunting and he was repulsed. He turned on his side, facing away from all of them, and stared at the wall. He could not wait for this horrible night to be over.

Joe woke with a start, his head pounding. Sally's thunderous snoring filled the room. Across the way, Mike and Betty were sprawled on the other bed. *Christ, what an idiot I am, falling asleep with a whore in the room. All that money from today's run...*

He checked his pocket, sighing with relief when he found

the cash still there. He shook Mike awake. "Let's get them out of here before they rob us blind."

After they had paid the women and sent them on their way, Joe fell back into a deep sleep. It seemed only minutes later when Mike was shaking him awake.

"Get up, Joe. The door was open when I woke up. All our money's gone—yours, too. I checked. Those broads must've stolen the room key and came back while we were out cold."

Joe's stomach dropped as he verified his empty pockets. A week's pay gone, including what they owed the boss.

"How we gonna pay the boss?" Joe asked.

Mike wouldn't meet his eyes. "You're the one who handles the money. You'll have to figure something out."

"You're not gonna help?"

"I'll help you pay it back," Mike said, but they both knew it was a lie.

Joe watched Mike drive away, sick with the knowledge of what the boss would do to someone who couldn't pay up.

Mike pulled away from the warehouse. Once he was certain Joe was nowhere in sight, he stopped and pulled a wad of bills from a hidden pouch sewn into the leg of his pants. He counted the money—their salaries and the boss's take, all intact except for the two dollars they had paid the prostitutes. *Poor dumb bastard,* he thought, *believing those girls would have the sense to come back and rob us. He'll learn the hard way you can't trust anyone in this business—if he survives not being able to pay the boss.*

TWENTY-NINE

When Joe arrived home, Gloria was in the front yard playing ball with the children. Her maple-colored hair was highlighted by the sun, and she looked carefree and beautiful. He stood watching her for a few minutes before he entered the house. It was quiet—Lily was probably resting upstairs. A flicker of guilt crossed his mind at the thought of his exhausted wife, her body strained by pregnancy. But the feeling passed quickly. He was hungry and needed a shower—everything else could wait. He could still smell Sally's strong perfume, and he longed to rid himself of that putrid odor before his wife caught a whiff of it and he had to explain.

As Joe let the hot water run over his body, he thought about the money he owed to the boss—Salvatore would be expecting him to deliver it by the end of the week. Joe silently cursed Mike for putting all this on his shoulders. Men who worked for the mob had been killed for less and he knew had to find a way to pay. Joe closed his eyes and let the water run over his face and hair.

After a long hot shower, Joe put on the smoking jacket he had purchased for himself after his first meeting with the boss of the syndicate, who had been wearing a smoking jacket. Then he went downstairs to see if he might catch another glimpse of Gloria. She was still outside playing with the children, her laughter as sweet as church bells and her smile contagious. Joe watched her longingly.

"She's so good with Mimi, isn't she?" Lily said as she walked into the kitchen. "How was your trip?" Her pregnancy had changed her, made her move differently. As Joe looked at Lily, he felt his old restlessness stirring. Gloria's fresh youth and energy called to something in him, made him forget the haunting shadows of war. Made him wish for different choices, different freedoms.

But panic gnawed beneath his wandering thoughts. The boss would be expecting his money and Joe had nothing to give him. He had seen what happened to men who couldn't pay up.

Once Lily had left the kitchen to join Gloria and the children outside, Joe slipped into the bedroom and went into his wife's jewelry box. He knew that her mother had given her an heirloom—a pin shaped like a rose, filled with large diamonds and emeralds. She never wore it, too afraid of losing it. He found it and stuffed it into his pocket. Tomorrow he would tell Lily that he had been robbed on this run and needed to pawn her pin to pay the boss. He would explain that his life was at stake and, although she might cry, she would insist that he sell it.

THIRTY

That night after dinner, Gloria gave the children their baths and put them to bed. Once the children were settled in their rooms, Lily said, "I'm going to bed, too," trying to stifle a yawn. "I've been so tired lately. I can't remember if I was this exhausted when I was carrying Mimi or not."

"You need your rest," Gloria said warmly. "I'm going to bed soon, too."

After Lily had left, Gloria felt Joe's eyes on her as she thumbed through a German cookbook.

She kept her eyes on the page, trying to look casual. Joe made her nervous. "What are you looking for? A special recipe?"

"Just something special that reminds me of my mom, today would've been her birthday. So, hopefully I can prepare something that the family will enjoy," Gloria said.

"I'm sure anything you prepare would be wonderful," Joe replied, gazing intently at Gloria.

Something in his tone made her skin prickle.

"Oh, that's not true. I've made plenty of meals that haven't worked out. Some, I'm ashamed to admit, were inedible. But now that I'm working here, I don't dare waste a morsel of food. So, I'm trying to find recipes I can trust."

"Lily is very pleased with you," he said, his voice dropping lower. "And... so am I. You sure are good with Mimi."

"I love kids. I always have." Gloria's fingers tightened on the cookbook. "And Lily is a wonderful person. I couldn't be more grateful to her."

"And..." Joe paused meaningfully. "What about me?"

Her stomach clenched. "I'm sorry?"

"Aren't you grateful to me? I mean, Lily may have hired you, but it's me who pays you. Lily doesn't have any money. The money is mine."

"Well, yes, of course I'm grateful." Gloria closed the cookbook, her hands trembling slightly.

"Why don't you show me just how grateful you are?"

Cold fear slid down her spine. "I don't understand. It's getting late and I should be going to bed." She struggled to keep her voice steady. "Goodnight, sir."

Gloria forced herself to walk normally up the stairs, feeling Joe's eyes on her back, grateful that Nick would be waiting in their room. But even as she climbed, dread settled in her stomach. She needed this job desperately—but at what cost?

THIRTY-ONE

Gloria lay in bed, her heart beating wildly. The fact that Lily's husband was showing her all this unwanted attention was the worst thing that could happen. Everything had been going so well since she met Lily. It felt more like they were good friends rather than employer and employee. Mimi was a delightful child and she adored her, as did Nick. In fact, she had never seen Nick so protective of anyone or anything in the way he was with Mimi. And finally, and most importantly, she no longer needed to worry about how she was going to feed her little boy. She knew that as long as they were living under Lily's roof, neither she nor Nick would go to bed hungry. Their room was warm, clean, and comfortable. It was the nicest place she'd ever lived.

Why did this man have to come home and try to ruin this for me? Gloria sighed. She knew men like him. Men who only cared about their own needs. *If I can do one good thing while I'm on this earth, it will be to teach my son to treat women better than I have been treated,* she thought.

Her mind drifted back to the beginning of her relationship

with Nick's father, Lenny. He was the first boy she had ever been out with. They met at a neighborhood dance. Lenny was a bit of a rebel. Everyone knew he gave the teachers a hard time and they said it was because he was very smart. He was wildly handsome with uncombed, wavy black hair and dark brooding eyes. Even though he was only two years her senior, he already seemed to be knowledgeable in the ways of the world. Rumors had been going around that he had had an affair with one of their teachers. Gloria didn't know if it was true. But she knew that the girls in her class swooned when he walked into a room.

When Lenny arrived at the dance the mood changed, and Gloria could feel it almost immediately. Her female classmates began to giggle and whisper. She caught them smiling at him and looking coy. Gloria wished she could somehow get his attention, but she didn't know how to look coy or flirt. Her mother, who was a strict Catholic, had raised Gloria and her sister to be modest and respectful. And Gloria had always listened to her mother. But that night was the first dance she and her sister had ever attended, and she wanted so much to fit in with the other girls. To Gloria they looked grown up while she looked childish in her simple pink dress. Yet when Lenny saw her, he turned all the way around to look her over from head to toe. By the time his eyes met hers, she was blushing so hard that she had to turn away. When she looked back to where he had been standing, he was gone.

Unlike Gloria, who had always been shy, her older sister Joan was popular with the other girls in their school. Girls liked Joan, and even though she was not permitted to dress like them or to wear makeup, she was allowed to join their clique. When Gloria asked Joan what her secret was— how she made and kept so many girlfriends—Joan laughed and said, "I don't look like you. You're gorgeous and they're all jealous. The boys all want to go out with you. I'm just an ordinary girl. They feel safe around me. They know their boyfriends won't be interested in me."

Gloria walked to the back of the room where a row of chairs had been set up and she sat down. She knew that this area of the dance was designated as the place for wallflowers: girls no one wanted to dance with. As Gloria sat staring at her shoes and waiting for the awkward evening to end, someone walked over and said, "Hello." It was a male voice. When she looked up and saw Lenny, her heart skipped a beat. He was standing right in front of her looking more handsome than she had ever imagined any man could look.

"Hi," she managed to stammer.

"I'm Lenny," he said confidently.

Gloria nodded, her heart fluttering. Everyone knew Lenny —the most handsome boy in school. When he asked her to dance, she nearly refused out of shyness, but something in his gentle persistence made her take his hand.

In his arms, Gloria felt herself transformed. He guided her gracefully around the floor, and when other girls from her class shot envious glances their way, she felt a flash of pride that she had never known before. Joan watched from across the room, her lips pressed thin with displeasure.

"Can I walk you home?" Lenny asked Gloria when the band played their last song.

Joan interrupted before Gloria could answer. "We need to get back before our parents start to worry."

But Lenny would not be deterred. He walked them both home, answering Joan's questions politely but keeping his attention fixed on Gloria. For the first time in her life, Gloria wasn't in her sister's shadow.

Before she met Lenny, Gloria had sometimes dreamed about the man she might someday marry, but never in her wildest imagination had she believed he would look like a

Hollywood movie star. She had always assumed that he would be a calm, studious boy who enjoyed books and quiet times the way she did.

When they turned the corner to the street where Gloria lived, she felt ashamed of her home. The buildings in her neighborhood were run-down. Clothing hung on lines outside tenement windows. She wondered where Lenny lived and whether he came from a better neighborhood or if he was just as poor as she was. Then she stole a glance at his clothes. *I don't see any fraying on the sleeves of his shirt or his suit jacket, and his suit fits him well, so it's probably not his father's, she thought. I'll bet he's not as poor as we are. I'm sure that now he sees where I live, he's going to lose interest in me.*

"Well, we're going to have to say goodbye to you here," Joan said when they were a few buildings away from their home. "If our parents look out the window and see us with a boy then we'll be in trouble."

"Sure. I can understand that," Lenny said with a smile and then he stopped and gently held Gloria's upper arm so that she would stop walking, too. Lenny turned her around to look at him. "Can I take you for an ice cream or a soda sometime?" he asked.

"Yes, I'd like that," Gloria said, feeling her heart flutter. Then she caught a glimpse of Joan's face. Her lips were pursed like she had just eaten a dozen raw lemons.

"Ma and Pa won't like it," Joan tutted.

"Well, maybe you could cover for your sister. I bet she'd do it for you," Lenny said, winking at Joan.

Joan gave him a look of disgust. "I suppose I could," she said.

"Oh, Joan. Thanks so much," Gloria said. She hadn't meant to gush, but the words just came flooding out.

Over the next few weeks, Lenny waited for Gloria after school each day, carrying her books and treating her to ice cream—a luxury she had never known growing up poor. The contrast between their worlds became clear when she saw his family's house, so different from her tenement building with its laundry lines and crumbling stairs. But Lenny made her feel like none of that mattered.

He showered her with attention and poetry about her beauty, took her to restaurants where he insisted that she order anything she wanted. Gloria had never felt so special, so cherished.

"I'd love to sit outside all night with you and count the stars," he said to Gloria one evening as they walked together. Joan had promised to cover for her again.

"Can you imagine?" she giggled. "My folks would kill me if I didn't come home."

"Yeah, but it would be real special, don't you think?"

"I do," she agreed.

"Yeah, me too." He smiled wistfully. "How many stars do you think we could count?"

"I don't know," Gloria replied, "the sky is full of them."

"If we stayed out here counting stars we could watch the sunrise. Have you ever watched the sunrise with anyone?"

"Me?" she asked, shocked. And then she laughed. "Never."

"Have you ever seen the sunrise at all?"

"Nope. I can't say that I have," she admitted.

"Well, I have and it sure is special. You know what? I'd love to see the first sunlight of the day shining in your beautiful eyes," Lenny said, looking at Gloria with a longing stare.

"You say the sweetest things."

"You inspire me to say beautiful things, because you're the prettiest girl I've ever seen."

Gloria looked down at the ground, a little embarrassed and shy but overwhelmed by Lenny's flattery. Not knowing what to say, she stayed silent, but her heart was soaring like a tiny bird through the clouds.

Looking back now, she could not pinpoint exactly when things changed—when the restaurant dates became hurried afternoons in his empty house, when his sweet words became demands. She had been too in love to see the shift, too eager to believe his unspoken promises of forever.

THIRTY-TWO

Even now, Gloria couldn't remember how she had ended up on the sofa in the living room of Lenny's house with her dress unbuttoned and her panties removed. It wasn't that he lied. He never actually said he was planning to marry her. However, he led her to believe that was the direction in which their relationship was headed. It was the unspoken words that she thought she heard, or wanted to hear anyway, that made her believe that someday she would be Lenny's wife. Lenny constantly told her that she was beautiful and he worshipped her porcelain-like skin and the soft waves in her hair. He said that her eyes glittered like topaz. Gloria had never seen topaz, but from the way Lenny said it, she knew it was a beautiful stone. *Ahh, Lenny,* she thought to herself. *He could be so convincing.* It had been so easy to fall in love with him and so easy to believe he was falling in love, too.

After the first time Gloria and Lenny were intimate, it seemed to be the only thing they ever did together. After school they rushed to his house. His parents were always out during the day. The maid was there, and Gloria was concerned about her telling Lenny's parents that they were in his bedroom with the door locked. But when she asked Lenny about it, he just laughed. "She'll never say a word. Don't worry about her."

So, Gloria didn't worry. She was too much in love to worry. And she loved lying naked beside Lenny in his bed every golden afternoon. She missed their weekly trips to the ice-cream parlor, and she would have loved for him to take her out for dinner again, but they never left his bed anymore. This went on for two months and during that time Gloria lived in a rose-colored bubble.

When Gloria missed her monthly cycle, she wasn't immediately afraid. Somehow, in her youthful innocence, she thought that Lenny would be happy about the baby. But his handsome face twisted with anger at her news.

"Are you sure it's mine?" Lenny's cruel words cut deeper than any physical blow.

"Of course it's yours! You know I was... you were my first."

He stopped meeting her after school. She waited an hour each day for a week before accepting the truth—he wasn't coming back.

By her fifth month, when her mother's eyes narrowed at her growing belly, Gloria knew she couldn't stay home. She packed a bag that night and walked until morning, finally gathering the courage to knock on Lenny's door.

His father received her in their elegant living room, smoking an expensive cigar while Lenny stood at the window, refusing to face her. They offered money—enough to "take care of it," they said. Gloria clutched her belly protectively. "This child is a gift from God," she whispered, but Lenny never turned around.

She took their money—she had no choice—but not for what they intended. In a distant neighborhood, she found a tiny room and work at a factory, hiding her pregnancy as long as she could. At first, she felt so alone. It was so quiet living by herself. She missed her home and her family, but she knew her parents would never allow her to return and so she decided to make the best of her new life. Not many of the other girls in the factory where she worked were willing to befriend her when they discovered that she was pregnant and unmarried. But she held her head high and forced herself to get up and go to work every day.

After Nick was born, Gloria scraped by on factory wages and determination until the day she met Lily. When Lily offered her the opportunity to be Mimi's nanny, Gloria was thrilled. That first night in Lily's house, kneeling beside Nick's bed in their clean, warm room, she had wept with gratitude. Finally, a real home, a chance to give her son the life he deserved. But now, watching Joe's eyes follow her through the house, she felt that old familiar dread. She wouldn't let another man's desires destroy everything that she had fought so hard to build. She couldn't—not with Nick's future at stake.

THIRTY-THREE

The following morning, Gloria got up early and prepared a breakfast of porridge for everyone. After the children finished eating and while Lily was showering, Gloria helped them to get dressed for a trip to the park. Just as she was 'laying out their clothes, Joe strolled into Gloria and Nick's room. "Where are all of you going so early in the morning?" he asked.

"I'm going to take the children out to the park so they can get some fresh air," Gloria said, nervously walking into the hall, trying to lead Joe out of their room.

"You look divine today," he replied, smiling.

Gloria shook her head. "Please don't," she said sharply, stilling the anxiety brewing inside her. "I'm very happy working here. I'm not looking for trouble. I need this job."

"Oh my goodness." He smirked. "What makes you think you're going to lose your job? I'm the man of the house here. I decide who stays and who goes. And I have no intention of firing you."

"I don't want to get involved with you, sir. I like Lily very much. I would never want to do anything that would hurt her.

Please try to understand," Gloria whispered, worried that Lily or the children would hear their conversation.

"What she doesn't know won't hurt her," Joe said, winking coyly.

"I'm sorry but I must make this clear to you. I am not going to get involved with you like this," Gloria said. Her voice was firm, but she was trembling.

"Then... I might just have to let you go," he said casually as he shook his head and smiled.

"Please, I need this job. I need a home for my son. I will do a good job for you. I will take good care of Mimi. I will love her like my own child. But I won't... I can't."

Joe's face darkened. "Then pack your things and get out. Take your kid and be gone before Lily finishes her shower. I'll tell her that you quit. I'll say you changed your mind about working here."

Gloria glared at him. She glanced back into the room at her son who was on the floor playing a game with Mimi. For the first time in a long time, he was so happy and healthy. And he had a playmate who he really liked. *Damn Joe. How could he be so despicable?* "Please?" she begged again. "Please just let me be."

"How about this? I'll give you a day to decide. You can either accept my invitation or go back to whatever hole you crawled out of."

Gloria couldn't lose this job. She just couldn't.

"You want to know what I see?" Joe said. "I see that you're attracted to me. I see it in your eyes."

She shook her head. *Whatever you think you see in my eyes is wrong,* she thought furiously. *I am not attracted to you. I hate you.*

"I'll give you a day to think it over." Joe leaned closer, his jaw tight, eyes cold. "Either you do whatever I ask and you and your brat get to stay here and live a good life. Or you keep your morals and you're back out on the street with a bad reference. I'll make sure that no one hires you." His lips curved into a cruel smile. "You choose." He straightened up, slowly adjusting his tie before striding from the room.

"Mommy, are we going to the park?" Nick asked.

"Yes, of course we are," Gloria said as brightly as she could, but she was still shaking. She felt hot tears sting the back of her eyes, but she didn't want Nick to see her crying. He always got so upset when she cried. Gloria managed to smile at her son. "Alright. We're ready to go. Come on, Mimi," Gloria said, extending her hand to the little girl. Mimi slipped her fingers into Gloria's grasp while Nick reached for her other hand; they formed a small chain as they walked. She smiled at her son and the three of them went out the front door.

The children played at the park until it was almost lunch time. It was a quarter to twelve when Nick walked over to Gloria and said, "I'm hungry."

Those words had always struck fear in Gloria's heart. That was, until now. Now, it felt so good to Gloria to know that when they got back to the house there would be food for the children. But at the same time, Joe's words were haunting her and making her miserable. She knew that if she wanted to take care of her son properly, she had no choice but to give in to Joe. If she didn't, she and Nick would be back in a dirty one-room flat in a rough part of town. And she would be scrounging for work that paid enough for her to pay her bills and feed her child. If either of them got sick and needed a doctor, there would never be enough money to spare. The very thought of that made her shiver. But Gloria really liked Lily, and she didn't want to betray her.

. . .

The following day Gloria didn't see Joe at all. She was hopeful that he had gotten busy with work. Perhaps he'd decided to let his pursuit of her go. But that night she was woken by a presence in her room. She opened her eyes and was alarmed to find Joe standing over her.

"So, what did you decide?" he whispered menacingly.

Nick was sound asleep beside her. Gloria's heart beat wildly.

"My answer is yes. I'll do what you want. But not here. Not in this room with my son asleep beside me." Gloria felt disgusted at the words she uttered.

"I'll rent a room in a hotel. I'll tell Lily that you deserve at least one day off every week. On your day off you'll come and meet me in that room I rent."

"What about Nick?" she asked.

"Tell Lily that you have to leave Nick with her for a few hours. She won't care. She loves kids."

You are a louse. A good-for-nothing louse. No better than a cockroach, Gloria thought. *You have a good wife. She is kind, loving, and beautiful—yet you still want something more. Something different. You don't care whose life you ruin. You don't care who you hurt.*

"Alright. Just let me know where to go and when," she said coldly.

"You're going to like it. You're going to like me," Joe said, smiling.

Gloria said nothing.

His voice was heavy with desire. "I can make life very comfortable for you and your son. I earn a good living, as you can see. So, a few extra dollars for you each week won't affect me at all."

"Thank you," Gloria said, trying to sound calm. But her heart was racing and she could hardly bear to look at him. "Please, can I ask you for a favor?"

"Oh." He smiled. "A favor? You have a favor to ask of me?"

"I need you to be very careful, because I just can't get pregnant again. Please, can you make sure I don't?"

"Sure, doll, anything you say."

After Joe left the room, Gloria lay beside her son trembling.

THIRTY-FOUR

Joe had been so consumed with thoughts of Gloria that the mob debt had slipped his mind. Until Zeb appeared at his door the next day. One look at the hitman's familiar face snapped Joe back to reality—and to what happened to men who couldn't pay.

"So, Joseph." Zeb dragged a chair across the floor with deliberate slowness, the scraping sound like nails on wood. He settled himself at the dining-room table, adjusting his suit jacket to reveal the telltale bulge beneath. "Boss had to interrupt my day off to send me here. Real inconvenient, if you know what I mean." His dead-eyed smile never reached his eyes. "Seems there's some confusion about the money from your last run."

"It was a mistake. I forgot. I've been real busy, but I promise you, I'll get it in today." Joe was flustered, beads of sweat beginning to form on his forehead. He knew that the boss took loyalty seriously and he had heard that men could be killed for such an oversight. For a moment he thought about telling Zeb the truth about what happened. But he could not trust that Zeb would not shoot him for being careless. *No, I can't tell him what Mike and I did,* Joe decided. *It's better if I just sell the pin and give the boss the money.*

"I'm going to give you the benefit of the doubt. Don't make me sorry that I did. You know what I'm saying?" Zeb narrowed his eyes at Joe.

"Yes, I know. I know exactly what you're saying. And I promise I'll take care of it today, Zeb."

"No need to show me out, Joe," Zeb said with a wink. He got up and walked to the door before pausing to turn and look at Joe.

Joe felt the hair on the back of his neck stand straight up.

"It was nice to see you again, Joe," Zeb said. "Let's hope you do what you're supposed to do, so I don't have to come back and visit you in a couple of days."

With a shaking hand Joe locked the door behind Zeb. Then he quickly stuffed the pin into the pocket of his pants and walked out the door.

The pawn shop was about a half-hour drive away in a much less affluent neighborhood. Joe drove there as quickly as he could. He had meant to tell Lily but hadn't found the right time. The pawnbroker was a heavyset man with unruly auburn hair and squinty blue eyes who sat behind a window. "How can I help you?" he asked.

"I need to pawn this," Joe said, pulling the pin out of his pocket and handing it to the pawnbroker through the opening under the glass.

The pawnbroker looked at it under a loop, but his face gave no indication of how valuable the piece actually was.

"I'll give you five hundred dollars for it," he said flatly.

"Five hundred dollars? Are you nuts? That thing is full of diamonds and emeralds. It's worth about five thousand dollars," Joe protested.

"Five thousand dollars?" the pawnbroker repeated and huffed. "I'll give you two thousand."

Joe stood his ground firmly. "Five thousand dollars or I can go to the next pawn shop down the street."

The pawnbroker ran his fingers over his chin before saying, "Alright. You run a hard bargain but five thousand it is."

Joe knew from the pawnbroker's eager agreement that he had still undersold the pin, but he needed the money, and he needed it right now. So, he nodded as the pawnbroker counted out five thousand dollars in large bills. "All set," he said

Joe stuffed the cash in his pants pocket. Then he left and got into his automobile. He drove right to the mob boss's office. Still out of breath from nerves, he knocked on the door.

"Yeah," the boss said. "Who is it?"

"It's me, Joe."

"Come on in."

Joe walked into the office. He noticed a gun on the desk in front of the boss and a shiver ran down his spine. Without saying a word, Joe pulled the money out of his pocket and laid it on the table. "I'm sorry, I forgot to bring this in last week."

The boss didn't count the money, he just picked it up and put it into the drawer of his desk. He nodded. "You can go now, Joey," he said, a menacing smile fixed on his face.

Joe walked to his car, the immediate relief of survival already curdling into something darker. His hands clenched on the steering wheel. *Who does the boss think he is, sending some thug to threaten me?* he thought, enraged. *I'm the one taking all the risks while he sits safe behind his desk, counting the money that I bring him. Mike and me do all the real work.*

A smile tugged at Joe's mouth as an idea formed. *Maybe it's time the books showed a little less profit.* Whistling, he turned the key in the ignition, already planning his revenge.

THIRTY-FIVE

As far as Joe knew, Lily had not looked at that pin since they arrived in the United States. He had thought about selling it before, in the beginning, when they were struggling. But in those days, he had still been madly in love with her and he just couldn't ask her to give it up. Now, however, he had been forced to steal her pin and pawn it. If he didn't, it could have easily cost him his life.

The following day Joe received a call telling him he was scheduled to make another run at the end of the week. He had not been called to do another job since he had not paid the boss. *Well, at least he was back in the fold,* he thought.

The pin's absence gnawed at Lily like a physical ache. She had been thinking of her mother all morning, reading Chloe's latest letter until the paper was soft at the creases. Without conscious thought, she had reached for her jewelry box, wanting to hold that precious connection to home.

But the pin wasn't there.

She searched with increasing desperation—through drawers, under papers, behind boxes. Her hands trembled as she emptied the entire drawer onto her bed. Nothing.

When Joe came home that Monday, Lily could barely get the words out. "The pin... Maman's pin is missing."

Joe's face remained carefully blank. "Missing?"

"I don't care about its value." Lily's voice cracked. "I would never sell it. But it's all I have left of her, of home. My grandfather gave it to my grandmother when—"

"I'll bet you Gloria took it," Joe cut in quickly.

The suggestion hit Lily like a slap. "Gloria?" She shook her head. "I can't imagine—"

"Well, who else?" Joe's voice hardened. "Let's ask her."

When Gloria entered Joe's study, Lily saw fear flicker across the other woman's face.

"Did you take my wife's pin?" Joe demanded.

"No!" Gloria's eyes filled with tears. "Never. Not from Lily. Please, you have to believe me. Nick and I love it here, I would never do anything to betray your trust."

Lily watched Joe watching Gloria, something in his expression making her stomach clench. Lily assured Gloria that she believed her, and asked her to go check on the children.

Joe reached for Lily's hand, his touch too gentle. "Lil, I gotta tell you the truth."

The story spilled out—the robbery, the threat, the pawn shop. With each word, Lily felt something inside her crack and splinter along with a terrible wave of guilt. She remembered her mother's tears as she had pressed the pin into her hands that last day on the dock. "Never sell it," Chloe had whispered, "as long as you have it, you have a piece of home."

"Can you get it back?" Lily heard herself ask, her voice strange in her ears.

"I promise, I will." Joe replied, not meeting her eyes.

Lily moved like someone in a dream, retrieving the money her mother had given her—meant for emergencies, meant to buy a ticket home if America proved too harsh. She pressed it into Joe's hands, watching him pocket it without counting.

That night, alone in their bed, Lily touched the empty space on her dresser where the jewelry box sat. She thought of her mother across the ocean, waiting for the ticket that Joe kept promising to buy. Had she made a terrible mistake trusting her heart to a man who could steal the one thing he knew she held sacred?

When Joe brought his money to the boss that week, he learned that it was easy to steal from the mob. As long as he didn't get too greedy and take too much the boss didn't seem to notice. Then he had an idea. Joe went to the pawn shop and explained to the shop owner that the pin belonged to the mob boss, and the boss was looking for it.

He offered the money that Lily had given to him, and while it wasn't enough to cover the full cost of the pin, the pawn shop owner explained that he wanted no trouble with the mob and reluctantly returned the heirloom to Joe.

Joe came home with the pin, but he still felt guilty for stealing it and selling it in the first place. But he continued to justify his actions in his own mind and that made him feel that what he'd done was all right.

Joe knew that he had broken trust with Lily, but she never made him feel like it was his fault. And, for that, he was grateful. As a reward, he brought her flowers or candy whenever he went into the city. She smiled and thanked him each time he brought her a present. But she didn't seem to be too thrilled with his gifts.

When he asked her what he could do to make her happy, she told him that she was missing her mother terribly and she begged him to send money to her mother in France, so that Chloe could take a boat and come to America.

He promised he would, but he never did. And when Lily asked him about it, he always gave her an excuse as to why he could not spare the cash at that time. She didn't argue, and he thought it meant that she understood. But when he looked into her eyes, he could see that she was disappointed and unhappy.

So, he promised himself that eventually he would send for her mother. However, he was afraid of what Chloe would say when she found out what he was doing for work, and so he decided not to hurry and send for her.

Perhaps, he thought, he would get promoted eventually and be given a job that appeared at least outwardly respectable. Then he could send for Lily's mother. Just not now.

THIRTY-SIX

One morning as Gloria was busy serving coffee to Joe and Lily, Joe slipped a note into the pocket of her apron. Gloria's hand was trembling as she glanced over at Lily. Lily looked up and smiled at her. She was busy stirring milk into her coffee. *She is so kind and so trusting,* Gloria thought. *I hate what Joe is forcing me to do to her.*

Gloria went back into the kitchen and pulled the note out. On the paper Joe had written the name of a hotel, along with a date and a time. That was all it said but Gloria knew exactly what it meant. She quickly stuffed the paper back into her apron pocket and then she went to the stove and took a pan with steaming scrambled eggs off the burner and scooped the contents out onto a plate which she delivered to the table. *My son had eggs and toast with real butter this morning for breakfast. If I lose this job, I'll be lucky to afford to feed him day-old bread again. I have no choice but to do what Joe asks of me. I just have to remember that I'm doing what I must do for my child.*

Gloria hated Joe. She couldn't bear to look at him. She finished serving and then left Lily and Joe to eat. Once they were finished Gloria cleared the table and cleaned the kitchen while Mimi and Nick played in Mimi's room.

Lily went to her bedroom after breakfast. Then Joe stood up, stretched his legs and said he had to go out for a while. Gloria felt her shoulders relax as the front door clicked shut. She found the children in Mimi's room, sitting cross-legged on the floor, building a castle from bright blocks. Nick's face was intent with concentration as he helped Mimi balance another block on top. Gloria leaned against the doorframe, watching them, so absorbed in their play that she didn't notice Lily had entered the room.

"They get on so well, don't they?" Lily said, cradling her stomach with one hand and rubbing the small of her back with the other.

Gloria smiled in agreement, a sharp stab of anger washing over her when she thought of Joe and the destruction he was creating.

"I've been meaning to say, you should enroll Nick in school here. It'll be much closer for him and I can help you if you would like."

"That would be wonderful," Gloria said.

"We'll do it this afternoon. We can dress the children and take them with us to the school."

"I want you to know that I appreciate everything you're doing for Nick and I," Gloria said quietly.

"I'm happy to do it. I'm just glad I can help and you're doing so much for us," Lily said, squeezing Gloria's arm affectionately.

"Lily," Gloria said in a soft voice.

"Yes."

"I have something I must confess to you."

"Oh? What is it?" Lily asked. She was trembling, afraid that Gloria was going to tell her that she had fallen in love with Joe. She didn't want to hear what Gloria had to say. She longed to put it out of her mind and forget that Gloria had ever brought it up. But she knew she couldn't do that. She knew it would haunt her until she heard whatever it was that Gloria had to tell her. Lily took Gloria's hand and said, "It's alright. Just tell me. What is it, please?"

Gloria took a long deep breath—she wanted to tell Lily about what Joe was demanding of her, but she couldn't bring herself to do so. So, instead she addressed another issue she had been wanting to talk to Lily about. "I lied to you when we first met. I told you that Nick's father was dead. He isn't dead. And... we were never married. I was so ashamed. I thought that if you knew the truth you would think of me as a fallen woman and you wouldn't want me in your home. I hated lying to you. And I am sorry. I am so sorry. Can you forgive me?'

"Oh, Gloria, of course I can," Lily said, hugging her friend. "Don't even think about it. It's alright."

"You don't know how much I appreciate everything you have done for Nick and I. I've felt so terrible about lying to you."

"Don't even think about it anymore. Forget it ever happened," Lily said and both women smiled at each other.

As Gloria dressed both children, she thought about how much she hated Joe for forcing her to betray her best friend and she wished she could find a way to stop his advances but she didn't know what to do.

Once both children were dressed Gloria and Lily made their way to the school with Nick and Mimi in tow.

Lily was so helpful. She signed all the documents that permitted Nick to use her address to attend the school in her district. And the kinder Lily was, the more Gloria hated herself for what Joe was forcing her to do.

After they finished with all the paperwork and Nick was registered to start school at the beginning of the next semester, they left and began to walk towards home. "Shall we stop for some lunch?" Lily asked.

"At a restaurant?" Gloria asked. "With the children?"

"Sure, why not? The place I'm thinking of isn't fancy. It's just a small café." Lily smiled.

Nick had never eaten out and Gloria longed to let him experience going to a restaurant, so she agreed.

Lily led them to a small restaurant with only five tables. Nick took Mimi's hand and held it for a minute. "We're in a restaurant," he said excitedly. "We're eating out like grown-ups."

Lily settled Mimi in a chair beside Nick, and for a moment Gloria's throat tightened watching them together—these two children, this kind mother who had opened her home to strangers. When the steaming bowls of soup arrived, both children fell silent, breaking off pieces of bread to dip in their broth. Gloria caught Lily's eye across the table, saw such trust there that she had to look away. The warmth of the soup turned bitter in her mouth as she thought of Joe's ultimatum—of how she would have to betray this woman who had given them everything. Such a simple meal, but it felt like her last supper.

THIRTY-SEVEN

On the date that Joe requested that Gloria meet him at the hotel, Gloria said she needed to take care of some personal business and requested a few hours off. Lily didn't pry. She never asked a single question, and Gloria felt a sense of deep betrayal eat away at her as she shrugged on her coat and left the house.

The hotel where Gloria was to meet Joe was a little over a mile away from the house. It was cold outside. There was a layer of ice on the sidewalks and she had to take extra care not to fall. The walk seemed to take forever. Gloria was certain that Lily would not suspect anything even though she and Joe were both out of the house at the same time. Joe was always going somewhere, or so he said, for business. So Gloria knew that Lily would think her husband was out working. As she walked across the snow-covered ground, she cursed Joe, not only because he had the comfort of driving in a warm car, but because what he was forcing her to do was causing her to hate herself.

Gloria entered the hotel. She knew that no one was really watching her and yet she felt as if everyone she encountered was aware of the sin and betrayal she was about to commit. She stood in the lobby for several moments listening to her own heartbeat. *Lily has been so good to me. I wish I didn't have to do this,* Gloria thought as her heart raced. She forced herself to climb the stairs that led up to the room number Joe had written in his note. Gloria knocked softly on the door, hoping that Joe had changed his mind and would not answer, but he opened the door immediately.

"Hello there, gorgeous," he said. "It sure is good to see you. Don't stand out in the hall, come on in." He smiled warmly. "Would you like a drink? I brought a bottle for us."

Gloria nodded. Joe quickly poured two glasses of whiskey and handed her one. She drank the entire contents of the glass in a single swig. The alcohol burned her throat. And she didn't really like it, but it was a burn she felt she deserved and it dulled her senses. She needed to feel numb to complete this task. Joe didn't seem nervous at all. In fact, he didn't even seem to be thinking about betraying Lily. Gloria wondered how he could put his wife out of his mind so easily.

When Joe reached for Gloria, she winced. Her body tightened up. But Joe was so excited that he didn't seem to notice this either. He unbuttoned her dress and it fell off her shoulders. Although she had given birth to a child and was certainly no virgin, Gloria still felt shy and ashamed. He reached over and undid her bra. She looked down at the stained hardwood floor in the hotel room and felt like she might vomit. But Joe pulled her close to him and kissed her roughly. Gloria flinched.

"Why don't you like me?" Joe bristled, his face suddenly flaring with anger. "Most gals think I'm pretty handsome. If you give me a chance, you're going to find out that I'm an amazing lover."

Gloria suddenly felt deeply afraid of the man standing before her.

"It's Lily. She is like a sister to me. Don't you understand how I feel? She's been so kind to Nick and me that I find it hard to betray her like this." Gloria could barely speak.

"She'll never know, so she'll never feel betrayed," Joe replied casually. "You and I are the only two people who will ever know what happens here in this room. If neither of us tell her, Lily will never know."

He's a monster, Gloria thought, appalled by Joe's lack of guilt.

"Can we turn off the light please?" she asked.

"No, you're too pretty for that. I want to see you," Joe said, lifting her hair out of the way to kiss her neck. Then he gently pushed her onto the bed and reached his hand under her slip. Gloria shivered with disgust. She tried her best to think about something else, but it was almost impossible. Joe got up on his knees and unzipped his pants. Gloria tasted bitter bile as it rose in her throat.

She lay there stiff, trembling, and unyielding. If Joe noticed her resistance, he never let her know. He didn't make any attempt at further foreplay, he just entered her. His penis felt like an unwelcome foreign object inside her body. Gloria closed her eyes, not wanting to see his face. She forced herself to swallow the bile that continually rose in her throat. After what seemed like a lifetime, it was finally over. Joe climbed off her. Without a word he turned away from Gloria and faced the wall. A few minutes later she heard him snoring.

Gloria picked up her dress from the floor where Joe had discarded it and pulled it over her head. Then she took a comb out of her purse and ran it through her hair; she put on her lipstick without looking in the mirror. *I should check the mirror. I should make sure I look alright, but I don't think that I can stand to look at myself right now after what I just did.* She quietly opened the door and slipped out of the room and into the hallway. Joe was still asleep. A man wearing a well-made suit walked by. When Gloria crossed paths with him, they both turned away from each other. *He's ashamed of whatever he did, just like I am. This run-down old hotel is a place of shame. People come here and do things that they should not do. I am no better than he is.*

The air in the hotel corridor smelled musty like dirty clothes or unwashed bodies. Gloria walked down the stairs as quickly as she could and almost ran to the front door, flinging it open. Once she was outside, Gloria breathed deeply, sucking air into her lungs and attempting to rid herself of the smell of Joe that clung to her skin. As she began to walk back to Lily's house where her son waited, she tried to clear her head.

THIRTY-EIGHT

Joe did not return home that night, but Lily did not seem concerned. She just assumed he had gone to work. "I don't worry about him. He's done this before. Sometimes he goes off to work and forgets to tell me," Lily told Gloria. "He has a difficult job so I must try to be understanding. He'll be back home in a few days. A week at most."

Gloria smiled at Lily, but deep inside she was glad Joe did not come home. She dreaded seeing him and yet she knew she would have to eventually.

During the quiet days when Joe was away on business, Gloria found herself relaxing. Without his heavy presence in the house, laughter came easier. She and Lily would sit together while the children played, sharing stories and confidences like sisters. One afternoon, Lily pulled Gloria into her bedroom, eyes bright with mischief.

"Try these on," she insisted, pulling dresses from her closet. "You never know when you might want to catch someone's eye."

"How would I ever meet anyone? I'm always working," Gloria said softly. "But I don't mind. I'm content as I am."

"You never know," Lily teased. "Love can find you anywhere—the market, the park..."

"Those places are all mothers and children," Gloria said with a smile.

"Then take a day off! Go to a dance with friends. Life shouldn't be all work."

Gloria's chest tightened with affection and guilt. "I'm happy here," she said. "Nick has a real home now and Mimi's like a sister to him." She hesitated, then added quietly, "And you've become like a sister to me."

The words tasted like ash in her mouth, Joe's shadow falling across this precious friendship. Someday, Gloria promised herself, she would find a way to make this right.

THIRTY-NINE

Joe did not even stop to greet Lily or Gloria when he returned home the following week. He went right to his room, fell into bed, and slept until the next morning.

It was a beautiful day, the sun was bright, and the sky was blue and cloudless. Gloria and Lily were sitting in the garden. Nick was patiently showing Mimi how to use a small shovel to fill a bucket with dirt.

"Can I confide in you?" Lily turned to look at Gloria.

"Of course." Gloria smiled but she felt her lips quivering. She was afraid that somehow Lily knew what she had done with Joe. *Joe is not a good man and someday he's going to hurt Lily badly,* she thought. *Whether it's with me or someone else, he's going to destroy her and I can't stop it. But how can I tell Lily that? She is his wife.*

"I wish I could go home," Lily said wistfully.

"Home? Isn't this your home?" Gloria asked curiously.

"It's not my real home. Don't get me wrong, it's a lovely house. But Joe is so distant and difficult to be married to. Sometimes I feel so lonely and insignificant in his life. I wish I could visit Paris. I'd love to go home to my mother. I miss her terribly..."

Oh, Gloria." Lily's smile was sad. "Joe loves the idea of us more than the reality. When we met, he was so passionate, so sure. But men like Joe... they're like wild creatures. The moment you try to hold them, they slip away." She looked out at the flowers in the garden and traced a pattern on the tablecloth that lay on the outside table with her finger. "He says the words—that he loves me—but his eyes are always searching for something else. And watching him drift further away, I've felt my love for him fading, too."

Gloria could not look into Lily's eyes. She wanted to say, "I'm sorry." She wished she could unburden herself and tell Lily the truth. But she knew that she couldn't, so she sat next to Lily and took her hand to reassure her. Then she watched the branches of the weeping willow tree sway in the wind. They sat together in comfortable silence until Gloria said, "Perhaps you might consider going out with him, like on a date? It might be fun, especially before the new baby is born."

"Do you really think so?" Lily sounded so hopeful that Gloria almost started to cry. Instead, she bit her lower lip and squeezed Lily's hand. Gloria was praying that she was right—*maybe Lily and Joe could rekindle their romance?*

"Why not try it? It can't hurt. And you don't have to worry about finding a babysitter for Mimi. You can go out anytime that you like because I'm here to help you and watch the children," Gloria said. "Maybe if you spend more time doing things with Joe that he enjoys he'll become more interested in your marriage again."

"I don't know if it'll work... but I'm willing to try."

Gloria hoped, more than anything in the world, that her plan would work. If only Joe could fall madly in love with his wife again, everything would be fine.

. . .

That night after Gloria placed dishes of piping hot food on the table, she went back into the kitchen. She sat down at the kitchen table with a small plate of food and began to eat. But from where she sat, she could hear Lily and Joe's conversation coming from the dining room.

"I was thinking," Lily said, "that I would really like to go to one of the speakeasies with you."

"How did you know that I go to speakeasies?" he asked. "I never told you. Who told you what I do for work? Or are you just guessing?"

"Of course, I know what you do. I know that you run liquor for the mob. And I know it's illegal. But I don't blame you for doing it, Joe. In fact, I am grateful to you. When we came here to America, we were barely able to survive. Your job has taken us out of poverty, and I am thankful every day for everything we have. So, I would love to go with you to a speakeasy or a party. You are my husband, and I love you, so I want to be a part of everything you do."

"You are quite the woman, Lily, and you never cease to amaze me. Alright, I have an idea. There's a party tomorrow night. It's being given by the boss, and I am expected to attend. Most of my coworkers will be there. Some of the wives will be there, too. Would you like to come to the party with me?"

"I would."

Joe called out to Gloria who was sitting in the kitchen listening. "Can you bring us some more water?"

"Yes, sir. Of course," Gloria said.

"Good. We'll try it." He let out a laugh. "I don't think you're going to like it. But what the hell do I know? We will go and see if we can have some fun together. You've been so serious since you've been pregnant again. It's like you changed from a fun-loving girl to a more serious one. But I must admit, you sure are a responsible mother," Joe said.

Gloria poured water into Joe's glass from a pitcher which

she then set down on the table. Joe gave Gloria a quick, but intimidating glance. She turned away and walked quickly back into the kitchen.

Gloria shivered and wondered if Joe thought she had told Lily about what happened between herself and Joe. She hoped not. Gloria would never tell, not because she wanted to protect herself or to protect Joe. She would keep this secret, because she cared for Lily and wanted to protect her.

"Well," Lily said sincerely, "I am older than I was before Mimi was born. And of course, being a mother forces me to be more responsible. However, I am still the same fun-loving girl I was when we met, and even more importantly, I want you, my beloved husband, to be happy. So, I say, let's go out. We'll go to this party and have a good time together," she said, smiling at Joe.

He returned her smile. Then he winked at her and began to laugh.

"What's so funny?" Lily asked him.

"You're just so adorable," he said.

Gloria caught a glimpse of joy radiating from Lily's eyes as she watched them from the kitchen. She sincerely hoped that Joe and Lily could find a way to bring the love and romance back into their marriage.

"Alright, you little minx," Joe said affectionately to Lily. She beamed like the light from a lighthouse. "I have to go out for a while. Why don't you see if Gloria can help you find something nice to wear tomorrow night? Maybe fix your hair up special?"

Lily's hand drifted to her rounded belly, uncertainty flickering across her face. None of her good dresses fit anymore.

Gloria had never seen Lily so giddy as she was when she suggested they go shopping. She was like a young schoolgirl, and Gloria wished Lily's joy could last.

"Shall we take the children and go together?" Lily asked Gloria.

"If you'd like," Gloria said. "I can watch the children so they don't distract you while you shop. Or I can stay at home with them. Whatever you prefer."

"I'd love it if you came with me. I'd really appreciate your opinion on which dress to buy. After all, you're my best friend," Lily said to Gloria.

"Alright, you two. You can work on logistics, but I have to leave now to make a quick run. I'll be home by seven tomorrow night. Can you be ready to leave by eight?" Joe asked Lily.

"Yes, of course I can." Lily smiled.

"I'll get the children ready to go into town," Gloria said as she stood up and smoothed her skirt. As she walked towards the playroom she thought, *I've never seen Lily so happy. She told me that she wasn't in love with Joe anymore. But I've always known that she was madly in love with him. He just hurt her so much that she had shut down her feelings. This could change things. And, if it's possible, I feel even worse about what happened between Joe and me. Perhaps if they start having fun together, it will be the end of Joe's interest in me.* She hoped so.

Gloria dressed the children. Then she quickly changed from her uniform to a dress she kept for going into town or to church. But when she went downstairs to find Lily, she saw that her friend was still in her robe and nightgown. Gloria glanced over at Lily. "Is everything alright?" she asked. She was suddenly afraid that Joe might have told Lily everything to assuage his guilt.

"Yes, everything's fine," Lily said, "but I need a favor."

"What is it? What can I do?" Gloria asked, holding her breath as she waited for Lily's answer.

"I was looking in the mirror and I think I look old because I've stopped following the styles. Do you know what I mean?"

Gloria shrugged, not knowing how to answer.

"Well, I decided that I want to cut my hair. I want you to do it. Cut it in a bob. Do you think you can cut it? Or should I make an appointment at a beauty shop?"

Gloria laughed. She was so relieved that Joe had not divulged their miserable secret. "Of course I can. I've been cutting my own hair my entire life. The answer is yes. But let's go and find a dress first. Then when we get home the children will be tired and ready for a nap. That's when we'll have some time, and I'll bob your hair and put finger waves in it. You'll look beautiful."

"I'm so excited. Joe has been growing distant from me for a long time, and I have been wanting to return to France and to my mother. My mother has only seen Mimi as an infant. She would love her so much and Mimi would love her *bubbie*. In fact, I was going to ask Joe if I could go home to Paris for a month and take Mimi with me. But now I don't think I'll go because he seems willing to try to rekindle things between us and I'm so thrilled about it. You're a genius for suggesting this."

"I'm not a genius, but I must admit I do think it's wonderful." Gloria smiled. "Now, let's hurry and get dressed so we can go into town and get back in time for me to cut and style your hair. I want to get it all done before the children get up from their nap."

"You're right. I'll get dressed right away."

FORTY

Joe entered the diner and glanced at the back where he and Mike had a regular booth. Mike was already there waiting. He sat nervously drumming his fingers on the wooden surface of the table.

"Joey, my boy!"

"Yeah," Joe said, "I'm here. What was so important that it couldn't wait until our next run?"

"I think the boss is on to us." Mike's voice was tight. "Word from the speakeasy boys is he's noticed bottles going missing. Money, too. He might overlook a broken bottle here and there, but Joe..." He leaned forward. "We've been skimming more than that. Now, I'm not sure he knows it's us, but we need to watch our backs."

"Don't get yourself worked up," Joe said, though something cold settled in his stomach. "It's pocket change to him. He's making a fortune off our risks—barely paying us half what we're worth. If he was really concerned, he'd call us in, give us a warning."

"I've been thinking about coming clean," Mike said, "and telling him we'll pay it back—"

"Don't be stupid," Joe interrupted. "We're running smooth operations. No trouble with cops, no rival gangs. He's not going to care about a few bottles and dollars here and there."

"Maybe you're right." Mike didn't look convinced. "Still, I'm glad we've got the next three days off. Those border crossings make me nervous every time."

"Yeah, me too, but I try not to think about it."

"You have any plans for the weekend?" Mike asked.

"Actually, I do. I'm going out tonight to see a girl I met last week. We'll have dinner than spend the night," Joe said. "I told the wife I had to make a quick run."

"She's a good woman, your wife," Mike said. "She never questions you too much. You're pretty lucky, Joey."

"Yeah, she's a good woman. And you're not going to believe this but I'm taking the wife to a party at the speakeasy tomorrow night. The boss is throwing a do for one of the real big bosses. It's his fiftieth birthday."

"Oh yeah? Which boss is celebrating his birthday?"

"Frank Segreto. Ya know him?"

"I've met him briefly, but I ain't never had a conversation with him or anything. I was invited to the party, but I'm not planning on going."

"If you were invited, you have to go. You know that," Joe said.

"Yeah, you're probably right." Mike's eyes darted nervously to Joe's face. "Just hope you're right about the skimming. Either the boss doesn't know it's us, or..." He left the rest unspoken; both men knew what happened to thieves in their line of work.

"What can I get you fellas?" the waitress asked wearily.

"I'll have a short stack of pancakes. Ya know what, actually make it two," Mike said. Turning to Joe, he added, "I hope you're hungry."

"Of course I am, gotta keep my energy up and my belly full."

After they finished their plates, Joe stood up and said, "I've got to go and meet that gal. I hope she doesn't wear me out." He laughed.

"Are you going to the party tomorrow for sure?" Mike asked. "Because sometimes you say you'll be somewhere, but you don't show up."

"The more I think about it"—Joe ran a hand through his hair—"maybe I should leave Lily home. She has no idea what's really going on at work—she could say the wrong thing. But I already promised her." He shrugged, a smile spreading across his face. "Hell, maybe it's better this way. Anyone stealing from the boss wouldn't show up at his party with his wife on his arm, right?"

"Yeah, buddy, you got it figured." Mike sounded like he was trying to convince himself. "See you tomorrow night."

"Yeah, see you then," Joe said, walking out of the diner.

FORTY-ONE

Lily sat on a chair in the living room while Gloria cut her long black curls into a fashionable bob. Gloria's hands trembled slightly as she worked, the weight of her secrets making every intimate gesture an act of betrayal. She longed to confess everything, but the thought of losing this friendship—this haven she'd found for Nick—kept her silent.

When Lily stood to examine her new hairstyle in the mirror, her mouth fell open. "Oh my," she said softly, "it's so short. I know it's the style, but after wearing my hair in a bun for so long—"

"You don't like it?" Gloria asked.

"No, I do. It's just different." Lily touched the curls framing her face. "Actually, I look younger. Fresher."

Suddenly, Lily turned and hugged Gloria. "I'm so glad I found you. You're like a sister to me and you're so wonderful with Mimi. The only other person I'd trust with her is my mother in France."

Gloria looked away, unable to meet Lily's eyes.

"I miss her so much," Lily continued wistfully. "She would love Mimi—that's where she gets her blonde hair and blue eyes.

My mother was quite the beauty—do you remember I told you that she was a ballerina in her youth? Her eyes are as blue as the summer sky."

"Yes, I remember. She sounds lovely," Gloria managed.

"I've begged Joe to let me visit, but he always has reasons why we can't." Lily's hand drifted to her growing belly. "I wish you could meet her. She's so wise and kind—she would love you."

Gloria's heart clenched at the trust in Lily's voice. "You should rest now. Pregnancy takes so much from the body. Not long now, and the little nugget will be born."

"I am tired," Lily admitted.

"Go nap. I'll wake you for dinner."

FORTY-TWO

Lily studied herself in the mirror as she got ready for the party, her hands shaking slightly as she pinned back her newly bobbed hair. The face that looked back seemed pale and hollow-cheeked, despite her careful makeup. "Joe will be home any minute," she murmured, pressing her palms against her swollen belly. "And I look like I haven't slept in weeks."

"You don't look drawn. I promise you, you look beautiful," Gloria said. "But if you feel you need a little boost, let me touch up your makeup."

"I'm not good with makeup at all," Lily explained. "Besides, I don't have much. I never know what to buy."

"Well, don't worry about that," Gloria said. "I have some lipstick and some mascara. That's all that you'll need. We can use lipstick as rouge, too. It will give you the lift you need to make you feel confident. Wait until you see it. It's a lovely shade of red. And when we're done, you're going to look even more gorgeous than you already do. Give me a minute and I'll go and get it."

Gloria returned with a little bag and began to apply makeup

to Lily's face. The cosmetics transformed her from a pretty girl to a glamorous vixen.

When Gloria was finished Lily looked in the mirror and gasped. "Oh my, would you just look at me? Why, with your help, Gloria, I'm almost beautiful."

"You're so silly. You're always beautiful—with or without makeup. The makeup just polishes your beauty the way a jeweler polishes a diamond."

They both giggled. Their laughter was interrupted by the sound of the front door opening.

"That must be Joe," Lily said, color rising in her cheeks as she smoothed her dress. Gloria watched her friend's face light up and felt her heart pounding with anxiety. The love in Lily's eyes made everything worse—she shares a bed with a husband whose desires had turned their household into a nest of secrets.

"Lily," Joe called out. "I'm home. I just want to wash up a little before we leave. It's getting late. I hope you're ready to go to the party."

"I am," Lily answered, then she turned and smiled at Gloria. "I don't know how to thank you for all your help with my dress, with my hair and makeup, and with the children. I could never have gotten ready for tonight without you."

"Don't be silly. I'm sure you could have," Gloria insisted. "Don't even think about me right now. It's time for you to get going. Go on and have fun."

"I'll try," Lily said, stealing once last glance in the mirror before turning to Gloria with a nervous smile. "I'm sure you'll be asleep when Joe and I get home, but don't worry, I'll tell you everything that happens tonight as soon as you get up tomorrow morning."

Lily kissed Gloria affectionately on the cheek, leaving a red lipstick stain. Then she walked out of the bedroom and into the living room where Joe was sitting on the sofa waiting after his freshen up.

"Wow, just look at you," Joe said. Gloria, who was still in the bedroom, heard him whistle in appreciation. *Maybe, just maybe, they'll be able to rekindle the flame in their marriage and he'll leave me alone,* Gloria hoped.

A few minutes later Gloria heard the front door close quietly as Joe and Lily left for the party.

The children were playing and Gloria sat down in the living room. She closed her eyes, imagining life in France—the streets that Lily spoke of with such longing. She thought of Mimi's delicate features, her golden hair, and summer-sky eyes. If the child truly took after her grandmother, that former ballerina must have been stunning indeed.

Gloria's mind wandered to images of France she'd seen in photographs—the Eiffel Tower rising above elegant crowds, narrow cobblestone streets lined with blooming window boxes.

A soft sigh left her lips as Nick called out, "Mother, I'm hungry." *Ahhh, time to put an end to daydreams,* Gloria thought, jolted back to reality by her son's request. *I'd better get up and get the children's supper started.*

Gloria put the soup on a low flame and then went into the living room where she found Nick sitting on the floor and talking to Mimi. "Alright, you two," she said. "Mimi's mother had to go out for a while. So it's just the three of us for supper tonight. We're going to have soup. It's already heating on the stove. After you both finish eating, I'm going to give each of you a bath. Then you can play for a little while before going to bed."

The children were surprisingly cooperative. They held hands as they followed Gloria into the kitchen. The soup was still on the stove. But it was already hot and before Gloria had a chance to stop her, Mimi had reached up to touch the pot. She let out a blood-curdling scream, holding her finger.

"Oh, Mimi! Let me see." Gloria gently pulled Mimi towards her.

Before Gloria could look at Mimi's little finger, Nick had already dipped a rag into his water glass then wrapped it around her hand gently. A few minutes later Mimi stopped crying. Neither of the children ate much that night. Mimi was too concerned about her finger and Nick was upset because Mimi was hurting. Gloria allowed them to play on the floor for a while before bathing. After bathtime they wanted Gloria to tell them a story.

Gloria told them a tale her mother had shared with her years ago—about a little bird who found its way home through a great storm. Her voice was soft and melodic, soothing the children to sleep. She watched as Mimi's eyelids grew heavy. Nick had already sprawled on the floor, fighting sleep.

"I'll be right back, little one," she whispered to her son, gently lifting Mimi. The child stirred as Gloria tucked her into bed, those blue eyes blinking up with such trust that Gloria's heart squeezed. She pressed a soft kiss to Mimi's forehead before the little girl rolled over and drifted off.

When she returned to the living room, Nick had surrendered to sleep in her bed, his warm weight familiar and precious. Once both children were settled, Gloria changed into her nightgown and retrieved the novel from her dresser drawer, savoring this rare moment of peace.

FORTY-THREE

When they arrived at the party, Joe's coworkers and bosses greeted them warmly, but something in the air made Lily uneasy. The room was heavy with smoke and the scent of illegal alcohol. Lily was concerned that the police might raid the place and arrest her and Joe. However, this was his world. These were his friends, and she wanted to make him happy, she wanted to make him love her again, and so she didn't let him know that she was feeling uncomfortable. As Joe made introductions, everyone remarked on Lily's beauty, seeming not to notice her swollen belly. They treated Joe like someone important and Lily felt a flutter of pride beneath her anxiety.

It had been so long since she had felt beautiful. She found herself blushing at the compliments she received; Lily wondered if Joe noticed how much his coworkers admired her. *Me, beautiful?* The thought seemed strange—her mother was the true beauty, and now Mimi had inherited Chloe's striking features. Lily had always deflected compliments with a humble smile, assuming they were mere politeness.

"Come over here," Joe said to Lily, indicating a small table for two. "Sit down and wait for me. I'll go and get us something to drink."

Lily nodded. She had never been to a place like this, and she wasn't used to drinking alcohol, but she wanted more than anything to rekindle things with her husband.

Joe brought two whiskey-filled glasses to the table. He set one down in front of Lily and the other in front of himself. "Taste this stuff. This is the same whiskey that I bring down from Canada every week," he said. "Go on and try it."

Lily raised the glass to her lips and drank. She hated the bitter, strong taste, but she didn't want Joe to think that he had made a mistake bringing her here. She was determined to finish the contents of the glass. Lily swallowed hard. Her throat still burned but she raised the glass to her lips and drank again. This time the whiskey didn't taste nearly as bad, so she forced herself to drink again and again. And by the time her glass was empty, she found she didn't hate it at all anymore.

A piano player was playing ragtime jazz and couples swayed and spun in the center of the room, their movements casting shifting shadows on the walls, cigarette smoke curling above their heads. "Would you like to dance?" Joe asked Lily. "I remember what a good dancer you are."

Lily smiled nervously. "I don't know that I'm such a good dancer, and it'll be hard to move with this to carry round," she said, cradling her stomach, "but I'd love to dance."

They got up and joined the others on the dance floor. Lily could feel eyes on them, but she assumed it must be because she was so pregnant; she felt foolish dancing at her size. Joe tried to teach Lily the Charleston, and having grown up watching her mother dance, Lily was a very quick learner but being large from the pregnancy she felt a little clumsy and ungraceful. Then they switched to a slower song, where she and Joe swayed to the music, and she was having fun dancing with her husband. It had been a long time since she and Joe had enjoyed each other's company. Finally, when he was out of breath from their energetic dancing, Joe turned to Lily and said, "What do you say we take a little break? Let's have another drink."

"Sure," Lily happily agreed.

They each had another glass of whiskey, and then another. Joe became so amorous that he couldn't keep his hands off Lily. She was embarrassed by his open displays of affection. But when he took her hand in his and kissed her palm, then ran his fingers across her cheek, Lily's heart sang. *It was worth all the preparations I had to make to come here: the makeup, the haircut, all of it. He still loves me,* she thought with relief. *He's acting like my old Joe again.* Joe leaned across the table and pulled Lily almost completely out of her chair. Then he kissed her. It was a long passionate kiss, and it reinforced the hope that she so desperately needed.

Lily's back ached, her swollen belly making it hard to find a comfortable position in the wooden chair. When Joe wasn't looking, she stole a glance at his watch—it was four in the morning. The sun would be rising soon. She thought of Mimi, who would be searching for her mother in a few hours, but things felt so right with Joe tonight. She could not bring herself to ask to leave, even as exhaustion dragged at her limbs.

Joe seemed oblivious to the time. He was full of passion as he leaned over and kissed her ear. Then he brazenly fondled her breast. Lily was glad it was dark, because she felt her face turn hot and she knew she was blushing. After all, they were in the middle of a crowded speakeasy, and he was touching her as if they were alone in their bedroom. Lily couldn't help but notice that people were looking, and she secretly wished he would stop. He whispered in her ear, "Let's go home to our bedroom where we can be alone."

"Yes, let's do that," Lily agreed, feeling self-conscious despite their years of marriage. Some part of her would always be a shy girl from France when it came to matters of intimacy.

. . .

As they walked to the car, Joe leaned over and took Lily into his arms and kissed her. She was elated and grateful to Gloria that their plan to rekindle Joe's interest in her seemed to be working. Joe was quite drunk. He was stumbling and Lily wished she knew how to drive. When he met her gaze, she caught a glimpse of that old fire, the look that had first stolen her heart in France. For this moment at least, she was his whole world again. He opened the automobile door for her and helped her get inside. Then he walked around to the other side of the automobile and climbed in. He leaned over and kissed her again.

Joe turned the key in the ignition, but the automobile did not spring to life. In fact, there was no sound at all. "Shoot, I think the car's dead. I'm pretty sure it's the battery."

"Do you think we should try to get a taxi or see if someone you know can give us a ride?" Lily asked, anxious to get home.

"Lily." He said her name softly and sighed heavily.

"Is something wrong, Joe?"

"No." He hesitated. "Well, yeah, I guess you could say something is wrong. It's nothing you did. It's me. I guess you could say that I realized something."

She was trembling. *Was he trying to end their marriage?* "You've had a lot to drink tonight. We can talk tomorrow."

"No, I want to tell you now. I know you think I've had a lot to drink, and I have, but I'm not drunk. I know exactly what I'm saying. So, please, just listen to me, alright? Will you?"

"Yes, Joe," Lily said. "Of course I will."

He nodded, then spoke softly. "Lily, it means a lot that you came here tonight. A refined French girl like you, in a place like this—but you did it anyway, to be part of my world. Even the darker parts." Joe touched her hand. "Not many wives would do that."

She touched his face. "When I married you, I knew that I

wanted to be by your side through thick and thin. No matter what, Joe, I'm your wife and I'll stand by you."

"Aww, Lily, I gotta say that I am sorry, I haven't been the best husband to you. You didn't deserve the things I've done. And... I realize that now. But... well..." Joe stammered. "Even with all the bad things I've done and even when I've ignored you or spoken harshly to you, I've always loved you. Always. No matter what I did, or where I went, I could never escape the fact that you are my one true love. I tried to leave you back when we were in France, do you remember? I didn't come back for months. But I couldn't think of anything else but you while I was gone. I finally knew I had to return. I just couldn't go on without you." His eyes glistened in the dim light; for a moment he looked like that young soldier who Lily had first fallen in love with.

She looked into his eyes. "Really, Joe? Sometimes I've felt like you just didn't care anymore. Like you lost interest."

"Nah, never. I always cared for you, Lily," Joe said. "I didn't want to need you as badly as I do, so I tried to push you away sometimes. But it was impossible."

"You haven't said loving things like this to me in a very long time," Lily replied. A tear slipped down her cheek. "I love you, too, Joe."

"I know that. I've never doubted you. It's me that I doubted. Not my love for you, but my ability to love and let myself be loved. Does that make sense?"

Lily nodded. "Yes. I understand."

"I hated feeling vulnerable and loving you so much always made me feel that way. But the truth is, I don't want to lose you." He took her hand in his and gently squeezed it. "I wouldn't know how to live without you." Joe cleared his throat. "Lil, can we start over? Will you give me another chance to prove to you that I can be the husband you want me to be?"

There was a moment of silence. Lily closed her eyes. *I love*

this man and he's finally saying all the things I hoped and prayed he would say to me. "Yes, Joe. Yes. Let's start over."

Joe pulled Lily close, kissing her with an intensity that made her dizzy. The automobile was hidden in shadows beside the building and the combination of moonlight and champagne made everything feel dreamlike. *This is my Joe*, she thought, *the one I left France for.* She closed her eyes, lost in a moment that felt like their early days together.

And because Lily's eyes were closed, she never saw the two men approaching the automobile from either side.

"Got a message from the boss, Joe." The hostile voice cut through their moonlit moment like ice. Lily's eyes snapped open to see Zeb at the window, his gun glinting in the darkness. With trembling hands, she clutched her dress to her chest, recognition hitting her like a blow—the same man who had smiled and called her beautiful just hours ago now stood transformed, his face a mask of cold intent.

"Zeb?" Joe's voice cracked on the name.

"He ain't so happy with you." Zeb's gun stayed steady. "And I think you know why."

Joe looked ashen. His hands shook against the steering wheel as he stared straight ahead, unable to even look at Lily. "Look, I don't know what you're talking about. I don't know why the boss is unhappy with me. I'd like to talk to him." Joe's voice was filled with panic.

Zeb shook his head. "Joey boy, you should know better than to steal from the boss. He always finds out. He wanted me to tell you that you made a big mistake. You hurt his feelings, you see. He says to tell you that he trusted you. He even gave you a good job when you couldn't find work anywhere. A job that paid you very well and what did you do? You didn't appreciate his kindness; you stole from him," Zeb said with an exasperated sigh. "Joe, you've been around for a while. You've been in the mob, and you've seen plenty of things like this. They always

end badly. I can't help you now. You should have known better. And I'm sorry to say you're going to have to pay the price."

"Joe, what's going on here?" Lily asked, her voice shaking. But Joe didn't answer. He slumped against the seat, his shoulders trembling with silent sobs, all his swagger gone.

"It's not true. It wasn't me. I didn't steal from the boss. It was Mike. My partner."

"Joe, you're embarrassing yourself. Don't sit there crying like a baby. Take your punishment like a man. The boss knows that it was both of you."

Joe looked defeated and afraid. "I'm sorry. I didn't take much. Can you at least tell him that?"

"Yeah, sure. I'll tell him if you want. But that doesn't change things. You should know that the boss can't have this sort of thing happening. If he lets you get away with this, other people will think they can get away with anything with him in charge. He can't let the guys think he is weak. So, Joey... I'm really sorry I have to do this." Zeb pointed his gun at Joe.

"Oh, come on, Zeb," Joe pleaded. His voice was full of desperation. "Come on, you and me are friends. Just let me go this one time. I promise I will never steal again."

In that last moment, Lily saw Joe's face transformed by terror. Suddenly she understood everything—the missing money, all the lies. Her final thought was of Mimi, waiting at home for a mother who would never return. Then the flash, and darkness.

FORTY-FOUR

Gloria had fallen asleep on the sofa and she woke up disorientated to see the sun high in the sky. She heard the children's laughter coming from Mimi's room. Nick and Mimi were giggling together; the sound was so delightful that it warmed Gloria's heart. She stretched and stood up. *Lily and Joe must have come in very late and decided to go to bed without waking me,* she thought, trying to understand why she hadn't heard them return from the party. *I hope Lily's plan worked. I'll keep the children quiet, so they don't wake them up.*

"Good morning, you two! I'll bet you're both ready for breakfast," Gloria said to the children.

"Yes, please!" Nick replied. He had been well-fed since they had moved in with Mimi and Lily, but he was always hungry. Mimi gave no response, she was still looking at Nick and giggling.

"Come on. You two can play again after breakfast," Gloria said. "But right now, let's all go into the kitchen. Do you want porridge?"

"Yes, I do," Nick said. He took Mimi's hand and they

followed Gloria into the kitchen. Nick entertained Mimi with one of her dolls while Gloria prepared breakfast.

After they finished eating, the two children went back into Mimi's room to play with her toys while Gloria cleaned up the kitchen. Gloria liked to cook in a clean kitchen, and she assumed that soon Joe and Lily would be awake and she would need to be ready to prepare their breakfast.

By noon, Gloria started to think that it was strange that they hadn't appeared. As she poured herself a cup of coffee, she looked outside the kitchen window. It was then that she realized that Joe's automobile was not parked in front of the house. A chill ran down her spine. *The automobile must have broken down,* she reasoned. *Or maybe Joe had to go into work late last night and he dropped Lily off then took the car?* Gloria tried to remain calm, but she could not shake the feeling that something was terribly wrong. As quietly as she could, Gloria opened the door to the master bedroom. The bed was untouched, it had not been slept in. The pretty floral bedspread that Lily loved lay perfectly on the bed. Their clothes hung neatly in the closet. Gloria bit her upper lip. She was no longer guessing; she could see now that something was not right. Lily and Joe had not come home the previous night. She was also quite sure that Lily would not have stayed out without calling to let her know.

Gloria did not know what to do. When she had been hired, Lily told her that because of Joe's job they must not ever call the police. What could she do now? Nothing but wait and pray that Lily and Joe would return soon. She could not eat or rest.

That evening, two police officers arrived as Gloria was serving the children their dinner. Gloria saw them striding up the walkway as she looked through the kitchen window. Her heart dropped. *I knew it. Something terrible has happened. I'm not sure what is going on, but I'm about to find out,* she thought with trepidation as one of the officers knocked on the front door.

"I'm coming," Gloria called out as she ran to the door.

Two young police officers stood outside. One of them asked, "Is this the home of Lily and Joseph Rosenberg?"

"Yes, it is," Gloria managed to say, trying to read their expressions.

"And who are you?"

"I'm Gloria, the nanny. Lily and Joe didn't come home from a party last night. I didn't know what to do. I was going to call the police, but I didn't want to cause any trouble. I was hoping they would come home this afternoon. Or if not, then by tomorrow." Panic rose in Gloria's chest.

The officer nodded. "I am afraid I have some bad news," he said solemnly.

Gloria did not want to hear what he had to say; she wanted to go on believing that everything would be alright and Lily would be home soon. Her hands were shaking, her knees weak. She felt hot and flushed as though she might pass out. But the officer didn't see how upset she was or if he did, he was ignoring her.

"Mr. and Mrs. Rosenberg were found shot to death in their automobile outside of what we believe is a speakeasy," he continued.

"No!" Gloria cried out. She felt her legs give way and she held on to the doorway for support. "Please come inside," she managed to say.

The two policemen walked into the living room. Gloria collapsed into a chair as Nick and Mimi walked into the room holding hands.

"Why don't you take Mimi into her room so that you two can play with the new puzzle her father bought her last week?"

Gloria said to Nick. She could barely look into Mimi's big blue eyes. *What am I going to tell her?*

"Alright, Mama," Nick replied hesitantly, sensing the tension in the room.

After the children left the room, the police officer turned his attention back to Gloria. "Do you know why someone might do this to your employers?"

"I... I don't know. I'm just their nanny. I live here with my son and I watch their daughter. I don't know anything else about their lives." Gloria was sure that he could hear her heart beating rapidly.

"I know you think you don't know anything, but even the slightest detail could be of help to us. Think hard, miss. Do you know anything at all about Joseph Rosenberg's job?" The officer looked at Gloria intensely.

"All I know is that he drives a truck and he's usually away from home a few days a week."

"Do you know what he transports?"

"I don't know. I'm sorry," Gloria lied. No one had ever actually told her that Joe was bringing liquor into America from Canada. But she had overheard conversations Joe had had on the phone and she had figured out that he transported illegal liquor for the mob.

"And the child?" the officer gestured with his thumb to Mimi's room.

"I could keep her with me," Gloria said, her voice breaking. The thought of losing Mimi, of the little girl being taken away to some cold institution, made her physically ill.

"No, you can't unless you are a blood relative."

Gloria's hands trembled as she thought of Mimi being torn away from everything familiar, everything safe. *Not after everything she's lost. I can't let that happen to her,* she thought. She drew in a shaky breath. "Mimi does have family. Mimi has a grandmother in Paris."

"I suggest that you make arrangements for the child to go to live with her grandmother in France then. Do you know if the Rosenbergs have a will?"

"I have no idea," Gloria replied numbly.

"Unfortunately, since Joseph Rosenberg was involved in illegal activities you will not be able to stay in this house. We need to close it up until someone can come out here to further investigate this homicide." The police officer cleared his throat. "I am afraid that you will have to leave. Do you know if there is enough money to send this little girl to France?"

"I... I don't know."

"I understand. And I'm sorry that you're going to have to find another place to stay. But don't go too far. The homicide detectives will probably want to talk to you so make sure you leave a forwarding address. Just jot it down and leave it on the kitchen table."

Gloria nodded. But she had no forwarding address. She watched the two policemen as they left the house. Once they were gone, Gloria put her head in her hands and wept. Lily was dead. Her dearest friend was gone in an instant. If only Lily had not gone out with Joe that night, she would still be alive. But there was no going back and Gloria blamed herself. After all, she had told Lily to go with Joe and try to rekindle the flame in their marriage. Now Mimi was left without her mother and father, and Gloria had lost her dear friend.

FORTY-FIVE

Gloria forced herself to get up and go into the bedroom. The children were playing, but Nick could sense that something was wrong because he stopped playing and looked up at her.

"Mama, are you crying?" he asked. The innocence in his voice touched Gloria so deeply that she couldn't speak. She just shook her head and tried to smile. But he continued to watch her as she began to pack the suitcases. She looked around Mimi's room and took some of her toys and clothes and placed them in the cases. She sat down on the bed, listening to Mimi's innocent giggles. The sound brought back Lily's voice, so full of longing when she had spoken of France and of her dreams that Mimi would get to know her grandmother. "Someday," she had said, "I want to take my little girl home."

Gloria walked into Lily's bedroom. She had always known that Lily kept a diary on the wooden nightstand next to her bed. Until now, Gloria would never have thought of opening it. But she had no idea where to find Lily's mother. *Maybe Lily's diary would hold some clues?* she thought. Gloria opened the diary, tears falling down her face as she read the lovely words that Lily had written about her. She wanted to put the book away and hide from the truth. Lily was gone and she would never be coming back.

Gloria was glad that Lily had never found out about what happened between herself and Joe. But even so, she was still overcome with guilt about what Joe had forced her to do. She had loved Lily, and even though sleeping with Joe had not been her choice, she did it. And now she was afraid that Lily's death was God's way of punishing her.

Gloria continued to search the diary for the address until she found what she was looking for. It was a letter. On the envelope was a return address that belonged to Lily's mother. It came from a little town just outside of Paris. Gloria stuffed the envelope into her pocket.

I will need money to take Mimi to France, Gloria thought as she opened Lily's jewelry box which sat on top of her dresser. Lily had never hidden her jewelry from Gloria. She had trusted Gloria implicitly. Joe had earned so much money that it was strange that he never bought jewelry for his wife. Gloria sifted through the contents of the box. There was an old love letter from Joe and a pair of earrings that didn't appear to be of any value. Then Gloria picked up the box and sat down on the bed to continue to look through it. That was when she saw the pin. She gasped. It was the most magnificent piece of jewelry that she had ever seen. Running her fingers over the jewels embedded into the bright yellow gold, she knew that if she sold this there would be enough money for her and Nick to take Mimi to France to live with her grandmother. Her heart ached and tears stung the back of her eyelids.

I will miss my friend forever and I will never forget her. She took my son and I into her home and trusted us, Gloria recalled fondly. *I loved her like she was my sister. It's my fault that she's dead. If I hadn't felt so guilty over that horrible afternoon with Joe and then tried to fix it by trying to fix the marriage, Lily would still be here. I owe her so much and I know that, more than anything, she would want me to take care of Mimi. I hate to sell this pin because by rights it should be Mimi's when she grows up.* She looked at the diamonds sparkling in her hand and felt sick to her stomach. *I wouldn't touch Lily's things if I didn't believe wholeheartedly that this is what she would want.*

The next morning Gloria put the pin in her handbag and started to get the children ready to leave.

"Where is my mommy? When will she be home?" Mimi sobbed.

Gloria soothed Mimi the best she could, but she had been struggling to tell the little girl the truth. It felt too painful, though she knew she must. Nick held Mimi's hand and they headed out to the pawn shop on the other side of town.

When Gloria had started working for Lily, Lily had given her so many pretty clothes. And because of this, even though she didn't realize it, Gloria looked like she was a rich woman. The pawnbroker, a very short and stout man, smiled at Gloria when she walked into his store, sizing her up. She could tell that he immediately took her for a naive young mother who was in some kind of trouble.

"Good morning, young lady," the pawnbroker said with a sickly smile that did not reach his eyes. "What can I do for you today?"

Gloria pulled the pin, which was wrapped in a handkerchief, out of her purse. The pawnbroker didn't speak. She laid it on a piece of black velvet on the counter. The man's eyes grew wide.

"How much can you give me for this?" she asked.

The pawnbroker looked at the pin. Then he picked it up and studied it under a loop. Gloria noticed that his hands were trembling. He said, "I'll give you one hundred dollars. That's a fair price, ma'am." His voice was confident; he thought this was going to be easy.

But he had misjudged her.

Gloria had been poor, so she knew how to bargain. That pin was full of diamonds which meant it was worth at least five hundred dollars. And she knew she would need every penny of it to travel to France aboard a ship with Nick and Mimi.

"Look at this pin," Gloria said. "These are diamonds and emeralds. From what I know of diamonds, the ones in this pin are very good quality. Not to mention the emeralds and that all the jewels are all set in gold. I'm sorry but one hundred dollars is robbery. If you want this piece of jewelry, you're going to have to make me a fair offer or I'll go somewhere else and find someone who is willing to do that." She looked the pawnbroker straight in the eyes.

He shifted his eyes to the floor. "How much will you take?" he asked.

"I'll need five hundred dollars. If you can pay that, then we can do business," Gloria said firmly.

The pawnbroker picked up the pin and looked at it again.

Please let him agree the price, Gloria thought.

"Five hundred dollars it is," the pawnbroker said as he pulled a roll of paper money out of his pocket. He began counting. When he reached five hundred dollars, he handed the money to Gloria. She folded the notes carefully, turning away from his beady eyes as she slipped the money in her bra before taking Nick and Mimi's hands and leaving the store.

"Where are we going now, Mommy?" Nick asked.

"We're going on an adventure. I'm on my way to buy passage for the three of us to board a great big ship that will take us to France. We're going to visit your grandmother, Mimi."

"Where is my mommy?" Mimi asked, her eyes brimming with tears.

Gloria was overwhelmed by the prospect of breaking the

awful news to Mimi. *I'm going to have to tell her. I just don't know how.*

"Is Mimi's mommy coming with us?" Nick asked.

"No, dear, I'm afraid not." Gloria bit her lower lip.

"Why not? Why isn't my mommy coming with us?" Mimi asked. "She wouldn't want me to go without her. I know she wouldn't."

"Mimi, your mommy and daddy have gone to heaven," Gloria said, shaking.

"I want her to come back. Why won't she come back? Tell her I need her."

"Sweetheart. She can't come back. But you have Nick and me, and you'll soon meet your grandmother in France."

"You mean my bubbie? The one whose picture is on the table in our living room?"

"Yes, that's who I mean. Your mommy loved her very much."

"I wish Mommy could come to France with us," Mimi said. Then she added, "Daddy, too."

"I wish for that as well. But she can't. I'm sorry, honey," Gloria said to Mimi as the three of them walked towards the bus stop.

"Where is France?" Nick asked curiously.

"France is far away. It's on the other side of the ocean in a place called Europe."

"Europe?"

"Yep. Europe. This is going to be a great adventure for all three of us," Gloria said, trying her hardest to make the journey sound exciting.

"I don't want to go without my mommy." Mimi started to cry.

"Oh, sweetheart. You must trust me to take care of you. I'll keep you safe, I promise," Gloria said.

"I want my mommy." Mimi was crying so hard that she sat down on the sidewalk and refused to move.

"Mimi, sweetheart." Gloria knelt beside the trembling child. "We need to catch the bus."

"I want my mommy!" Mimi's scream pierced the air, raw with terror. Her small body shook with sobs that seemed too big for her chest.

Gloria's hands trembled, anxiety creeping up her neck in red patches. She reached for Mimi and then pulled back, horrified at the impulse to shake sense into her. "I'm so sorry," she whispered, tears burning her eyes. "Please, darling, please be brave for me."

Nick settled quietly beside his friend. He took Mimi's small hand in his, waiting until her huge, tear-filled eyes met his.

"Remember when you were scared of the thunder last month?" he said softly to Mimi. "And you came to sleep in our room? My mom made us hot chocolate and told stories until the storm passed." Nick squeezed her hand. "She'll take care of us now, too. And I'll stay right beside you, Mimi. I promise."

Mimi's sobs gradually quieted to hiccups. She leaned against Nick's shoulder, her fingers still gripping his. "You won't leave me?"

"Never," Nick whispered, meeting his mother's grateful eyes over Mimi's bowed head.

"Are you sure?"

"Yes, I'm sure." Nick smiled. "Now, come on. Get up and walk with me to the bus stop so that we can go home."

Mimi put her small hand in Nick's and then she looked up at him and smiled through her tears as they walked hand in hand to the bus stop.

"Where is Mimi's mother?" Nick whispered to Gloria. "She hasn't been home for a long while."

"I can't explain just yet. But I will. Thank you for helping me with Mimi," Gloria said. She was proud that her son was so grown up and resourceful.

"You will tell us soon?" he asked.

"I will. I promise," Gloria replied. "Now, that's enough questions. I have a lot of money in my purse so I must be careful and watch out for us until I can pay for our tickets to get on the ship."

But Nick didn't stop asking questions. He was excited but also nervous and he wanted to know everything. "How much will it cost? And when will we leave?" he asked.

"I don't have any answers to those questions yet, I'm afraid," Gloria explained. "I don't know when the next ship is leaving, all I know is that when it leaves, we're going to be on it. Now, come on, walk a little faster, we have places to go."

After Gloria purchased tickets for the voyage, she decided that she would indulge the children and buy them each an ice cream. Lily had always been the one to buy the children little toys or ice cream when they went out to do errands. She would have been happy to give them whatever they wanted, especially today. Gloria counted the coins in her purse, each one precious, each one meant for bus fare or bread or rent, and especially because she didn't know when or where more money would come from. But when she looked at Mimi's tear-stained face, she remembered another girl who had lost everything—herself, not so many years ago, clinging to the kindness of strangers. Some comforts were worth more than money could measure.

"Would you like some ice cream?" Gloria asked the children softly, already knowing that she would find a way to make up for the expense later. The way Mimi's face lit up, even through her grief, made the decision feel right.

As the children ate their ice cream quietly inside the pharmacy that doubled up as a soda shop, Gloria took the tickets to board the ship out of her purse and looked at them. The money she had made from selling the pin would only be enough to sustain them if she remained frugal. She would have loved to book a nice stateroom, but she dare not splurge just in case they needed the money later. So the three of them would be traveling in steerage.

They would be taking the next ship scheduled to leave New York City at the end of the week. This gave Gloria four days to get everything packed and ready to go. She had not been able to find a boat that was going directly to France. This one would dock in Hamburg. When she asked the man who sold her the tickets for the ship how to get to Paris, he explained that she could easily catch a train in Hamburg that would take her.

FORTY-SIX

Gloria and the children returned to the house that night. Relieved that the police had not yet returned, Gloria began packing up the last things the following day. She moved through the house like a ghost, touching familiar things—Lily's silver hairbrush on the vanity, her half-finished embroidery still in its hoop, Mimi's height marks penciled on the kitchen doorframe. In Lily's bedroom, she had found a tiny knitted bootie, half-finished, the needles still holding the delicate white yarn. Two lives lost, not just one—Lily and the baby she had never been able to hold.

She knew that she could only take as much as she could carry with two small children in tow.

"I want to bring my rocking horse," Mimi insisted.

Gloria bent down so that she was the same height as Mimi; she looked into the little girl's eyes. "Sweetie, I know you love your rocking horse, but it's too big to carry. And there won't be enough room for it on the boat. Maybe you should bring your stuffed rabbit. I forgot his name, what was it?" Gloria asked gently.

Mimi started to cry. She wasn't listening to Gloria. "I want to take my rocking horse. My daddy got it for me," she said. "I can't leave it!"

"You're a big girl now, Mimi," Nick said. "You don't need a rocking horse anymore—they're for babies." He picked up the well-worn stuffed rabbit that was lying on Mimi's bed. Mimi watched Nick as he turned to his mother and said, "Mom, this is Fluffy. I don't think you two have ever formally met."

"Hello, Fluffy. It's nice to meet you," Gloria said.

"I think Fluffy likes my mom." Nick smiled at Mimi.

Mimi giggled.

Nick has a way of making her smile, that's for sure, Gloria thought, relieved. *He knows how to calm her down when I can't. What a good boy he is.*

In the middle of the afternoon there was a knock on the door. At first Gloria tried to ignore it, but the knocking was persistent, and she was afraid it might be the police. "Who is it?" she called nervously. Her hands were sweating as she walked over to the door.

"My name is Anthony," a male voice shouted from outside. "I worked with Joe, and I still work for Joe's boss. The boss sent me here. Please open the door."

Gloria opened the door just a crack and glanced at the man who stood on the other side. He was well-dressed, wearing a suit that fit him so perfectly that it must have been tailor-made. Anthony looked Gloria over and smiled at her. His teeth were the whitest she had ever seen, and she had to admit he was very handsome. But when she looked at him the hair on her arms stood on end; all of her instincts told her to be careful around him.

"What do you want from us?" Gloria asked, trying to keep her voice even.

He gave her a smile as he removed his hat respectfully.

Although his face was hard, when he smiled his eyes seemed to soften.

"I'm sorry that I had to be the one to come here and tell you this, but unfortunately, it's part of my job. I just hadn't expected you to be so pretty."

She felt the color rising in her cheeks. However, if the man saw Gloria blush, he pretended not to. He was still smiling warmly when he said, "You see, I knew Joey pretty well. Joey and me worked for the same boss."

His suit was expensive, his voice soft as velvet, but his eyes were cold when he explained that the house belonged to the boss. The mob owned everything—the furniture that Lily had chosen so carefully, the garden where she had taught Mimi to plant sunflowers, even the walls that held the echoes of her laughter.

"You'll need to vacate in a few days," the man said, straightening his silk tie. "The boss is being generous, giving you that long."

Gloria clutched the kitchen counter, remembering Lily's last morning in this room, how she had smiled over coffee, talking about taking Mimi for an ice-cream that afternoon. How could she tell that sweet child that they were losing her home, too, so soon after losing her mother? She thought of Chloe across the ocean, waiting for letters that would never come, unaware that her granddaughter's inheritance was being stripped away by men who dealt in whiskey and blood.

"The police were here yesterday," Gloria said. "They plan to close up the house while they investigate the murder."

The well-dressed man smiled. "No need to worry about the police. We have them under control. They won't be coming around again," he said. "But you need to take these children and move out."

Gloria was no stranger to organized crime. She had grown up in a poor Irish neighborhood ruled by crime bosses. She had never had any problems with them, but that was because she had never questioned their authority. Gloria studied the man before her, weighing her next words carefully. He had the boss's ear—maybe even his trust. She had learned how to read men like him, how to make herself seem smaller, less threatening. Her hands trembled slightly as she smoothed her skirt.

"Please," she said softly, letting vulnerability creep into her voice. "I'm taking Joe and Lily's daughter to France, to the little girl's grandmother." She glanced up through her lashes, then quickly down again. "The tickets are bought. The ship sails in at the end of the week. I only need a little more time."

Gloria held her breath, watching his reflection in the polished surface of the hall mirror. Three weeks might as well be three years to men like him, men who measured time in profits and payments. But Mimi's future hung on his answer.

He smiled at her and nodded. "I think that can be arranged," he said. "When exactly is your ship sailing?"

"Saturday, May 26th."

"Alright. I'm a reasonable man. Just make sure that you and the children are out of the house by the first of next month," he said.

Gloria could see from his eyes that he meant what he said. "We'll be gone by then," she replied.

"Good. Well, it was a pleasure to meet you, ma'am. And now, I'll be on my way." He stood up, put his hat on, and began to walk towards the door.

Gloria's mind raced with thoughts about the future. *I was hoping to come back and stay at the house until I could find work. But now I'm not sure if I'll return to America. Perhaps the best thing for me to do is to try to find work in France? I just wish I could speak French. Maybe Mimi's grandmother will help me?*

As the man from the mob turned to leave, Gloria felt a question burning in her throat. Her hands knotted in her skirt, then released. *For Lily,* she thought. *I have to know for Lily.*

"Wait." The word came out louder than Gloria had intended. He paused, one hand on the doorknob, and Gloria forced herself to meet his cold eyes. She had faced worse fears than this man, hadn't she? She had to ask—for Lily, who had given her shelter when the world had turned its back. For Lily, who had treated her like a sister, not a servant.

"Sir"—her voice barely wavered now—"I know I have no right to ask this. But Lily was family to me, and I need to know—"

"What is it? What do you want to know?"

"Well, do you know who killed Joe and Lily? And... do you know why?" she stammered. "If you tell me, I won't go to the police. I just want to know what happened to my friend."

He cleared his throat. "Now, you're a pretty lady and I sure would like to answer all your questions. However, I think you should take my advice, and don't ask questions like that. If I did give you answers, those answers could get you in trouble and you sure don't need that." His smile had vanished. His face was hard and when she looked at him, Gloria shivered, knowing for certain that this man had a dark and dangerous side. A side that was hiding just under the surface of that handsome face. His eyes were warning her to leave things alone. And she knew it was best to heed that warning.

If Gloria could have one wish granted, it would be to bring Lily back to life. Before this happened, things had finally been going so well for her. For the first time since he was born, Nick had been growing up in a nice home in a safe neighborhood. And now in the blink of an eye it was all over. She had enough money left over after buying their tickets to France to return to America if she chose to. But before she returned to America, she would try to find work in other cities in Europe if she couldn't find a job in France. It was strange how everyone who came to America believed the streets were paved in gold, but Gloria knew better. She remembered the dingy apartment where she and Nick had been living before they met Lily. She remembered how the paint was chipping off the dirty walls and how dangerous the building was for children living there.

"I'm going to leave now," the man said, interrupting Gloria's wandering thoughts. "But since we have no real answers, if I were you, toots, I'd assume that the murder was a robbery since your friends were at an illegal speakeasy in a rough neighborhood."

There was no doubt in Gloria's mind that he was lying. He knew who did it and why, but when she looked into his eyes, she saw the warning again and decided not to ask anything more.

"A robbery. Yes, I'm sure that's what happened," she replied quietly.

"Yes, I'm sure it was," he said. "You have my sympathy for the loss of your friend." He paused before asking, "Do you need a little extra money? I figure you probably don't have any."

For a moment Gloria was frightened; after all, she had taken Lily's pin and sold it without permission. That was stealing. She wondered if the boss that this man had spoken about owned the pin, too. *He could do something terrible to me and then what would happen to the children? They would end up in an orphanage. I'll keep my mouth shut for now, and soon we'll leave here and be far away from all of this in France.* "Money? No, no. I am alright," she replied.

"Don't be proud. I can give you some money to help you get back on your feet. Now, I don't know how you afforded to pay for passage on a ship for three of you. But I'm sure you need any money you can get right now. Take it please," he said, offering Gloria several bills.

He doesn't know about the pin and he's assuming I don't have a penny, Gloria realized. "Well, yes, some money would certainly help."

The man handed Gloria the notes. She didn't look at them

to see how much he had given her before stuffing them into her dress pocket. "Thank you," she whispered.

He nodded. "I'll be back in two weeks. You should be out of here by then."

"Yes," she promised. "We'll be on our way to France."

After the man's footsteps faded down the front path, Gloria sank into Lily's favorite chair by the window. Her hands trembled as she withdrew the money from her dress pocket. Two hundred dollars. She spread the bills across her lap; each one represented a chance for her and Nick in France; each one was stained with the grief of how she had gotten it.

Through the window, she watched the man's black automobile disappear down the street as she slipped the money back in her pocket. He hadn't been cruel, exactly. His voice had stayed soft, his manner almost courteous. But she had recognized something in his eyes—the same cold calculation that she had seen in Joe's during that terrible night at the hotel. These were men who could smile while they broke your world apart.

She pressed her palm against her racing heart, feeling the money crinkle beneath her dress. In the kitchen, she could hear Nick and Mimi's quiet voices, the children still unaware of how completely their lives were about to change. A few days to pack up a home full of memories—to prepare Mimi for a journey across an ocean, to see a grandmother she had never met. Four short days to leave behind every trace of Lily except the precious burden of her daughter's future.

Gloria closed her eyes, breathing in the lingering scent of Lily's roses from the garden. *Watch over us,* she prayed silently. *Help me to take your daughter home.*

FORTY-SEVEN

From his vantage point on the ship's first-class deck, Friedrich watched a flock of seabirds wheel against the darkening sky. He knew he was handsome, and not because he spent a lot of time staring at his reflection in a mirror. Friedrich Wagner was far too busy enjoying the benefits of being the only son of a wealthy family to spend even a few moments a day marveling at his tall, well-built frame, his blond hair, bright blue eyes, and winning smile. But he had learned early in life that his looks were pleasing to others, especially women who always seemed to fall at his feet.

When he first met a woman, they had a lot of fun, but then after a few weeks he got bored. And at nearly forty, as he grew older, he found himself yearning for something more meaningful. He was tired of the same old quick sexual trysts, the wild parties, the excessive drinking followed by waking up in strange beds beside women whose names he had forgotten as soon as he heard them.

Friedrich longed for a partner who he could talk to. A smart woman who would share the love he had for his country of origin, Germany. He didn't want to start a family in America.

He wanted to marry, have children and raise them in his homeland. The Alps perhaps.

For as long as he could remember, his parents and neighbors had been trying to introduce him to eligible women from good, wealthy families. They hoped that he would marry one of these well-connected, affluent women. His father often told him that he wanted him to run the family-owned factory in America. But since his family still owned a business in Germany, Friedrich made it clear that someday he wanted to take over the German factory and live there.

Some of the women he was introduced to were very pretty, others were less attractive, but one thing they all had in common was that they were all very rich.

Money had never impressed Friedrich—it was too familiar to excite him. He had watched the parade of hopeful women at Manhattan's finest parties, some offering their bodies, others their social connections. They spoke of family names and influential friends like merchants displaying their finest wares. But Friedrich had long since grown weary of such transactions masked as romance.

His mother understood, in her way. "You're an idealist, *liebchen*," she would say, a shadow crossing her beautiful face. "But it's easy to dream of love when you've never known hunger." She had been a poor girl with a pretty face when his father proposed, and she had counted herself lucky. Yet Friedrich had seen the price of such bargains in the quiet moments when his mother thought no one was watching.

No, he wanted something different. *Something real.* As he gazed across the Atlantic's gray expanse, he thought of Germany—his true home, despite its current troubles. The country might be bowed by defeat, its economy in shambles, but Friedrich saw opportunity in the chaos. He dreamed of finding a woman who would see it, too—someone who would choose adventure over security, who would help him build something new from the ashes of the old world.

Over the past few years, he had met women who were willing to move to Germany with him. But he never felt that they loved him or his country. In fact, he was sure they were more in love with his money than with him. Friedrich knew that if he was ever going to marry, the woman would have to be special, different from the others. And if he didn't find her, he was resigned to spending the rest of his life as a bachelor traveling back and forth between Germany and America so that he could oversee his family's assets in both places.

He had to admit, he liked America. It was a young and idealistic country. For some people, like his father, it had fulfilled their dreams, but for others it had turned out to be filled with empty promises. However, as much as he enjoyed being a wealthy German-American, he knew that his heart lay in his native country across the Atlantic. And from what his friend, Bernhard Kohler, had been telling Friedrich in his letters recently, Germany was in the midst of growing political turmoil. Radical parties were gaining support, promising to bring change to Germany and rebuild it as a world power following the disastrous loss of the Great War.

Friedrich had been impressed when Bernhard told him that this new government was going to get the Jews who lived in Germany under control. Friedrich was tired of the Jews who he met in his business. They seemed to be taking over everything. He would never tell anyone else how he felt, but he had to admit to himself that these Jews were smart. He also found them to be arrogant and not to know their place. They spoke out of turn and thought they were equals to the Germans who they interacted with. This behavior grated on his nerves. *I'll probably be forced to endure an entire voyage with lots of Jews who are also staying in first class, even though they don't belong there,* he thought. *They're a lesser species and, no doubt, they should be in steerage.*

Bernhard had begged Friedrich to come to Germany and meet some of his friends who were members of a group called the National Socialist German Workers' Party. Friedrich never passed up a reason to return home and so he was on his way. He tapped his foot impatiently; he was about to go to the front of the line and use his family name to enable him to board immediately when he caught the gaze of an old family friend, someone he had known his whole life—Agnes Lange.

Agnes's family owned factories that made frames for eyeglasses. She came from money and both of their parents had been hopeful that one day they might marry. But Friedrich was not attracted to her in that way. Even so, to appease his mother, he had gone on a few dates with Agnes when they both came of age. She was bold and very willing to please him. Consequently, his first sexual encounter had taken place with her. She was sixteen at the time, he was seventeen. It was pleasant enough. They had gone out to dinner and had sex a handful of times. But it was far from magical and soon Friedrich had lost interest.

"Fancy meeting you here," Agnes said. She looked as sophisticated as ever in a traveling suit that must have come from Paris. The sea breeze caught her dark hair, and for a moment he saw the girl that she had been during their childhood summers in Baden-Baden.

"Agnes." Friedrich smiled. "Don't tell me you're bound for Germany, too?"

"Following in your brother's footsteps, it seems." She joined him at the railing. "How is your dear friend, Bernhard? I haven't seen him since... well, since before the war changed everything."

"Neither have I." Friedrich's smile turned wistful. "But you know Bernhard—he's probably still charming his way through Berlin's social circles, war or no war."

Agnes laughed, but there was something brittle in it. They both knew that the Germany they were sailing toward was not the one that they had left behind. "Yes, I imagine Bernhard is," she said. "Anyway, I'm going to live with my aunt and uncle in Germany for a while. My sister got herself into a bit of scandalous trouble, and because of her I've been forced to leave America for a while. Why are you going home?"

Friedrich knew that Agnes was hoping he would ask her what kind of trouble her sister had got into. If he did, she would have plenty to talk about. But quite frankly, he didn't care about her or her sister. Friedrich had been taught good manners, and he was doing his best to be polite, but he wished she would go away and leave him alone. He didn't want to tell her why he was going to see Bernhard. It was none of her business. He also knew that she wasn't blessed with intelligence and consequently he didn't want to discuss German politics with her.

"I'm just going home to visit our factory and to see Bernhard. No other reason. I was bored at home and I needed a bit of a change."

"That's understandable," Agnes said, smiling. She cocked her head. "We should get together while we're both in town."

"We'll see. I'm not sure I'll have time. Bernhard has made all sorts of arrangements for me. You know how he is. But I'll try," Friedrich replied.

"Well, a girl can't ask for more than that," Agnes said. She saw her maid signaling for her to come back. "It looks like I'm boarding. I hope we'll see each other on the ship. Perhaps we might have dinner in the dining room together?"

"Perhaps," he said.

Agnes smiled. "It's so good to see you. It's been such a long time, and you're just as handsome as I remember."

Friedrich merely smiled. *And you're as unattractive as I remember,* he thought.

FORTY-EIGHT

Gloria stood in the long line of people who were waiting to board the ship that was heading to Hamburg in Germany. She held Mimi and Nick's hands as they stood on the dock at Ellis Island and watched ragged but excited immigrants disembark from another large ship. Gloria watched as Nick guided Mimi to a shaded spot on the deck; she noticed the way that he positioned himself protectively between Mimi and the rushing crowds of passengers. At barely nine, he had already developed such gentle instincts—checking if Mimi was tired, making sure she had enough water, telling her stories to keep her mind off the endless ocean. Sometimes Gloria caught glimpses of Lily in the way that Mimi's face would light up at Nick's small kindnesses; it reminded her of the same trusting smile that her mother had given them when she had first opened her door to two relative strangers.

The newly landed immigrants looked exhausted but full of hope as they left the ship. Guards led the new arrivals inside the building. Gloria watched the bright faces of immigrants crowding the ship's railings, straining for their first glimpse of America. She remembered Lily telling her that when she, Joe, and Mimi had first come on a ship to America, she'd had that same yearning in her own heart—that belief that a new world meant a new life. Now Gloria was sailing away from those golden dreams, knowing too well how they could tarnish. She thought of the factory girls working themselves to the bone, the veterans begging on street corners, the desperate mothers in breadlines. Even Lily, beautiful Lily who had married for love, had found only heartbreak on those promised streets. The people getting off this ship with their worn clothes and broken suitcases had left behind everyone and everything they knew in hopes of finding a better life. Gloria wondered how many of them would. Most of them would end up in poor and over-crowded neighborhoods like the one where she had lived until Lily had given her an opportunity to see what life could be like.

The line at Ellis Island barely moved, crowds pressing against each other in the warm breeze. Gloria studied the women around her—hollow-eyed mothers clutching children's hands, young girls with pinched faces, elderly *babushkas* dabbing at tears with threadbare handkerchiefs. Some wore tags marking them for deportation: TB, heart trouble, mental defi-ciency. Others simply hadn't passed the officials' stern interro-gations about their finances, their politics, their morality.

Each tear told a different story of a dream dying. A seam-stress whose fingers were too arthritic to prove she could work. A widow whose savings had been stolen on the crossing. A young mother whose cough had betrayed her at the wrong moment. Gloria held Mimi closer, grateful that their papers—purchased at such cost—would carry them safely onto the ship, away from this island where America's promises had turned to dust for so many.

It was a hot day, and the sun was high in the sky. Beads of perspiration formed on Gloria's forehead and the hair at the nape of her neck was wet with sweat. She was tired and wished she could lie down, but they had to stand in line until they were boarded onto the ship.

"I'm hungry, Mama," Nick said.

"I'm sorry, I don't have anything for you to eat," Gloria said sadly. She had packed whatever food was in the house, but there was not much, and she needed to keep it for the children's dinner that night. *Nick is growing so fast, he's always hungry,* Gloria thought, worrying about the long journey ahead. *Little Mimi hardly eats so she'll be no trouble on this voyage, but Nick is a growing boy, and he needs food. Even though I have a little money left over from selling Lily's pin and the money from the mob, it won't last forever, and I don't know how we're going to get along once we get to France. I don't speak the language, but I'm going to need to find some kind of job.*

"Excuse me, miss." A handsome young man was standing in front of Gloria. She could tell that he was wealthy from his clothing, and she assumed he had probably booked a stateroom.

"Yes?" she answered.

"It's none of my business, but I heard your little boy say that he's hungry and it just so happens that I have a sandwich, a few cookies, and an apple. Would it be alright with you if I gave him this food? I'm not very hungry and my sister always has the maid pack a snack for me when I travel."

"I'm hungry, Mama. Can I please have the food? I'll share it with Mimi," Nick pleaded, gazing longingly at the sandwich and cookies.

How can I deny Nick this food? I don't know who this man is, but I'll have to hope and pray that it's safe. Gloria nodded cautiously. "If you're sure you don't want it?"

"I'm quite sure. I had a big breakfast before I left."

"Well, it's very kind of you. Thank you so much," Gloria said.

The man reached into his bag and took out a small package that was carefully wrapped in white kitchen towel. He opened it and presented its contents to the children. Nick immediately grabbed the sandwich. He tore it in half, dividing it between himself and Mimi. Then he began eating. But when Nick looked over at Mimi, he saw she was not eating the sandwich he had given her. She was hiding behind Gloria's skirt, looking scared and shy.

Before he took another bite, Nick walked over to Mimi. "It's alright. Eat," he said gently, but she refused. "Would you prefer a cookie?" he asked, picking one up and handing it to her. Mimi nodded. She took it and began to stuff it into her mouth.

The handsome young man smiled at Gloria. "My sister would be so pleased," he said. "She always accuses me of throwing away the food she packs. And to be honest, I often do. If I ate everything she tried to give me, I'd be working as the fat man in the circus."

Gloria laughed. "Well, I appreciate your kind gesture," she said. "And the children appreciate it, too."

He smiled. "I'm glad to be of help," he said. "I'm Friedrich Wagner. Pleased to be at your service, madam." Friedrich winked. "And I hope it's not too presumptuous of me, but may I be so bold as to ask your name?"

"Gloria," she replied, smiling. "Wagner?" she asked. "Any relation to the composer?"

"I'm afraid not," Friedrich said.

"I'm Nick and this is Mimi," Nick chimed in proudly.

"Well, it certainly is a pleasure to meet the three of you. And you are quite the eloquent young man," Fredrich said, looking directly at Nick. "How old are you, son?"

"Nine," Nick said, holding up seven fingers.

"You're very mature for your age, aren't you?" Friedrich asked.

"Yes, sir." Nick smiled.

"May I ask what brings you on this journey across the ocean?"

"Oh, yes," Gloria stammered. "Mimi has a grandmother in France. I'm taking her to visit her grandmother." She was uncomfortable giving a stranger too much information about herself, but he seemed so kind. "How about you, why are you going overseas? Your accent tells me that you were born in Germany. Is that true?"

"Yes, actually, it is. My family is from Germany, and I am one hundred percent German."

"I'm of German descent, too. My parents came to America from Düsseldorf," Gloria said.

"And what does your family do for a living?" he asked.

"Not much. Whatever work we can get," she said. "What about you, what does your family do for a living?"

"We own two clothing factories."

"I see. Clothes for men or women?"

"Women. Ready-to-wear. We have one factory in America and another in Munich where we make ready-to-wear skirts and blouses for working girls. We also have a division that produces very expensive custom clothing. So, we must always keep up with the latest fashions."

She smiled at him. "That sounds like fun."

Friedrich laughed. "I wouldn't call it fun. It's definitely work, but I have to say the business has been good for us. It's very lucrative."

"You must be happy about that," Gloria said, intrigued by the man but also willing him to leave them alone.

"Of course," he admitted. "May I ask you another question?"

"Yes, please do," Gloria said. *I have to be polite and friendly,* she reminded herself. *After all, he gave the children his snack.*

"I know this is rather bold of me, but I hope you won't take offense," Friedrich said.

"Please, go ahead and ask me whatever you want to ask me," Gloria said, hoping he was not going to say something offensive.

"Do you have a stateroom on the ship or are your tickets for steerage?" he asked.

"We're in steerage," Gloria admitted.

"I feel it's my duty to tell you that it is not a good idea for you to travel in steerage on a ship heading back to Europe. Most of the people who will be traveling with you have been rejected at Ellis Island because they were sick. Some of the diseases they have, or are carrying, are life-threatening." Friedrich hesitated for a moment before continuing. "To make matters worse, many of these people are very contagious. That's why America is forcing them to go home."

"I see, but steerage was all we could afford," Gloria explained. "And we must take a ship to Europe. I owe it to this little girl's mother to make sure she is delivered safely to her grandmother. Her mother was my friend. My best friend. She passed away, and I know this is what she would have wanted."

"I'm not saying don't go to Europe. Of course, I understand, you must go. But not in steerage. Perhaps you wouldn't mind if I put you in a stateroom with the children?" he asked tentatively.

"Your stateroom?" Gloria said. *I knew this was coming,* she thought. *Men always expect something for their kindness.*

"Oh, no. Of course not. I would never expect a lady to stay in a room with a gentleman who is not her husband. I want to purchase a stateroom for you and the two children. Hopefully, it will be close to mine so that we might see each other on the ship. Perhaps you and the children might like to dine with me one evening?" Friedrich said.

"But staterooms are so expensive, and quite frankly, I couldn't let you do that," she said.

"I must do it," he replied firmly. "Don't you see, as a gentleman, I can't possibly let you and these two adorable children board this boat and go downstairs to steerage where you'll be in close contact with people who have cholera, tuberculosis, trachoma, and who knows what other diseases. Believe me, there will be many sick people on this ship, especially in steerage. Are you familiar with any of these diseases?"

"I know of them," Gloria said.

"Well, these two beautiful children are so young and vulnerable. They could easily contract one of these horrible diseases. If that happened, I'd never be able to forgive myself because, right now, I have the opportunity to prevent it."

Gloria did not answer. She had no idea what to say. *If I accept this man's generosity, I'll owe him and he'll expect me to go to his bed*, she thought, recalling her awful experiences with Joe.

"So, what do you say? Shall I purchase a stateroom for you?"

"Really, it's not necessary."

"But it is," Friedrich insisted. "It is a matter of life and death. Do you have any idea how terrible trachoma is?"

Gloria shook her head. "I have no idea."

"Well, I'll tell you so you can make an educated decision as to whether you will accept my gift." He smiled at her, a warm and caring smile. After clearing his throat, Friedrich continued, "First, the eyes begin to itch and then they burn. Next, pus oozes out of them."

She shivered a little. She hadn't considered any of this when she bought the tickets for steerage. This man's description was making her nervous.

Friedrich carried on describing the awful disease. "You'd think this disease would only cause blindness and that is certainly bad enough. However, trachoma is fatal. And I have a feeling it's going to run rampant in steerage, because many of the passengers down there already have it. You see, if the people who run the immigration program at Ellis Island even suspect that an immigrant has any one of these diseases, they're immediately put back on the ship that brought them here. They are not allowed into America. So, I'm quite certain that many of the passengers in steerage are ill and that's why they are being deported."

"That's horrible," Gloria said. "Those poor people. I know it means the world to them to get to America. I'm sure most of them have spent every penny they have to make this journey. How can they ever pay for their passage back to Europe?"

"They don't have to pay for that. The law says that the shipping line that brought them to America must pay for them to be sent back to Europe. And, as you can imagine, the shipping line wants to transport them as cheaply as possible. So, they pile them into steerage. It's dirty and overcrowded. It would warm my heart if you would allow me to help you. I promise you that I will ask nothing of you in return except perhaps your friendship."

Gloria stood still for a moment, letting her thoughts take over, then she looked down into Nick and little Mimi's eyes. *I can't let anything like that happen to them.* "Thank you for your generosity. I will accept your offer. It's very kind of you and I must protect the children the best I can," Gloria said. She was certain that he was lying about not expecting anything from her. Years of survival had taught her the true cost of men's "kindness." But with two vulnerable children in her care, she couldn't risk the dangers of steerage—the disease, the predators, the crushing crowds. She owed it to Mimi and Nick to keep them safe, whatever the price might be.

FORTY-NINE

True to his word, Friedrich upgraded Gloria and the children to a clean and comfortable state room. Gloria was surprised to find how luxurious it was. And the following morning when Gloria passed the entrance to steerage on her way to the dining area, she looked in. When she saw the wretched conditions within, Gloria knew that she would do anything to keep the children away from such misery. Her heart ached, remembering Lily's stories of her own desperate journey to America. *Oh, Lily,* she thought, *you should have had this. You deserved so much better than the life that Joe gave you.*

When Gloria and the children entered the dining room, Friedrich was already seated at a lovely mahogany table with a white tablecloth. He smiled and waved to Gloria, indicating that he would like her and the children to join him. They headed over. "Good morning," he said. "How did you sleep?"

"Very well," she replied, watching Nick help Mimi on to her seat with brotherly care. When Gloria settled next to Friedrich, she caught the subtle scent of his cologne.

"And the little ones? Did they sleep alright?" His voice held genuine concern.

"They were exhausted—slept like angels." Gloria smoothed her skirt, aware of his attention.

"Well, that's good." Friedrich's smile was warm, but something shifted in his expression as he studied her. "Tell me, how is it that a pretty young lady like you is traveling alone?"

"I'm not alone," she said softly, gesturing to the children. "We're taking Mimi to her grandmother in Paris."

"Yes, but..." His eyes held hers. "I was wondering about your husband."

Gloria hesitated, then lifted her chin. No point hiding what he would learn eventually. "I don't have one."

"Is the little boy yours?"

"Nick is my biological son. We've been alone since his father passed away," she lied. She didn't feel comfortable sharing her story about Nick's father with a stranger. "Mimi has no one but me and her grandmother in France," Gloria added, watching the children. "I was her nanny when her parents died. Her mother was..." She swallowed hard. "She was my dearest friend."

She stroked Mimi's hair as the little girl leaned against her. "But I can't afford to raise two children on my own. I need to find work and no family will take a nanny with two children in tow." Gloria's voice softened. "That's why I'm taking Mimi to her grandmother in Paris."

"That's awfully kind of you. Most nannies wouldn't make this trip. After all, the child is no longer your responsibility. Most people in your position would just abandon their charge. Believe me, I know," Friedrich continued, his voice taking on a bitter edge. "My mother had plenty of nannies look after me when I was young. She became quite the society lady and she really didn't want to be bothered with me, so she hired women to come in and take care of me. Not one of them truly cared. If my parents had died or stopped paying them..." Friedrich shook his head. "They would have vanished without a second thought about what might happen to me."

"How terribly sad. I'm so sorry," Lily said, her heart breaking a little for the young Friedrich.

He shrugged. "What does it matter? It was a long time ago."

"And now, would it be alright if I asked you the same question you asked me?" she said, turning to him.

"Of course, my life is an open book," he answered, smiling and spreading his arms wide as if he was welcoming any questions she might have.

"Are you married?" Gloria asked.

"Me? Nope. I've never been married."

"Why not? You're a handsome man and quite charming."

"I like my independence. I've enjoyed being able to pack up and travel whenever I like."

"I can understand that. So, where is your destination? Where do you plan to go after this voyage?"

"Well"—Friedrich smiled again—"once we hit land, I'm planning to stay in Munich. A boyhood friend of mine who I've kept in contact with over the years has joined an organization called the National Socialist German Workers' Party. I'm very interested in learning more about it. From what he tells me, I like their doctrine and I may join as well."

Gloria hadn't kept abreast of the political situation in Germany and was curious to know more, but before she could ask another question a waiter wearing a black tuxedo and white gloves walked over to the table. "May I take your order?" he asked.

She looked at the waiter nervously, cleared her throat, and said, "Just some warm milk for the children."

"Nonsense," Friedrich said. "All of you must be famished." He turned to the waiter and commanded, "Make it a full English breakfast for each of us."

"Yes, sir." The waiter nodded before walking off briskly.

Gloria was embarrassed, but she had to ask, "Is the cost of food included with the stateroom?"

"No, the ship will keep a running tab of everything we spend. Then at the end of the voyage, we pay the entire bill. But don't worry, I intend to pay for the food on this voyage for all of us. After all, how could I allow a beautiful lady like you and her lovely children to go hungry?"

"Are you sure you want to do this? I feel so indebted. I do have some money of my own," Gloria said.

Friedrich laughed. "It's really my pleasure. And you aren't at all indebted to me. In fact, I hope it's alright to tell you that I'm enjoying your company."

She smiled back but inside she felt panic begin to take hold. *What if he expects me to give him what every man wants? What will I do then? The small sum of money I have left won't go very far on a ship like this, especially if we're not in steerage.*

Heaped plates of eggs, sausage, bread, and baked beans arrived a few minutes later. Nick helped Mimi to put her napkin on her lap and handed her a fork. The children were starving and so was Gloria. She hadn't eaten since the previous morning and her instinct was to wolf down the food, but she forced herself to eat slowly.

"There's a masquerade ball on the ship tonight," Friedrich said as they ate. "May I be so bold to ask you to attend with me?"

"A masquerade ball? I don't have a costume. And besides, I can't leave the children alone in the stateroom. I'm sorry, I must decline," Gloria replied.

"First off, you won't need a costume, only a mask that I'll purchase for you. And, as far as the children are concerned, I'll find a sitter for them. There are plenty of young women on this boat who would love the opportunity to earn a few American dollars."

"But can I trust someone I don't know to care for the children? It seems rather irresponsible," she said, shaking her head. "I'm sorry, but I really don't think it's a good idea."

"Very well then. I completely understand."

"I am sorry," Gloria said softly.

"Do you know how to play any card games?" Friedrich asked.

"I do. But I haven't played cards in years," she admitted.

"That's alright. We won't play for money, of course. We'll play for fun."

"I'm not sure I understand. You want to play cards with me?" she asked, cocking her head.

"I was wondering if you'd be willing to play cards with me in your stateroom this evening instead of attending the masquerade? That way we can all be together, and you and I can keep an eye on the children."

"Oh," Gloria stammered, feeling uncomfortable at the idea of him joining her in her stateroom.

As if reading her mind, he smiled a warm and embracing smile that reached all the way up to his twinkling eyes. "You can be assured that I will be a perfect gentleman. I wouldn't think of taking advantage of the situation. And, if you would like, I'll retire to my own cabin as soon as the children go to bed. That way, you don't have to feel uncomfortable about us being alone together."

Gloria smiled. *He is a stranger, but he seems so kind—so refined and understanding.* "Alright," she agreed, "but are you sure you want to miss the party?"

"I've been to millions of parties. But it's not every day that I can spend some time getting to know a beautiful young woman and the two lovely children with whom she is traveling."

"That's awfully kind of you to say."

"It's true. It's exactly how I feel." He smiled. "So, why don't we meet right here at this table for dinner? Would seven this evening be alright? And, of course, you will bring Nick and Mimi with you.

Mimi was making a mess as she tried to eat without any grown-up help.

"Oh dear," Gloria said as Mimi accidentally dropped a sausage on the floor. "I'm so sorry. She's still very young." Gloria bent to pick up the sausage.

"Please, let it be. The staff in the dining room will clean up after every meal. You'll see that when we come back for dinner tonight, the place will be spotless."

"I'll help Mimi," Nick volunteered as he began to cut her other sausage into small enough pieces for her to pick them up with her fingers. Then Nick turned to speak to Friedrich. "Mimi isn't very good with a fork yet."

"It's alright, son. I understand. And it's very grown up of you to help her. You are quite the little gentleman."

Nick smiled broadly, clearly taken with Friedrich.

After they finished eating breakfast, Nick gently wiped a crumb off Mimi's cheek. She smiled up at him. *They're like brother and sister.*

Gloria noticed a tall woman in an expensive blue silk dress approaching their table, her face pinched with disapproval. Even before she spoke, Gloria recognized the type—she had the same look of superiority that she had seen on Lenny's mother's face years ago.

"My goodness, Friedrich. I was hardly expecting to see you here in the first-class dining room with a wench from steerage and her two little urchins," Agnes said coldly.

Gloria looked away. *The woman knows we're poor because of our clothing,* she realized. Suddenly she felt ashamed sitting in the dining room. Gloria had been so entranced by Friedrich that she had not noticed anyone else. But now, as she looked around, she registered the fine clothes that the other people were wearing.

Friedrich gave Agnes a look of disgust.

"It seems you've made time to have breakfast with them," Agnes continued. "Since you have time to spare, you could arrange to have dinner with me this evening if you so choose."

"I'm sorry, Agnes." Friedrich kept his eyes on his coffee cup. "I have other plans."

"Tomorrow perhaps?" Agnes laid her gloved hand on his shoulder.

"Perhaps." His tone was noncommittal.

Agnes straightened, her lips pressed into a thin line. She looked through Gloria and the children as if they were invisible, focusing only on Friedrich. "I'd really love to spend some time with you. We could catch up on old times." With a rustle of expensive silk, she turned and glided away, her spine rigid with wounded pride.

A few minutes later, the waiter brought the bill and Friedrich signed it. Then he turned to Nick. "Would you like to take a tour of the ship? We can go and see the kitchen and meet the chef. And I'm sure I can talk him into giving you two some cookies."

"Really? Do you know him?" Nick asked excitedly, his eyes wide.

"I've been on this ship before, so yes, we've met. I also know the captain and I can introduce you to him, too. He's a very nice fellow who will be happy to tell you exactly what it's like to run a large ship like this. What do you think? Would you like to do that this morning?" Friedrich was speaking directly to Nick.

"I would love to meet the captain," Nick admitted. Mimi was too young to understand Friedrich's offer. She just grabbed Nick's hand and held it. He smiled and gently pinched her cheek, making her smile.

"So, what are we waiting for? Let's go and explore the ship. Shall we?" Friedrich said as he winked at Nick then turned to

Gloria with a gentle smile that erased any lingering tension from Agnes's visit. "Shall we?"

Gloria felt something like hope unfurling in her chest. Here was a man who saw beyond circumstances to the heart of things, just as Lily had done.

FIFTY

They spent the entire morning and early afternoon meeting everyone who was of any importance on the ship. As Friedrich promised, the chef gave the children two large sugar cookies each.

"Here, Mimi. Save one for later," Nick said, tucking the extra cookie in his pocket.

Gloria noticed both children's eyes growing heavy from their morning of exploration. "I think we all need a rest before dinner."

"Not yet," Mimi protested, but her words dissolved into a yawn.

"Is anyone hungry first?" Friedrich asked.

"Yes, please," Nick said, already at ease in Friedrich's presence.

"How about a quick lunch in the dining room, then?" Friedrich led them to a table, ordering cheese and bread. The children ate heartily while Gloria declined, still full from breakfast.

After walking them back to their stateroom, Friedrich paused at the door. "Shall we say seven tonight for dinner?"

"That would be perfect," Gloria said.

Back in the stateroom, Gloria tried to lose herself in her book, but Friedrich's voice, and his gentle manner with the children, kept intruding. She lay down on the sofa, pressing her palms against her eyes, but rest would not come. Every time that Gloria closed her eyes, she saw Friedrich's smile. Finally, exhaustion pulled her under.

A little while later, Gloria was woken by Nick's gentle touch on her shoulder.

"Mimi and I are hungry," he whispered.

"What time is it?"

"It's almost nighttime. It's getting dark outside," Nick answered. Gloria sat up and ran her hands through her hair. "Where's Mimi?" she asked.

"She's still in her bed."

"Alright. Why don't you help Mommy? Can you go and get Mimi and help her to wash her face and hands? And you must wash yourself, too." Gloria studied Nick. "Oh dear, your shirt is very wrinkled." She shook her head, conscious of trying to avoid further judgement from first-class passengers. "I'll leave a clean shirt on the bed. Make sure you change after you wash up. Then we'll go and meet Friedrich for dinner."

But a few seconds later, Nick returned. His face was pale and his eyes were wide. When he spoke, his voice shook as if he might start crying. "Mimi is gone," he said.

"What?" Gloria stood up, startled. "She has to be here."

"She's not. I've looked all over the stateroom. I've looked everywhere," Nick said. He was wringing his hands.

Gloria felt herself starting to panic. *How did Mimi get out of this room? The door is very heavy, too heavy for her to open. She's such a little thing. If she's alone on deck, she could easily fall off the ship and drown in the ocean. I must find her quickly.*

"Nick"—Gloria could hear her voice shaking as she checked the clock—"it's a few minutes after seven and Mr. Friedrich will be waiting for us in the dining room. I need your help and you must be very grown up. Can you help me?"

"Yes, Mommy." He stood straighter, his small face serious.

"Listen carefully." Gloria gripped Nick's shoulders, her heart racing as she knelt down to his level. She tried to steady her voice. "Go straight to the dining room. Don't stop and talk to anyone. You must do exactly as I say. This is very important. Do you remember where we were sitting in the dining room?"

"Yes." Nick nodded solemnly, already backing towards the door.

"Alright. You must go there directly and tell Mr. Friedrich that we need his help. Explain that Mimi is missing, and that we must find her quickly because she is too young to understand the dangers of being on a boat like this. Can you do this? Can I count on you, Nick?"

"Yes, of course I can. I'm so worried about Mimi, Mommy," he said, his voice quivering. "Do you... do you think we'll find her?"

"Dear God, I hope so," Gloria said and then caught herself, registering the fear in Nick's face. *I must put on a brave face for my son.* "We'll find her, sweetheart. You go tell Mr. Friedrich. I'm going to knock on the doors of everyone on this floor to see if they've seen her."

Gloria ran from stateroom to stateroom knocking on the doors, her breath catching in her throat. "Have you seen a little girl—blonde hair, blue eyes?" But each shake of the head sent fresh panic through her veins. *Lily trusted me with her child. Oh God, please.*

When she knocked on the next door, a maid answered. Through the opening, Gloria caught sight of Agnes lounging on a silk-covered sofa. The woman rose with fluid grace, her lips curving into a cold smile as she approached.

"Well. If it isn't Friedrich's breakfast companion. Do come in, dear," she said to Lily. Her voice was honey over steel. "I believe we need to have a conversation."

Gloria hovered at the doorway. "I don't have time to sit and talk. My little girl is missing. Do you remember her? Have you seen her?" She spoke quickly, desperate to continue searching for Mimi.

"I do remember her. Such a pretty child." Agnes's smile never reached her eyes. "But no, I haven't left my room all afternoon. However"—she moved to block Gloria's path—"there are things you need to hear about Friedrich. I've known him for years, you see. And if you're imagining some fairy-tale ending..." She gave a soft, cruel laugh. "Friedrich enjoys his little diversions. Especially with women who are... beneath him. You're merely entertainment for the voyage, my dear. Nothing more."

"Thank you for the advice. But right now, I'm looking for my little girl." Gloria felt her blood boiling. "She is missing, so if you don't have any information about her, I'm going to leave so I can find her."

"Well, my dear, just keep what I told you in mind. Because if you trust Friedrich, I can assure you he'll most definitely break your heart," Agnes said coolly before heading back into her room.

Gloria didn't answer. She backed into the hall, preoccupied with finding the little girl. *Where are you, Mimi?* She felt light-headed and gripped with panic.

A few minutes later, Nick returned with Friedrich.

The three of them searched the entire ship, but they couldn't find Mimi. Gloria sank into a deck chair, her legs finally giving out. "What if she..." She couldn't finish the terrible thought.

"We'll find her," Friedrich said softly, but the growing darkness beyond the ship's rails made his words ring hollow.

Nick pressed against his mother's side, his face streaked with tears. "Mama, what if—"

"No." Gloria's voice cracked. "This is my fault. I fell asleep, I wasn't watching them. Oh God, I promised Lily I'd keep her safe." Her hands trembled as she covered her face.

"Come on," Friedrich said, taking Gloria's hand. "Let's go back to your stateroom. You can wash your face and dry those tears. We'll find her. You'll see. Once you're ready, we can go and speak to some of the ship's crew. I'm sure they'll be able to help us."

Gloria could barely stand, her legs trembling beneath her. Friedrich's arm around her waist was the only thing keeping her upright as they hurried to the stateroom. She was beyond caring about propriety now.

They burst into the stateroom and Gloria's heart stopped. There, curled up small on the sofa, was Mimi—thumb in mouth, stuffed rabbit clutched tight, tears streaking her face. For a moment, no one moved. Then Gloria rushed forward with a sob, gathering the child into her arms so fiercely that Mimi's stuffed rabbit tumbled to the floor.

"Where were you, sweetheart?" she whispered into Mimi's hair, her voice raw. "We've been so worried."

Mimi pointed a tiny finger toward the closet, her lower lip trembling. "I was sleeping in there."

Nick launched himself at his friend, wrapping her in a protective hug. His small shoulders shook with relief as Mimi buried her face against him, her tears soaking his shirt while he gently wiped her cheeks with his sleeve.

Gloria caught Friedrich's eye over the children's heads. The tension of the last hour seemed to drain from the room with their shared exhale.

"You gave us quite a scare, little one," Friedrich said softly, but Mimi was already drifting off against Nick's shoulder, exhausted from her adventure and their worry.

"Are you alright?" Friedrich asked Gloria. His gentle question made her realize that she was still shaking.

"I am now," she said, pressing her hand to her heart and feeling it slowly return to a normal rhythm. "Though I thought... when we couldn't find her—"

"But we did." Friedrich touched her shoulder lightly. "Now, I think we could all use some dinner. What do you say?"

"I'm hungry," Nick piped up, still holding Mimi close.

"Give me a moment to compose myself," Gloria said, touching her tear-stained cheeks. "Then we can go to dinner."

FIFTY-ONE

The stress had left Gloria famished and at dinner she cleared her plate for the first time in days.

Back in the stateroom, the children changed for bed while Friedrich settled into an armchair to read one of their books. His warm voice brought the story to life, both children leaning in closer with each page.

"Alright, you two." Gloria smoothed Mimi's hair. "It's been quite a day. Remember—no one leaves this room without telling me first. Understood?"

"Yes, Mama," Nick said. Mimi nodded, her thumb creeping toward her mouth again.

"Into bed now."

"Please, not yet." Nick's eyes were bright despite his obvious fatigue. "I want to stay up with Mr. Friedrich."

Friedrich leaned forward, touching Nick's shoulder. "We'll have plenty of time tomorrow, young man. And if you're good, I will show you my record player. But, right now, you need sleep."

"You promise?"

"I give you my word."

. . .

Once the children were settled, Gloria sat down beside Friedrich in the living room. The lamplight cast soft shadows across his face. "I can't thank you enough for everything today," she said.

"No need," he replied softly, his smile reaching his eyes.

"But you dropped everything to help search for Mimi." Gloria's voice wavered. "I can't tell you what that means."

"I'm just glad we found her."

"So am I. That was very scary."

"I know... Nick was so helpful," Friedrich said. "You've done a good job raising him."

Gloria smiled at the compliment. "He's a good boy."

"Yes, he is." Friedrich's voice softened. "And that bit about making me promise to return—that went straight to my heart."

"Everyone Nick's ever grown close to has disappeared," Gloria said quietly. "Except for me and Mimi."

"Speaking of disappearing acts..." Friedrich gave a gentle laugh, though his eyes were serious. "Little Mimi certainly gave us all a fright today."

"She certainly did." Gloria laughed a little, too, but it sprang from relief rather than amusement. She looked into the bedroom where both children were sleeping. Nick was hugging Mimi. "Aww, look at how sweet that is," Gloria said to Friedrich, indicating the sleeping children.

"Yes, it's very sweet," he agreed. "He's only nine and already he's in love."

Gloria laughed again, but more heartily this time. "Yes, I believe Mimi just might be his first love."

"Will you and the children meet me in the dining room tomorrow morning for breakfast?" Friedrich asked.

"We would love to," Gloria said.

"Is eight o'clock too early?" Friedrich asked.

"No, not at all. The children are awake by seven so that will give us an hour to get ready. It's perfect," she said. "I hope you don't mind, I know I promised to spend the evening with you playing cards, but it's been a long day, and I'm not in any mood to play cards tonight. I'm afraid this whole incident has exhausted me."

"Quite understandable." He smiled. "Why don't you and the children get some rest, and I'll see all of you in the morning?"

"Very well. Good night then."

Friedrich took her hand and kissed it. "Until tomorrow," he said before he left Gloria's stateroom, closing the door softly.

FIFTY-TWO

The following morning, Friedrich was waiting at their table when Gloria and the children entered the dining room. He greeted them warmly as he stood up to pull out the chair for Gloria. Then Nick pulled out a chair for Mimi and helped her to climb up.

"Just look at Nick, he's growing up to be a little gentleman," Friedrich said.

"He emulates you," Gloria said. "I noticed it yesterday."

Friedrich leaned forward, his hands clasped together. "I hope you won't think I'm overstepping..." He hesitated.

Gloria tensed slightly, drawing back into her chair. "Go on."

"It's not me teaching him those wonderful manners—it's you." Friedrich's voice softened. "You're an extraordinary mother. That's plain to see."

Gloria looked down at her hands, warmth rising in her cheeks. "I just... try to give him what I never had."

"However, I can see that Nick is badly in need of a father to help him navigate the world. It's only natural for a boy."

She didn't say a word. But she knew he was right. Her son needed a man to mold himself after.

Friedrich and Gloria fell into silence as they sat at the table watching the children. Nick straightened in his chair, mimicking Friedrich's posture. Then Nick turned to Mimi and asked, "What do you want to eat for breakfast? If you tell me, I'll order it from the waiter the way that Friedrich orders my mother's food for her."

Mimi leaned close to Nick's ear, her blonde curls falling forward. Nick's face brightened as she whispered; her request was too quiet for the adults to overhear.

"Alright. I'll get it for you," Nick said, already signaling for the waiter with all the gravity of a small gentleman.

Gloria smiled at Friedrich. "You're right. He does need a father figure."

The waiter walked over and asked to take their order. Nick spoke up immediately, "Mimi would like hotcakes. I would like the same full English breakfast that we had yesterday. And we would both like some milk."

"Excellent ordering, young man," Friedrich said warmly. Nick's cheeks flushed pink with pride. "Now, how about you, my dear?" he said to Gloria. "What would you like?"

Gloria told Friedrich that she would also love some hot cakes. So, Friedrich ordered Gloria's hotcakes and some scrambled eggs and toast for himself.

It was a beautiful day with a crisp ocean breeze. Once everyone finished eating, Friedrich suggested they all go and sit up on the deck where they might enjoy observing the water for a while. Gloria was looking forward to the fresh air.

First, they strolled along the deck. As they did, they passed Agnes and her maid, who were both sitting in the sun. Agnes was reading a book and pretended not to notice Gloria. But she smiled at Friedrich. "Good morning, Freddy," she said coyly.

"Morning, Agnes," Friedrich replied curtly, steering them to the far side of the deck. Gloria noticed the tightness in his jaw as they settled into their chairs.

The children sprawled on the deck with their jacks and ball, their laughter carried away by the wind. Gloria tilted her face to the sun, letting the salty spray kiss her lips, savoring this moment of peace. Everything felt right—the children's happiness, Friedrich's steady presence beside her.

"Gloria." Something in Friedrich's voice made her open her eyes. He had turned to face her, his expression intense. "I know we've only known each other days, but..." He drew in a deep breath. "I have something important to ask you."

She turned toward him, her heart suddenly racing.

"Gloria, would you consider marrying me?"

She sat stunned, her mouth dry. "I'm honored, truly. But I need time—time to get to know you better before I could answer something like that."

"Of course," he said gently. "Take all the time you need."

FIFTY-THREE

That evening after dinner, they followed Friedrich to his stateroom to see the record player he had described to them. Nick could hardly believe that music could come from a piece of metal, but Friedrich's eyes twinkled as he ruffled the boy's hair. "It's called an Orthophonic Victrola," he explained, "and I promise you it will play."

Gloria watched Nick gazing up at Friedrich with shining eyes, her heart both warming and constricting. This man's tenderness with her son touched something deep within her, but experience had taught her cruel lessons. If Friedrich proved to be false like the others, it wouldn't just be her heart breaking this time—it would be Nick's, too.

The children were sat down beside Gloria, but as soon as Friedrich started his music machine, Nick rose to his feet. He marveled at the machine as he listened. Mimi giggled and clapped her hands. Even Gloria, who had heard of such music machines, had never seen one before. It was wonderful to sit on the sofa and listen to music without needing to go to a ballroom to hear a live band.

For half an hour, the children were mesmerized by the spinning disk, while Gloria watched their wonder with a mother's pleasure. Nick pulled Mimi to her feet and soon they were twirling wildly to the rhythm. Then Friedrich rose and turned to Gloria, extending his hand. "Would you dance with me?"

Something in his gentle request made her pulse quicken. She stood, placing her hand in his. As they began to move together, Gloria found herself aware of every point of contact—his hand at her waist, firm but respectful, the light touch of his fingers against hers. It had been so long since she had been held like this, with such care. The scent of Friedrich's cologne mingled with the salty air drifting through the window, and for a moment, she allowed herself to forget her doubts and simply feel the music moving through them both.

The children watched in awe as the adults danced in perfect unison to the melody filling the room. When the second song came on, Nick took Mimi's hand and led her to the middle of the room. Then to the best of his ability he began to imitate the dance he had seen his mother and Friedrich do.

Mimi twirled around the room with surprising grace, following their steps. Watching her, Gloria remembered Lily's stories of her mother, the ballerina. The child moved with such innate elegance, a gift that must have been passed down through blood.

The sight squeezed Gloria's heart. *Oh, Lily.* Her closest friend, closer than even her own sister, taken so cruelly. Joe had forced her hand, made her betray the one person who had shown her true kindness. *If only you were here now, Lily,* she thought. *You'd know whether I could trust this caring man who makes your daughter laugh, who treats my son like he matters. You'd tell me if it's safe to hope again.*

As the music continued to play, Nick led Mimi around the room. He was trying to waltz with her as Gloria and Friedrich watched. The children were so adorable that they had to laugh. In fact, they laughed so hard that they had to stop dancing and sit down to catch their breath. When Gloria looked over at Nick, she saw that he was smiling. *Friedrich is right. It is obvious that Nick needs a father figure. He thrives whenever Friedrich is around. He imitates him and wants to do everything Friedrich does.*

Every night of the voyage after their music-filled evening, they all went to Friedrich's stateroom after dinner. Sometimes they played cards, other times they danced. Usually, the children fell asleep on Friedrich's bed. But he never seemed to mind. And at the end of the night, Friedrich walked Gloria and the children back to their stateroom. At the end of one of their evenings together, when they arrived back at Gloria's stateroom, the children ran into their bedroom while Gloria and Friedrich stood just outside the door. "Would you like to come in?" she asked him.

"I don't think so. It's late. You and the children should get some rest. I'll see you in the dining room in the morning," he replied softly.

"Yes, we'll be there," Gloria said affectionately.

As she reached for her door, Friedrich leaned in and brushed his lips against hers—gentle, questioning. When he pulled back, uncertainty flickered across his face.

"I hope you're not offended."

"No." Her voice was barely a whisper.

"Every evening with you, with the children..." His eyes held hers. "You've made this voyage something special."

Gloria felt warmth rise to her cheeks; she dropped her gaze.

"Those two are quite extraordinary," Friedrich said, glancing towards the children's bedroom.

"They are, aren't they?" Pride colored her voice.

"Thank you, Gloria. For making these days the sweetest I've known at sea."

. . .

Throughout the long voyage, Friedrich remained true to his gentle nature. Each evening ended with nothing more demanding than a soft kiss, his hand warm in Gloria's as they watched the children play on deck. It was so different from what she had known before—this patient tenderness that asked for nothing more than she was ready to give.

FIFTY-FOUR

The Hamburg docks bustled with activity as their ship eased into port. Nick and Mimi pressed against the railing, their eyes wide at the forest of masts and smokestacks, the strange German calls of the dock workers, the bustle of porters with their laden carts. It was their first glimpse of Europe, and Gloria watched their wonder with a mix of joy and apprehension. But as Gloria looked out at the harbor, she suddenly felt very nervous. She wasn't sure what she was going to find at the end of her search for Mimi's grandmother.

I rushed away so quickly, terrified of Joe's boss and the police, she thought. *But I should have written to Lily's mother first, prepared her somehow. Now I must tell this woman that her daughter is dead and appear on her doorstep with a grandchild she hasn't seen for years. What if she no longer lives at that address? What if she's too frail to take care of a child? Or worse...* Gloria's throat tightened. *What if, after this long journey, we arrive to find that Mimi's grandmother has passed away, too?*

Friedrich put his arm around Gloria's waist as they looked at the port. "Are you all packed?" he asked.

"For the most part. I have a little left to do. Not much."

"Come on. Let me help you finish packing," he said. "We should be disembarking soon."

"Alright," Gloria said. "Time to get ready to leave."

Back in the stateroom, she settled the children on the sofa. "Stay right here, both of you. No wandering off." The warning in her voice made them both nod solemnly.

As she and Friedrich gathered scattered toys from the bedroom floor, he caught her eye. "Are you feeling alright?"

"Yes. Do I look unwell?" Gloria asked.

"You're rather pale." Friedrich's concern made her realize how tightly she was gripping the jack-in-the-box.

"I'm alright." Gloria's hands trembled as she sank into the chair. "Just..." The weight of everything—the threats, the escape, the children's safety—suddenly pressed down on her chest, making it hard to breathe.

Friedrich listened silently as the tears that Gloria had been holding back for weeks finally spilled over.

"They sent a man to the house," she whispered. "One of the mob boss's men. So polite in his expensive suit, but his eyes..." Gloria shuddered. "The same men who killed Lily and Joe. The same ones who..." Her voice broke. "They wanted us out. No witnesses, you understand? And Mimi... God help me, who knows what they might have done to Mimi—"

"Really? Why do you say that?" Friedrich looked shocked.

"Joe was involved in illegal activity. I think it had something to do with transporting alcohol."

He gave a knowing nod.

"I was so nervous and in such a hurry to get away that I never even sent a letter to Mimi's grandmother telling her that we were coming before embarking on this journey."

"Feeling uneasy after making such a long journey is normal. And doing what you did, leaving quickly, I would have done the same thing. Anyone would have. You did the right thing, Gloria. You kept yourself and the children safe," he said, smiling warmly and gently taking her hand. "If you'd like, I would be happy to accompany you and the children to Paris to find Mimi's grandmother. But I cannot go right away. I won't be able to leave Germany for a week or so. I came here to attend a meeting of a political group that an old friend of mine has arranged and I must stay in Germany until the meeting is over. My friend said there are some important fellows who would like to make my acquaintance. Although I think I know why they're so keen to meet me. I'm pretty sure they need money and they know that I have plenty of funds. They figure that if I like them, and I like what they stand for, I'll be able to help them."

"The political party you mentioned before?" Gloria's voice caught as she remembered Friedrich's passionate speech about rebuilding Germany. "The one you said would change everything?"

"Yes." Friedrich's eyes lit with that same fervor that she had glimpsed on deck. "The National Socialist German Workers' Party. We're growing stronger every day. Soon everyone will know our name."

Gloria shifted uneasily in her chair. Politics had seemed so distant in Lily's warm kitchen, in the safe bubble of their daily routines with the children. But here in Germany, with its hungry crowds and bitter veterans, with its whispered conversations that stopped when strangers passed, she could feel something building—something that made her throat tight with unnamed fears.

"I haven't heard of it," she admitted. "In America, we were too busy surviving to follow German politics."

Friedrich's smile didn't quite reach his eyes. "You'll learn soon enough. Everyone will. Is it possible that you and the children can come with me to Munich where I am meeting with the party? Then once it's over we can all leave from there and go to Paris together. Can you wait a week before you go to Paris?"

"We can wait. In fact, I don't mind waiting. But I must

admit, we have nowhere to stay. I don't know anyone in Germany but you."

"I have plenty of room for you and the children in my home. Of course, you would have a private wing and, as I think you already know, I will be a gentleman in every sense of the word."

She laughed. "I do know that you are a gentleman. However, my reputation would be soiled if anyone found out that I was staying with a single man alone in a house."

"I don't care what people say. I never did," he said confidently, a smile playing his lips.

"You don't understand because you have that luxury. You're a man." Gloria's voice hardened with bitter experience. "When men are called promiscuous, they're admired, even envied. But a woman? One whisper of impropriety and we're ruined. It's not just me I'm concerned about, but anyone connected to me. The children." Her hands clenched in her lap. "These German neighbors of yours, they'll judge us before they know us. And their judgment will fall hardest on Mimi and Nick."

Friedrich nodded, but Gloria could tell that he didn't truly understand.

"I can't risk their future for convenience," she pressed on. "Do you have any respectable female friends who could offer us shelter?"

His smile held a touch of arrogance. "Any woman I know would see you as competition. You see, I'm considered quite a catch." He glanced down with practiced modesty. "Not for any particular merit of my own, but money has a way of making a man suddenly fascinating to every eligible woman in Germany."

"I'm sure it does," Gloria said carefully. Something in his tone made her uneasy. "Which makes me wonder—what exactly do you see in someone like me?"

Friedrich tilted her chin up with one finger, his touch too intimate for comfort. "What do I see?" His voice dropped to a husky whisper. "I see starlight in your eyes, sunshine in your smile—"

"Be serious," she cut him off, fighting the urge to pull away. They still needed his help, but Gloria's instincts warned her to be careful.

"I am serious. I do see all of those things. But I also see a woman who is independent. A woman who isn't after my money. A woman who has character and integrity."

"You hardly know me. How do you know I have character, or integrity?"

"The honest truth?" Friedrich asked.

"Of course. Tell me what you really think."

"Well." He hesitated. "I know you're not wealthy because when we first met you had purchased accommodations in steerage. However, when your friend died, she left you enough money to take this voyage with two children, isn't that right?"

"I sold a piece of her jewelry to pay for the voyage."

"You could have taken the money and abandoned Mimi to an orphanage. But you didn't. Instead of keeping that money for yourself, you decided to fulfill your friend's wishes and take her daughter all the way to France to live with her grandmother."

"Of course. How could I do anything else? It wouldn't be right, and I knew I couldn't afford to raise two children on my own. I wanted to do the right thing by her."

"But a lot of women I know would not have been so honorable if they were in your position."

"I could never do that to Mimi or to any child. Her mother was my dear friend, like a sister to me, and I know... I feel she's watching from heaven." Gloria could feel her voice cracking as she tried to continue. "And I could certainly never do that to Lily. She took Nick and I into her home and helped us when we were very down on our luck. I owe her this."

"And that's exactly what I'm talking about," Friedrich said. "You have character. Integrity."

Gloria smiled sadly and shook her head, a dark memory of what she did with Joe suddenly flashing through her mind. "I've done bad things I'm ashamed of. Things that make me wonder about my integrity."

"Do you want to talk about them?"

"No. I never want to talk about them. The truth is, I wish I could forget them."

He nodded. "It's alright. You don't need to tell me. I won't pry."

"Thank you, really."

Friedrich smiled. Then he sighed and said, "So, when we get off the ship, can you agree to wait for me to finish my business in Germany before you go to France?"

"Like I said, I would wait, but I don't have anywhere to go for a week. I think it's best for me to take the children straight to Paris and find Mimi's grandmother. Then once you are available, if you would like, you can meet us in France."

Friedrich nodded. "Please know that I am quite serious about my marriage proposal to you. And I plan to help you in any way I can. I have an idea," he said. "How does this sound? If you'll allow me to, I'll rent a hotel room for the three of you for a week. I'll make sure it's near my home so that I can bring you and the children anything you might need. Then once I've met with these gentlemen from the party, I'll be free to travel with you and the children to France. What do you think?"

"That sounds good," Gloria said. "But are you sure you want to do this? I mean, well... it's really very kind of you."

"You know that I have feelings for you. I really believe that if you agreed to marry me, we would be very happy together."

"What about Nick? I have a child, and I must consider his needs before my own."

"I realize that. And you must have seen from the way that Nick and I get along that I've taken a real liking to your son. He's a good boy, a strong boy, and anyone can see that he is of

FIFTY-SIX

The train wound through the German countryside, past rolling hills quilted with spring green. Gloria watched the landscape unfold; it was so different from the grimy tenements of New York. Something about the fresh air and open spaces made her chest expand with a sense of possibility. For the first time in years, she could imagine a future beyond mere survival.

The train came to a stop and whistled loudly to indicate that they had arrived at the station in Munich. As Gloria disembarked from the train onto the platform she was filled with excitement. The smell of fresh sausages filled the air of the train station, along with the hope for a new future.

Once again true to his word, Fredrich suggested a nice, respectable hotel that was not far from his home in Munich. He promised to rent a suite of rooms for Gloria and the children. On the way to the hotel, they stopped at a small restaurant where they had sausages and sauerkraut with a heaped bowl of potato salad. Then they walked a few streets until they came to a large, well-kept building with a doorman standing at the front wearing a uniform that fascinated Nick. Friedrich told Gloria to wait in the lobby while he made the arrangements.

Once Friedrich returned, they walked up two flights of stairs to the rooms he had rented for them. A few minutes later, they were followed by a bellman carrying their luggage. Friedrich unlocked the door to a suite that was bright and airy. It was nicer than any place, except for Lily's home, that Gloria had ever stayed. The bellman never flinched as he put Gloria's old, worn luggage down in the main room.

"Thank you," Friedrich said, handing the bellman some money before he left.

"Since you've never been to Germany before, I'm planning to take you all to dinner at this quaint little place tomorrow night," Friedrich then said to Gloria and the children. "It serves traditional German food and it's really quite charming."

Gloria smiled. "I'm sure we'll love it."

She could tell that he was slow to leave. He sat on the sofa for a few minutes before he finally stood up, stretched, and said, "Well, I'm going to go home and get some rest."

"No, Uncle Friedrich," Nick said, tugging on his arm. "Stay with us. You and Mama can play cards. If you stay, I promise not to bother you."

Lately Nick had taken to calling him "Uncle Friedrich"—Gloria suspected that Friedrich may have suggested this, given how much her son's face lit up whenever he used the name.

"Bathtime for both of you," she said, noticing Nick's reluctance to let Friedrich leave. Something twisted in her chest at seeing their bond deepen. *Maybe I'm being too cautious,* she thought, watching Friedrich ruffle Nick's hair in goodbye. *He's everything my son needs—gentle and patient, the kind of man I'd like Nick to become. And for a woman like me, with my history...* She caught Friedrich's warm glance. *It's not just security he offers, though God knows we've never had that. There's something about him that makes me want to trust again, despite everything.*

Eventually, Nick stood and stretched. When Friedrich held

out his arms, the boy ran to him, burying his face in Friedrich's coat. "Be a good boy for your mother and I'll see you tomorrow," Friedrich said softly.

Nick nodded against his chest, then stepped back with a brave smile.

After Friedrich hugged Mimi, he turned to Gloria. His embrace carried the scent of cologne and promise, making her heart flutter. "Sweet dreams," he murmured, and then he was gone.

FIFTY-SEVEN

The following evening, as he had promised, Friedrich took them all to the lovely restaurant that he had mentioned. It was only a short taxi ride from their hotel. When they arrived, the owner of the restaurant recognized Friedrich immediately.

"Friedrich Wagner!" the heavy-set man said with a winning smile. "I thought you were in America."

"I was," Friedrich replied warmly. "But I've returned to my homeland. I couldn't stay away. I love Germany and German food far too much."

"Of course you do! So do I. There's no food as good as German food."

"And no beer as good as German beer," Friedrich replied.

"That's true," the owner said before asking, "Is this your lovely wife and family?"

"Not yet, but I hope they will be one day," Friedrich admitted.

"I'm sorry? I'm afraid I don't understand." The restaurant owner looked at Friedrich skeptically.

Friedrich smiled. But he didn't answer. He was in no mood to explain, and the restaurateur did not press for answers. He knew that Friedrich was a wealthy man, and it was best not to ask him uncomfortable questions. So, the owner returned Friedrich's smile and then seated them at a private table in the back of the restaurant. He brought over special pretzels for the children, immediately declaring that he wouldn't charge for them.

As they watched Nick and Mimi delight in tasting their first pretzels, Friedrich turned to Gloria and said, "I'm afraid I won't be available tomorrow night. I'm meeting with the gentlemen from the National Socialist German Workers' Party."

The waiter set steaming plates of *sauerbraten* and *späetzle* before them, along with tall mugs of dark beer. Gloria inhaled deeply, memories of her mother's cooking flooding back.

"Oh good, your meeting's tomorrow," Gloria replied. She tried to ignore the small pang she felt at the prospect of missing his company.

"Yes, though I regret that I must spend the evening away from you." His eyes held hers, making her cheeks warm.

"I look forward to hearing about it," she said, focusing on her plate to hide her flush. The tender meat reminded her of childhood and the rare occasions when her mother could afford such luxuries.

"How do you like the food?"

"It's wonderful. My mother used to make German dishes, when we had the money." Gloria caught herself—she shouldn't remind him of their poverty.

Friedrich nodded warmly. "You'll enjoy plenty of wonderful German food here in Munich."

"And the beer is superb," Gloria said with a smile. She took a grateful sip, letting the rich flavor steady her nerves.

"Munich's famous for it. Wait until Oktoberfest—we have some of the best beer in the world."

"Thank you," she said softly. "You've made our voyage so lovely." *More than lovely*, she thought, *you've given us hope.*

"I hope so." He hesitated, a vulnerable expression crossing his face. "And I hope you'll still be in Germany when Oktoberfest comes around."

Her heart stuttered at the gentle pressure of his words. Part of her wanted to promise that they would stay forever, while another part whispered cautious warnings about moving too fast and trusting too easily.

FIFTY-EIGHT

The following evening, Friedrich arrived at the tavern where the meeting was scheduled to take place. He was half an hour early because he had arranged to meet with his friend Bernhard Kohler before everyone arrived. When he walked in, Bernhard, a short and stocky man with a large belly, was sitting at a table in the back of the room. As soon as he saw Friedrich he called out to him, "Freddy! Freddy!"

Friedrich waved and walked over to the table where Bernhard sat. Bernhard immediately stood up. His napkin fell on the floor as he took Friedrich into a bear hug of an embrace. "It sure is good to see you."

They spoke in German to each other.

"It's been a heck of a long time," Friedrich admitted.

"Too long," Bernhard said, smiling. "Sit down. Have a beer."

Friedrich sat down and looked around. The bar was almost empty. "Is the meeting we're attending tonight taking place here?" he asked, curious as to why there were so few people there.

"Yes, but this meeting is private. Only those who are invited will be permitted to come in. Didn't they ask you at the door who you were here to see?"

"Actually, someone did approach me. I assumed he was just being polite, since you'd mentioned waiting for me."

Bernhard's expression darkened. "No. He was following orders to ensure your attendance."

"I see," Friedrich said. Bernhard's voice had gone flat, and a cold sensation settled in Friedrich's stomach.

"Anyway," Bernhard continued. "I'm so looking forward to introducing you to the rest of the fellows in our group. They are quite impressive."

"I'm looking forward to it," Friedrich replied, looking around. The walls behind the bar were lined with bottles of German beer and intricately hand-painted beer *steins*. Friedrich found the workmanship on the *steins* lovely and meticulous. He was especially fond of one *stein* that he had noticed. It had been painted with a landscape of flowering trees, a green river, bright sunshine, and a mother bear lovingly cradling her baby.

Friedrich and Bernhard reminisced about funny events from their childhood as the room gradually filled with men. "I have so many people I want you to meet," Bernhard said. "Let's go up to the bar and get a couple more beers so I can introduce you to everyone."

Friedrich followed Bernhard; they both carried their mugs with them. After they ordered more beer, Bernhard put his arm around Friedrich and led him over to a tall, slender man with dark hair and glasses who was standing quietly in the corner. "Heinrich!" Bernhard said. "How are you?"

"Very well, and you?" he replied.

"Quite well!" Bernhard said. "I hear congratulations are in order. You're a married man now?"

Heinrich smiled. "Yes, Margarete and I were married a couple of months ago."

"I'll bet you're happy."

"As happy as a married man can be." They both laughed. "But, on a serious note, I'm very happy. She's a perfect Aryan wife," Heinrich said.

Then Bernhard put his arm around Friedrich's shoulder. "This is my friend, Friedrich Wagner," he said.

"Any relation to the composer?" Heinrich asked.

"Everyone asks that," Friedrich said, chuckling. "And I wish I could say yes because I love his music, but unfortunately, no. I'm not related to him."

"Friedrich, this is Heinrich Himmler, he's currently the personal assistant to Gregor Strasser, the Reich propaganda leader. He's an important man and a true asset to the Nazi party," Bernhard said.

"Oh? Sounds impressive. But I'm not sure what this Nazi party is or what it's all about."

"Of course, that's because we've renamed the National Socialist German Workers' Party. We're now calling it the Nazi party." Bernhard smiled. "And Heinrich is a very close friend of our leader, Adolf Hitler."

"I've heard a great deal about Herr Hitler," Friedrich admitted. "He has some very good ideas about how we can bring our country back to its rightful place as a world power."

"Last year Heinrich, and several other members of our group, myself included, marched against the current government in Germany," Bernhard explained. "We're all very hopeful that Hitler will be appointed chancellor. Things will be so much better if he is."

"I can see why you'd say that," Friedrich said.

"Just between us," Bernhard whispered to Friedrich as Heinrich turned away to greet another party member, "Himmler is from the working class. That gives him an edge with the people. He understands them. In fact, I heard that he was working in a manure processing plant before Röhm found him."

"Röhm?"

"Yes, Röhm is a very important member of our group. I'll introduce you to him soon. He's our Sturmabteilung chief of staff. Look over there. That's him." Bernhard indicated a man standing on the other side of the bar. "He's talking to someone at the moment, but as soon as he's free, I'll introduce you. You'll like him. He's a brilliant man and I truly believe that his talents, like Himmler's, would have gone unnoticed had it not been for Hitler."

"Bernhard Kohler!" A heavyset man walked over to Bernhard and Friedrich. "I haven't seen you in a while. Is everything alright?"

"Yes, I'm fine. I've just been busy," Bernhard said. "I'd like to introduce you to a friend of mine. This is Friedrich Wagner. Friedrich, this is Hermann Göring."

Friedrich studied the man before him—tall, broad-shouldered, with an air of military bearing despite his expensive civilian clothes. "It's a pleasure to meet you," he said, matching the man's practiced smile.

"The pleasure is all mine." Göring's handshake was firm, commanding. "But if you'll excuse me, I must make my rounds and greet the others before Herr Hitler arrives and begins his speech."

"Of course. I completely understand," Bernhard said.

Just then Röhm waved to Bernhard from across the bar. Bernhard waved back and motioned for Röhm to come and join them. "I'll buy you a beer," Bernhard called over. Röhm nodded and walked over. He was a strongly built man who reminded Friedrich of a grizzly bear. He gave Bernhard a welcoming hug, and although Bernhard was not a small man, he looked small compared to Röhm.

Bernhard turned to Friedrich. "This is Ernst Röhm, the great man I've been telling you about.

He is married to the most beautiful woman: Carin. She's a Swedish baroness. How is Carin?" Bernhard asked.

"She hasn't been feeling well actually," Röhm said, shaking his head. "She's a delicate girl, often ill. But I must admit, I do adore her."

His words were cut short by a sudden hush falling over the tavern. A man of slight build entered, his dark hair neatly combed, a small mustache as precise as a paintbrush stroke above his lip. The crowd surged to its feet, erupting in thunderous cheers.

"That's him," Bernhard whispered, his face transformed with fervor as he stared at the newcomer. "Our leader—Adolf Hitler."

FIFTY-NINE

After the crowd quieted, Hitler took his place at the front of the tavern. Friedrich watched in amazement as the unassuming man seemed to grow taller, his presence filling the room. His voice started soft, almost intimate, then built like a gathering storm. His hands carved the air with passionate gestures as he spoke of German pride, of destiny, of greatness to come. The crowd swayed forward as one, caught in his spell. Even Friedrich found himself leaning in, swept up in the electric atmosphere as Hitler's words thundered through the tavern, his face transformed by intensity, his eyes burning with conviction.

Hitler explained the pressing need to be careful of Jews and anyone else who was not a pure German. He referred to pure Germans as Aryans. Hitler explained the superiority of the German race and how all other races were put on earth to serve the Aryans. Then he warned his audience that Jews must never be trusted, blaming them for Germany losing the Great War.

"They stole everything they could from the German people," Hitler said. Friedrich could see the men in the tavern growing angry and preparing to defend their country.

But Hitler didn't stop there. He told them all that for the preservation of the Fatherland, he was eventually planning to create a Jew-free Europe. Friedrich had never known many Jewish people, but as he listened to Hitler speak, he was consumed by the man's fervor, believing every word he said. Hitler acknowledged that they must also be careful of the communists, who were usually Jewish, and that they must keep their eyes on all the political unrest in the Fatherland. He declared that for Germany to reclaim her rightful place as the premier world power there would need to be an extermination of her internal as well as external enemies: communism, socialism, liberal democracy, and most of all the Jews. "The Jews," he said, "are the most dangerous."

As Friedrich listened to this little man speak, he felt his heart swell with pride. *I am an Aryan. I am a pure German— part of the superior race that he is speaking of. When I first saw him, I thought he looked like a joke,* he thought. *But now that he's spoken, I can feel his power. Every word he says resonates with me. I feel honored to be in his presence.*

Once Hitler had stopped speaking, Friedrich and Bernhard made their way over to him. "I doubt you'll remember me," Bernhard said shyly. "We met at a rally some time ago."

"Of course, I remember you," Adolf said as he patted Bernhard warmly on the arm. "You're Bernhard Kohler? Am I correct?"

"Yes, I'm so flattered that you remembered my name," Bernhard replied.

Adolf smiled. "And who is this?" he asked, referring to Friedrich.

Bernhard proudly stuck his chest out and smiled. "This is a childhood friend of mine," he said. "His name is Friedrich Wagner. Like the rest of us, he's a pure Aryan, and a true German patriot."

"Very good! I like to see that," Hitler said. "We are the superior race and together we will take our country back from all of these anarchists who would try to destroy us."

"I agree," Friedrich said.

Hitler's hand landed heavily on Friedrich's shoulder. "Welcome to our group," he said, holding Friedrich's gaze for a moment that seemed to stretch into eternity.

As Hitler moved through the crowd, touching each man like a priest bestowing blessings, Friedrich watched the transformation on the men's faces and noticed them react with the same fierce devotion that he had felt stirring in his own chest during the speech. The tavern hummed with an energy he had never experienced before, as if they all stood on the cusp of something momentous. Something that would change Germany forever.

SIXTY

Hitler only stayed at the bar for a few minutes after his speech. The other party members soon began to say good night to each other and leave the tavern.

Once Bernhard and Friedrich had said their farewells, they walked outside. "Are you hungry?" Bernhard asked.

"Actually, I am. I was in such a rush trying to get to this meeting on time that I forgot to eat," Friedrich admitted.

"I know of a lovely beer garden right around the corner from here. Shall we go and have some dinner?" Bernhard asked.

"Yes, that sounds good. Let's go."

The two men walked to the beer garden and sat under the canopy of a large oak tree. After they placed their order Bernhard asked, "Did you like it? The meeting, I mean."

"I did. You were right. I needed to come home to Germany. I loved the group, and Hitler is the perfect leader. It's been such a long time since I've been around other people who share the same love for our Fatherland that I feel."

"Yes, these men, like us, do love Germany. And they want to see Germany heal from the Great War and prosper again."

"I can see that. You were right, this is a good thing," Friedrich said.

"Yes, of course it is," Bernhard replied with conviction. "But there will be some casualties along the way. I mean, let's face it, we can't rebuild our country with all the Jews who live here. They'll surely sabotage us. Just like they did in the Great War. We can't trust them."

Friedrich nodded. "I suppose you're right. I don't know many Jews, but I remember one family. Do you recall Fritz and his wife? The old couple who owned the candy store? Don't you remember how they always gave us a few pieces of chocolate even when we didn't have any money on us? Would you believe me if I told you that I found out that they were Jewish?"

"Yes! I remember them. They had a beautiful daughter who was only a few years older than us. I even had a crush on her." Bernhard laughed.

"Wasn't her name Elke?"

"I believe it was," Bernhard said. "At the time I knew they were Jews, but I was too young to realize that Jews were dangerous to Germany. Did you know that Jews were dangerous back then?"

"No, I didn't," Friedrich said. "At the time I was just a child and quite frankly none of it mattered to me. All I cared about was the chocolate."

"Of course not. We were just children. But now we must be more careful. We can't allow any Jews to get close to us. Now, we must accept that they're our enemy."

"Yes, you're right," Friedrich said. "However, I wonder if there are other good Jews like Fritz and his family. I find it hard to believe they were enemies of our country."

"I'm sure there are, at least on the surface," Bernhard said. "But, believe me, Jews are only pretending to be patriotic to our Fatherland. All they really care about is money. Money they can steal from the German people. And I'm sure that the Jews probably behave in the same way in America."

Friedrich nodded. In America, he'd observed Jewish families in Manhattan from afar, noting how they kept to their own neighborhoods, their own customs. He'd never had reason to speak with them - nor had he wanted to. But sometimes, on Friday nights or Saturday mornings, he would see Orthodox Jews walking on the streets of Manhattan, with their long beards and sideburns. Someone had told him that Friday night and all-day Saturday were Jewish holy days, and on those days, they walked to the synagogue. The Orthodox Jewish men had always frightened him a little because they wore strange long black and white shawls that hung across their shoulders. The women dressed in long skirts that covered their ankles and some of them wore wigs to cover their hair.

"I've never personally had any bad experiences with the Jews either here in Germany or in America," Friedrich admitted. "But I heard the rumors about them and always kept my distance. My father hired some Jews to work in our factories in both countries. He said they're good workers and they learn fast. He told me that he likes to hire them."

"I've heard this before about how they are hard workers. But you must not allow yourself to believe that they are good for your business. They may be hard workers, but they're also thieves. Please, my friend, don't fall for their facade. They are very dangerous," Bernhard whispered confidentially. "And you can believe Hitler when he says that the Jews are behind a lot of the political movements, like communism, that intend to destroy Germany and its Aryan people."

Some of Bernhard's comments sounded far-fetched to Friedrich. But frankly, he didn't care at all about the Jews. He had truly enjoyed the camaraderie he had felt when he was with the men he had just met. And he had to admit, he was still feeling high and hopeful for Germany after Hitler's speech. "So, how do I join your group? How do I become a Nazi?"

"I was hoping you would ask," Bernhard said. "Unfortunately, you'll have to endure some testing to make sure that you're of pure Aryan blood. But it's just a formality. I can vouch for you. So, don't worry, you'll be accepted into our group with open arms." He smiled. "After all, even though your family moved to America, you were born here in Germany and your blood is still pure Aryan. I've known you since we were children and both of your parents were pure Germans." He took a swig of beer.

"That's good news," Friedrich replied. "I've been feeling a bit lost lately. I know this might sound crazy, but I've been searching for something I can devote my life to, something I can believe in, something that will give my life meaning. Do you know what I mean?"

"Of course, I know what you mean. You're searching for your life's purpose. I've found mine in Adolf Hitler. I believe he will lift Germany back up to her rightful place in the world. And I want to be a part of that. A part of the new Germany, so to speak."

"Yes, I agree," said Friedrich. "I want that, too."

"What did you think of Hitler?"

"He's a compelling speaker, that's for sure. And he has good ideas. I am a little concerned about the racial purity issue. I mean, I don't know how he could possibly create a Jew-free Germany. It seems like an impossible task. Why not just ignore them? There aren't as many of them as there are of us. Besides, I find it hard to believe that they're as diabolical as he claims. I have a feeling that they're just people and probably quite harmless."

"Perhaps they've convinced you of this," Bernhard said skeptically. "But I know better. They must be controlled. You see, the Jews are very sneaky. You may think that they are just people like us, but they aren't. They're more like the devil."

"So, how does Hitler propose to do this?"

"Do what?"

"Get them under control. Have you heard him explain his plan?"

"Hitler has plenty of good ideas as far as how we can control them. But really, Freddy, you need not concern yourself with any of it. You're not a Jew so it's not your worry."

"But I wouldn't want to see anyone being mistreated in any way," Friedrich said.

"I understand. But listen to me, as you know, the Great War took a toll on our country. I don't know how long it's been since you disembarked in Hamburg, but you're going to see that many German people walk around in a state of depression. That's because we gave it our all in the war and we lost everything. To make matters worse, Germany was forced to sign the Treaty of Versailles. That weakens us even more." Bernhard shook his head in disgust. He took a long deep breath, put his arm around Friedrich's shoulder and said, "The pride of the German worker, as well as the German family, has been diminished in every way. Most of the men who returned from the war are unable to find work. They have no money to support their wives and children, so they're forced to join soup lines in order to eat. It's humiliating."

"Yes, I'm sure it is."

"Especially since many of these men were war heroes. Hitler was a soldier—a war hero, in fact," Bernhard said.

"Really. That's impressive. I had no idea."

"Oh yes, he fought in the war. He knows how hard it can be to serve in the army. Hitler loves our Fatherland as much as you and I do. To hell with the Jews. Who gives a damn what Hitler does with them? Let them fend for themselves. They're not your friends anyway," Bernhard said. He lit a cigar. "I'm glad you are going to join us, Friedrich. You can help us to rebuild our country."

"I look forward to becoming a member," Friedrich said, smiling.

"Do you want another beer?" Bernhard asked.

"Of course. I can never get enough of our good German beer. It's nice to be back home. I've been gone far too long."

"How long will you be staying here in Munich?"

"Indefinitely. I'm moving back to Germany permanently. I plan to only return to America for visits. My home is here in the Fatherland."

"What about your factories in America?"

"My father and stepbrother will be in charge of the American factory, and I'll manage the factory in Munich. Until now, my cousin was running it, but in my opinion, he's a bit daft. I'm confident that the company will be more profitable under my direction."

"Of course it will. You've always been a brilliant businessman."

"You flatter me," Friedrich said, letting out a short, embarrassed laugh.

"It's true. I would never lie to you, Friedrich. You're quite brilliant."

Friedrich smiled. He could feel himself blushing. "I hope that I can be of help to our Fatherland. Even if it is in some small way."

"I have faith in you, and I know you'll be very helpful to Germany," Bernhard said, patting Friedrich on the back. "By the way, on behalf of the Aryan race, welcome home, my friend."

SIXTY-ONE

After Bernhard and Friedrich separated at the corner of the street to go their separate ways back home, Friedrich was still feeling elated. It was a crisp night, and the stars and full moon were shining brightly. The streetlights cast haloes on the walkway. He longed to go to Gloria's hotel room. He was excited about everyone he had met and all he had learned. He wished he could tell her everything about his evening. But when he looked at his watch it was almost eleven thirty and he knew the children would be asleep. *She'll probably be asleep, too*, he realized.

It was difficult to contain his joy at having finally found his life's purpose. He felt like he was walking on air and the only person he longed to share his feelings, his hopes, and his dreams for the future with was Gloria. How wonderful it felt to have found the right woman, and at the same time to have discovered a cause that was so close to his heart. Friedrich whistled a song that was written by Wagner, the composer. He smiled as he recalled how often people asked if he was related to him. *Well, not by blood maybe, but even though Richard Wagner is dead he still inspires me to see beauty, love, and romance with his music,* he thought. *I'm certainly glad to share his name.*

When Friedrich arrived home, he thought about his cousin who had been running the family factory in Munich. *It is going to be difficult to tell him that he is being replaced, but it must be done. The factory hasn't been producing enough inventory and it's not earning up to its potential. Everyone in the family is aware of it. But no one wants to hurt his feelings. Meanwhile, our business is suffering. It has fallen into my lap to tell him... I'll give him the option to accept a demotion. But it's quite simple, things cannot continue the way they have been. It's time I took control of our family interests here in Germany. I realize he's probably going to try and put up a fight, but there's no use. I've made up my mind. And he can choose to stay or leave the company. It really makes no difference to me. I'll go and speak to him as soon as Gloria and I return from France. Hopefully, she'll be able to get rid of Mimi once we get to her grandmother's house. The child is young and therefore she is nothing but a pest. I must admit, I don't mind the boy so much. He's more mature and he'll be prime to join the National Socialist German Workers' Party in a few years. If Gloria marries me, I'll offer to adopt her son. I'll teach him everything he needs to learn. I'll make sure he learns to love the Fatherland, and we'll become best friends as we work together to bring about the new Germany.*

Friedrich smiled as he thought about how life would be if he and Gloria were married and if Nick was his son. Then he thought of Gloria's devotion to Mimi. He had never met Mimi's mother, but he knew that Gloria had loved her enough to travel all the way to Europe to deliver her child to her grandmother. And he had to admit these were the things that he found attractive about Gloria. She was loyal, devoted, honest, and good. *But little Mimi is really of no value to me or to Germany even if she is a pretty child. I'm willing to take Nick because he's Gloria's child, but hopefully Mimi's grandmother will want her.* He sighed aloud as he began to get undressed for bed. Then he remembered Agnes and what she had said about him and Gloria. *Agnes has always been after me like a lion chasing a zebra. She tried to ruin things between Gloria and me. And, I must admit, I hope she doesn't try to befriend Gloria, because I don't trust her. She thinks she knows me, but she was wrong when she said I would grow bored with Gloria. I'm never bored when I'm with her.*

Friedrich sank into the familiar comfort of his childhood bed, surrounded by the elegant furnishings of his family home. As he closed his eyes, thoughts of Gloria flooded his mind—her gentle smile, the grace in her movements. He ached to have her here beside him, to build a life together within these walls. Sleep was long in coming.

SIXTY-TWO

The following day Friedrich woke up early. He ate a light breakfast of bread, which he had purchased the day before, with strawberry jam. Then he got dressed and put on his coat. It was still early, too early to go to see Gloria, so he went for a walk to pass some time. After walking for a little over an hour he looked at his watch. It was just after eight. *The children will be awake, especially the little one. This is a reasonable hour to go and see Gloria,* he thought. He was bursting with news, excitement, and energy, and he would have liked to run all the way to the hotel where Gloria was staying. His feet seemed to have wings, but he knew it wasn't acceptable for a gentleman to run through the streets, so he forced himself to walk as slowly as he could.

When he arrived, he knocked on the door to Gloria's room. It took a few moments for Gloria to answer. Her hair was down and just messy enough to accentuate her beauty. She wore a dark red robe over her nightgown. "Friedrich!" she said. "You're here early. But I am glad to see you. It's been a long, difficult night. Won't you come in and sit down?" She beckoned him in. "Please excuse my appearance. Mimi wasn't feeling well, so I was up most of the night with her. Nick refused to go to bed until he was sure Mimi was alright. And even then, he wouldn't leave her side until she was asleep. I'm worried because I don't know what's wrong with Mimi and if what she has is contagious, I want Nick to stay away from her. But he refused. He said he'd rather come down with whatever she has than leave her to suffer alone. My poor little boy is just a child himself, but he was worried all night. Sweet little Mimi was vomiting. I don't know how many times she threw up, but it finally stopped at around midnight. Even so, she was still unable to rest. She finally fell asleep a few hours ago. I'm worried about her, too. I hope she'll be alright and Nick doesn't catch this."

"Was she just vomiting, or did she have any other symptoms?"

"She had a stomachache that started at about seven last night, and she said she had a very bad headache, too."

"Aww, the poor child," he said. "But try not to worry too much. Children are very resilient. They are stronger than you think. She probably just ate something that didn't agree with her. She'll be fine. You'll see."

Gloria smiled at him, but her lips were quivering and he thought she might cry. He hated it when women cried. It made him feel so helpless. "I hope you're right," she said.

"I know I am. And I intend to stay here with you so I can help you with anything you need."

"You don't know how much that means to me."

It didn't seem like the right time to tell Gloria about his meeting, or how wonderful he felt about his future with the party he had decided to join. He longed to tell her how impressed he was with Herr Hitler and describe the new friends that he had made. But she was far too nervous and worried about Mimi to appreciate being bombarded by details of the meeting. He knew that as long as the little girl was sick, Gloria would not be as enthusiastic about his future as he was.

Gloria and Friedrich sat holding hands but not speaking

very much. A little while later, Mimi woke up. The first thing she said was that she was feeling much better, and she was hungry.

"Like I told you, it had to be something she ate," Friedrich said. He was glad that his prediction turned out to be correct and that Mimi seemed to have recovered. "Are you hungry?" he asked Gloria. "I'm sure you haven't eaten anything."

Nick came out of the bedroom rubbing his eyes and over-heard the conversation between Friedrich and his mother. He answered before Gloria had time to speak. "I don't know about my mother, but I sure am hungry," he admitted. "And I'll bet that Mom and Mimi are, too." Nick smiled broadly. "Mimi is feeling so much better."

"I'm so glad," Friedrich said. "She had me a little worried."

"Yes, me too," Gloria said.

Then Nick looked at Friedrich and spoke directly to him. "I'm so happy to see you. I'm glad that you're here."

"I'm happy to see you, too, young man," Friedrich said. "Now that everyone is awake and feeling fine, why don't I go to the bakery across the street and get us some breakfast?"

"That would be wonderful. Thank you," Gloria replied.

"Do you think you can pick out what Mimi might like?" Friedrich asked.

"Anything with chocolate," Nick said, smiling again. "Me too. I like anything with chocolate."

Friedrich and Nick returned less than fifteen minutes later with a bag filled with pastries and two cups of coffee, one for himself and one for Gloria. "I would have bought juice for the children, but they didn't have any," Friedrich said.

"It's alright. Mimi and I will drink water. We prefer it," Nick said as he selected two pastries with thick dark chocolate on top. Then he turned and began walking to Mimi's room. "Thanks so much for the pastries," he said to Friedrich.

SIXTY-THREE

Mimi was feeling fine by noon. In fact, it was as if she had never been ill. So, everyone got dressed and went out for a walk to explore the town. Friedrich tried to purchase a handmade sweater for Gloria at one of the small shops, but she refused to allow him to do so. He tried to insist. "These are very beautiful," he said as he reached up and took a hand-knitted cardigan off the shelf.

"Yes, they are quite lovely. But they are also very expensive. And I don't need one. Thank you for your kindness, but I have a sweater," Gloria said.

Friedrich nodded and they left the shop.

As they rounded a corner in the main part of town, Nick spotted a toy store. His eyes lit up. "Can we go inside?" he asked.

"Sure, why not?" Friedrich said.

"Nick, I don't have money to waste on buying toys," Gloria said.

"I know, but can't we just look?"

"I suppose we can," she said.

The children were excited and as soon as they entered, they

started running through the store. Friedrich took them both by the shoulder and said, "You must behave or we'll have to leave."

Nick nodded and took Mimi's hand and said, "We can't run around here. We have to be careful not to break anything."

She nodded at him and smiled.

"Is it alright if they play with the toys a little?" Gloria asked the shop owner.

"It's fine, so long as they don't break anything. If they do you will be forced to purchase it," he said sternly.

"Of course," Friedrich said.

The children sat on the floor. Nick was spinning a wooden top for Mimi who was clapping her hands and saying, "*Dreidel, dreidel.*"

"*Dreidel?* What does that mean?" Friedrich asked Mimi in a gentle voice.

"*Dreidel,*" she repeated.

"I think it means top," Nick said. "She had one of these when she lived with her parents. She and I used to play with it. She loves it when I spin it."

"Where is this top now?"

"My mother said we had to leave it behind in America. We couldn't pack everything," Nick said, sighing.

"Well, that's alright. How about we buy this one? What do you think?" Friedrich asked.

"Really? Can we? My mother said we don't have any money to buy toys."

"It will be a gift from me," Friedrich said. Then he took the top up to the store owner and paid for it before handing it to Nick. "Here, you can carry it."

Nick nodded. Then he showed it to Mimi. "Look what Uncle Friedrich bought for us," he said.

"Dreidel," she repeated with an innocent smile.

Friedrich felt a creeping sense of unease. The word nagged at him, triggering a memory he couldn't quite grasp. *Dreidel?*

Then it hit him—he had heard it in the Jewish quarter. His eyes fixed on Mimi, studying her honey-colored hair, her perfect Aryan features. *It can't be.* But the word echoed in his mind, raising questions he wasn't sure he wanted answered. He forced himself to keep his voice steady. *Perhaps she had learned it from a servant? Yes, that must be it.*

They left the store and began to walk again. Mimi was getting tired, so they stopped at a local restaurant for a late lunch of traditional German sausages with sauerkraut and potato salad. By the time they returned to the hotel, both children were exhausted and Gloria put them to bed.

Returning to sit with Friedrich in the living room a little while later, Gloria asked, "How was your meeting last night?"

"I was afraid you might have forgotten that I went to that meeting with all of the chaos going on here with Mimi," he said.

"I never forgot about it." Gloria smiled. "I just wanted to talk about it when we were alone so the children wouldn't interrupt us. Tell me, how did it go?"

"It was actually quite wonderful. I truly believe that Adolf Hitler, the leader of the National Socialist German Workers' Party, is going to be our next chancellor. He's brilliant. I made so many new friends who share my patriotism and deep love and loyalty for our Fatherland," Friedrich explained. He told her all about the meeting—except the part about the Jews. He wasn't sure what Gloria felt about Jews and it was such an unpleasant subject that he decided to avoid it. At least for now.

Friedrich watched Gloria's face brighten as he spoke, her visible trust in his judgment making his chest swell with pride.

"It sounds like Herr Hitler will be a wonderful leader," she said.

Something flickered in his chest—a shadow of doubt that he quickly pushed away. If only Gloria could have been there, felt the electric energy in that tavern. But of course, she would understand in time. They all would.

"Yes, I truly believe he'll be a great leader," Friedrich said. Suddenly he could sense Gloria's distraction as he spoke about the party. Her thoughts were clearly elsewhere.

After a few awkward moments of silence, she cleared her throat. "Do you think we can leave for Paris soon?" Gloria's voice was soft, hesitant. "I need to get Mimi to her grandmother."

He smiled, charmed by her uncertainty. "Whatever you want," he said, watching color rise in her cheeks. "How about the day after tomorrow? Does that give you enough time to prepare?"

"Yes! That's perfect," Gloria said. The relief in her voice made Friedrich's heart skip, even as something nagged at him about her eagerness to leave Germany.

SIXTY-FOUR

PARIS, FRANCE, 1930

Two days later, they boarded the train to Paris, the children bouncing with excitement over another adventure while Gloria's stomach churned with anxiety. The night before, she had tried to explain that they were going to find Mimi's grandmother, but Mimi was too young to understand and Nick cared only about the promise of the journey ahead.

Watching them now, heads bent together over a picture book that Friedrich had bought them, Gloria's heart ached. She hadn't found the courage to tell Nick that this search would end in separation—that his precious friend would probably stay behind in Paris with a grandmother she had not met since she was a baby. *Oh, Lily,* she thought, *how do I tell your mother what happened to you?*

The countryside rushed past the window, each mile bringing them closer to Paris and the moment of truth. Friedrich sat beside her, occasionally touching her hand, his thoughts clearly still full of his new political passions. But Gloria could think only of the elderly ballerina waiting somewhere in Paris, not knowing her daughter was dead, not knowing her granddaughter was coming. Not knowing any of them—this odd little family that they had cobbled together on their journey.

Nick pointed out all sorts of interesting things to Mimi as the train sped by. There were cows and horses; there were young people who stood on the side of the tracks and waved. Mimi giggled as she and Nick waved back. A little while later the children were hungry, and they ate the sandwiches that Gloria had purchased from a vendor before they boarded. After lunch, both children fell asleep, Mimi leaning on Nick's shoulder.

Gloria was quiet during the entire train ride. She went over and over different scenarios in her mind trying to figure out the best way to tell Chloe what had happened to Lily and Joe. But by the time the train pulled into the station in Paris, Gloria had still not come up with a plan.

When the train arrived in Paris, a loud whistle pierced the morning air. Gloria gently awakened the children while Friedrich handled their luggage. Stepping onto the platform, she was overwhelmed by her first glimpse of the city Lily had described so lovingly in their late-night talks. The elegant architecture, the flower sellers with their bright bouquets, the melodic flow of French voices around them – it was exactly as Lily had painted it, yet somehow more vibrant, more alive.

Walking through the station, Gloria caught the scent of fresh bread from a nearby boulangerie. "Oh, the bread!" Lily had always said, her eyes dancing. "Nothing in America compares to Paris bread." Now that simple aroma brought tears to Gloria's eyes. Every corner seemed to hold echoes of Lily's stories - the café where she'd practiced her ballet, the park where she'd played as a child, the bridges over the Seine that she'd crossed each morning on her way to dance class.

How am I going to do this? Gloria thought, the weight of her mission pressing down. How could she walk these beautiful streets, knowing each step brought her closer to telling Chloe about her daughter's fate?

They made their way to a hotel in the heart of the city, where Friedrich, ever the gentleman, arranged two rooms – one for himself and another for Gloria and the children. As Gloria unpacked their few belongings, she stood at the window, watching the play of light on the pale stone buildings. Somewhere in this city was the mother who had shaped Lily into the extraordinary woman she'd become. Somewhere was the home where Lily had grown up, full of love and music and dance.

"It's late and the children are hungry and tired. Let's find a restaurant and have dinner," Friedrich suggested. "Then we can all get some rest and start searching for Mimi's grandmother tomorrow. Do you have an address for her?"

"Yes, I do. I found the address in Lily's desk drawer. But I can't be sure that she still lives there or even if she's still alive," Gloria said anxiously.

"Well, no matter what happens, I'm here to help you." Friedrich patted Gloria's hand. "Don't worry about anything. Tomorrow we'll find out where Mimi's grandmother is," he promised.

Friedrich was right, the children were hungry and tired. They found a cafe where Friedrich, who surprised Gloria by speaking fluent French to the waiter, ordered green salad with steak and *frites* for everyone. "I ordered something plain because I wasn't sure if the children would enjoy the rich food here in France. I was afraid it might make them sick," he explained.

When the steak arrived, Nick cut a piece into small bite-sized pieces and served it to Mimi. The food was undeniably delicious.

"I'd heard that the food in France was wonderful. But this is even better than I expected," Gloria said.

"I'm glad you're enjoying it." Friedrich smiled. "Now, let's try some *crêpes* for dessert. Does everyone like apples?"

"Yes," both children said.

"I do, too!" Gloria said, smiling.

"Then we'll have apple *crêpes* with vanilla ice cream and caramel drizzle. What do you think?"

"Yes!" Mimi and Nick said excitedly. Their voices were a little too loud and some of the other patrons in the restaurant turned to look, but Friedrich didn't seem to mind.

"You're so good to us," Gloria said. "I've never met a man like you."

"You're making me blush," Friedrich said. They both laughed.

"What's so funny?" Nick asked.

"Adult conversation," Friedrich said, but his voice was gentle and kind and Nick didn't take offense. He just turned his attention to Mimi and the two of them spoke to each other in whispers.

After dinner, everyone returned to the hotel. Gloria and the children went to their room. She gave each child a quick bath and put them to bed. She was tired but she could not sleep. Friedrich's proposal played on her mind. *He's a good man and I'm very fortunate to have met him. I don't know how I'd have ever managed without his help. Besides that, he's very handsome and if I married him, he'd adopt Nick and be a father and an excellent role model for him. I could use a man like Friedrich in my life. But I can't honestly say that I love him. I've been through so many bad experiences with men that it is difficult for me to trust or fall in love with anyone. However, I know that Friedrich is kind. And if we marry, I will do my best to learn to love him.*

. . .

The next morning, Friedrich knocked on Gloria's door. He brought pastries from the bakery across the street. In America, the children had eaten porridge for breakfast and they had not been permitted to have sweets early in the morning, so they were very much embracing Parisian life and food. Gloria's heart filled with joy as she watched the children eating—Mimi had sticky chocolate all over her face.

After breakfast, Friedrich asked Gloria for the address that she had for Mimi's grandmother. Gloria found the piece of paper listing Lily's mother's name and address in her purse and handed it to him.

"Alright." Friedrich nodded his head. "This shouldn't be difficult to find. If my calculations are right, it's not too far at all. I believe it's only walking distance from here. Shall we go?"

"Yes," Gloria said, then she whispered so only Friedrich could hear her, "I am just so nervous about meeting Lily's mother, Chloe. I have heard so many beautiful stories about her from Lily. Oh, Lily. I miss her so much. Mimi is all I have left of her memory. I am going to miss little Mimi and Nick will, too. But I know this is what is best for her."

"Yes, I'm sure you and Nick will miss her. However, I agree that she should be with her family. If her grandmother is alive, I believe the old woman will want her granddaughter to live with her," Friedrich said, and he hoped it was true. He took Gloria's hand and gently squeezed it and smiled. She returned his smile, but her lips were quivering and Friedrich was afraid she might cry.

They all began walking; Nick and Mimi were holding hands in front, and behind them were Gloria and Friedrich.

When Friedrich found the house at the address Gloria had given him, she was charmed by the lovely little stone structure with the large picture window in the front. The window shutters were lavender-colored and on the ledge there was a window box filled with miniature roses. For a moment Gloria didn't move. She stood and stared. *It's a quaint and beautiful place. But once this door is opened and Mimi's grandmother learns about her daughter's death, she'll probably take Mimi to live with her.* The reality of what was about to happen began to sink in. *That is what I want, of course, but things will never be the same. I must remind myself that this is what is best for everyone.*

Gloria still did not move. The door was made of wood that had been painted a deep shade of burgundy. She stared at the woodwork where the door had been carved. Then she noticed there was a gold *mezuzah* nailed to the doorframe. Gloria reached up and ran her fingers over the cold metal. She knew what it was because there had been a similar one on the door at Lily's house, and she had once asked Lily about it. For a moment she closed her eyes and remembered how Lily told her the story of the Jewish people on Passover.

She missed Lily so much at that moment that she felt hot tears stinging her eyes. Friedrich noticed Gloria stroking the *mezuzah*, but he said nothing. Gloria was too emotional for him to ask her if she realized what that metal thing on the door was. She was shaking as she tried to smile at Friedrich. Then she reached over and squeezed his hand. "I'm nervous," she admitted. "I know this is what's best, but I'm afraid that I'll never see Mimi again."

"If we're married, I promise you that you and Nick can come to visit Mimi whenever you want," Friedrich said, squeezing her hand back.

His words comforted Gloria and gave her the courage to knock on the door.

"It will be alright," Friedrich promised. "No matter what happens once this door is opened, I'll make sure that everything is alright for you and Nick."

A slender woman, with soft white hair coming down in tendrils from a bun that sat on top of her head, opened the door.

"Can I help you?" the old woman asked. Her eyes were as blue as the most azure blue jay Gloria had ever seen.

"Hello, my name is Gloria Schuster and this is my friend, Friedrich Wagner. I'm looking for Chloe Levin." Gloria's heart was beating wildly.

"I'm Chloe Levin," the old woman answered cautiously.

"Good afternoon, Mrs. Levin. It's a pleasure to meet you. I am your granddaughter Mimi's nanny. I work... worked for your daughter, Lily."

"You're my granddaughter's nanny. Lily told me about you in her letters," Chloe said to Gloria. "She spoke very highly of you. In fact, she said you were like sisters. I must say that I was glad to hear that she'd made such a good friend."

Chloe's voice trembled as her eyes found Mimi, drinking in every detail of the child's face. "But where is Lily? Where is my daughter?"

Gloria felt the weight of what she had to say press against her chest, making it impossible to meet Chloe's eyes. The moment she'd dreaded for weeks was finally here.

Gloria's tears came then, unstoppable. Friedrich pressed his handkerchief into her hand but remained silent, understanding this moment wasn't his to share.

"My daughter?" Chloe's voice cracked. "Where is she?" She moved to Mimi as if drawn by an invisible thread, kneeling to meet her granddaughter's eyes. "My baby," she whispered, more to herself than anyone else. "I haven't seen you since you were just a pitzel, a small infant."

When she reached to embrace Mimi, the child shrank back with a small cry of alarm. "It's alright, it's alright," she soothed, her voice gentle as spring rain. "I'm your bubbie."

Mimi tilted her head, studying the woman before her with Lily's same thoughtful gaze. Gloria notice something passed between them – a recognition deeper than memory – and the child's tension eased. In her grandmother's face, she found echoes of the photograph her mother had kept beside her bed, the one she'd kissed each night before sleep.

"My daughter?" Chloe said again

"I'm sorry. There was an accident and..."

"Oh, dear God, no... no... not my Lily. Not my Lily." Chloe began to cry. And then to her surprise Mimi put her arms around her grandmother's neck

"Don't cry, Bubbie. I remember you. My mother used to tell me stories about you all the time," Mimi said.

Chloe lifted Mimi in her arms and held her close to her.

Gloria could not believe how much Mimi resembled her grandmother. *Mimi never looked anything like her mother or her father, but now I can see that the resemblance between Mimi and her grandmother is uncanny. They look exactly alike,* she thought.

Chloe had Mimi on her lap. Then she took Mimi's hands in her own and she studied her face. "You are such a beautiful little girl. My Lily? Oh, dear God," Chloe said softly as she put her hand on her heart.

"Lily and I were good friends, best friends." Gloria could barely get the words out between sobs. "Since she passed away, I have been taking care of Mimi. I brought her here to France because Lily loved you so very much. She would have wanted you to know what happened. And I also know she would have wanted you to see your granddaughter again."

Gloria watched as Chloe swayed slightly, her face draining of color at the news of Lily's death. The older woman's hands trembled as she gripped the edge of the sofa, but even in her devastating grief, she gathered herself with a dancer's grace.

Gloria recognized that same strength she'd seen so often in Lily – the ability to push through pain for the sake of others.

As Chloe spoke softly to Mimi, Gloria could see where Lily

had learned her gentle nature. Despite the tears sliding silently down her cheeks, Chloe's voice remained steady, welcoming. Mimi, sensing perhaps what children sometimes do, cuddled into her grandmother's embrace as if making up for all the years they'd lost.

"Mama had a picture on the table next to her bed of a lady who looked like you," Mimi said. "She said that lady was my bubbie. That's how I knew it was you."

Gloria's heart clenched watching grandmother and grand-child together – so alike with their golden hair and summer-blue eyes. In Chloe's face, she could read both the magnitude of her loss and the miracle of this unexpected gift: her daughter's child, returned at last to Paris.

"I am your *bubbie*. I am your mama's mama," Chloe replied. A single tear ran down her cheek. She gently squeezed Mimi. "And I love you with all my heart."

"You do?" Mimi looked up at her wide-eyed.

"Yes, little one. I do," Chloe said to Mimi then she said aloud, speaking more to herself than to the others in the room, "Mimi is a wonderful little girl. She's so lovely and so affectionate."

"Yes, she is," Gloria agreed.

Then Chloe sighed and said, "I would like to take her in to live with me. She can have her mother's old room. It's exactly the way Lily left it."

Nick shook his head violently. He balled his hands into fists. "No, no, Mimi is not staying here. Mommy, you can't do this. I won't let you do this." He began to cry.

"Nick, listen to me. Mimi should be with her family. It's what her mother would have wanted."

"It's not what I want. If we leave her here, I'll never see her again."

"Oh yes, you will. I'm going to purchase an automobile. It's only a day's drive from Munich to Paris. We'll come to visit her often. I promise you," Friedrich said to Nick.

"How often?" Nick sucked his bottom lip.

"Every couple of months. That is, of course, if your mother is willing to stay with me in Munich."

Gloria saw the look on her son's face and her heart was breaking. *I feel terrible about separating Nick and Mimi. But it's the only way. Mimi should be with her grandmother. I'll make a promise to myself that I'll find a way to bring Nick back here to France to visit Mimi.*

"I will stay with you in Munich and marry you, Friedrich— that is, if your marriage proposal is still valid?" she asked tentatively.

"Of course it's valid. I want to marry you more than anything," Friedrich said.

"Then let's stay in Paris tonight. We can get married tomorrow morning, that way both children can be there with us. Perhaps Chloe will join us, too. Maybe we can create some good memories in Paris and leave on happier terms." Gloria looked at Chloe who was still shaking from the news about Lily, but she nodded, agreeing to attend the wedding.

Friedrich kissed Gloria on the lips. He turned to Chloe and said, "We'll be back here tomorrow morning with Mimi and Nick. Then we can all go to the city hall where Gloria and I will get married. Afterwards, I'll take us all out for a big, delicious French breakfast to celebrate."

"I'll be looking forward to it," Chloe said. But even though she was happy about Mimi, Gloria could see that under her smile Chloe was ready to cry, and she knew that the old woman's heart was breaking. *She is grieving the loss of her daughter.*

Nick was still holding Mimi's hand as they walked out the door of Chloe's home. As they were leaving, Friedrich paused at the mezuzah, his expression curious. "Do you know what that is?" he asked, pointing at the small metal case on the doorframe.

"Yes," Gloria said. "It's called a mezuzah. Lily had one on the door at her house, too."

"Do you know what it's used for?" Something shifted in his voice, just slightly.

"Yes, Lily once told me the story of Passover."

"Passover. So you know that's a holiday for Jews and that thing is something that Jews put on their doors."

"Yes, I knew that," Gloria said. "Lily and Joe were both Jewish. Her parents, too."

Friedrich was quiet for a moment, then his familiar warm smile returned. "How interesting. You'll have to tell me more about their traditions sometime." But something in his eyes made Gloria shiver, despite the mild spring air.

He took her hand, squeezing it gently.

Gloria pushed away her unease. She was being silly—Friedrich had shown nothing but kindness to her and Nick. And he'd promised they would visit Mimi often. That's what mattered now.

They walked back to the hotel, Nick and Mimi still hand in hand ahead of them. The setting sun painted the Paris streets gold, and Gloria let herself believe in the future Friedrich described—a comfortable home in Munich, Nick with a father figure, regular visits to Paris. If sometimes his passion for his new political movement seemed to burn too bright, well, all men needed a cause to believe in, didn't they?

Looking at the children walking ahead, Gloria thought of their long journey—from New York to Hamburg, Munich to Paris. So many miles, so many changes. Tomorrow would bring more, taking them away from Mimi toward their new life in Munich. Yet something whispered in her heart that this wasn't the end of their story. That somehow, someday, they would all find their way back home—wherever that might be.

For now, she chose to trust in the path ahead. After all, what choice did she really have?

A LETTER FROM THE AUTHOR

I always enjoy hearing from my readers, and your thoughts about my work are very important to me. If you enjoyed *The Last Lullaby*, please consider telling your friends and posting a short review. Word of mouth is an author's best friend. To hear all about my releases with Storm Publishing, you can sign up here!

www.stormpublishing.co/roberta-kagan

Also, it would be my honor to have you join my personal mailing list. As my gift to you for joining, you will receive three free short stories and my USA Today award-winning novella complimentary in your email! You can sign up here: www.robertakagan.com

You can review my book!

This story was born from my long-standing fascination with the period between the two World Wars—that fragile time when hope and darkness wrestled for Europe's future. While researching Jewish families who fled Germany in the 1920s, I discovered accounts of women who made impossible choices to protect their children. One story particularly moved me—a mother who sent her daughter back to relatives in France, sensing the gathering storm in Germany years before Hitler's rise to power.

In writing Lily and Gloria's intertwined stories, I wanted to explore how ordinary people navigate extraordinary times. How does a mother's love transcend borders? What price do we pay for the choices we make? And most importantly, how do we find our way back to what matters most when the world seems to be falling apart?

This novel is the first in a new series that follows these characters through one of history's darkest periods. While *The Last Lullaby* ends in 1930, the seeds of tragedy are already being planted. Through Gloria, Nick, and Mimi's continuing story, I hope to show how the bonds we forge in times of peace become our anchors in times of war.

I'm deeply grateful to my readers who continue to trust me with these difficult but important stories from our shared history. If you'd like to learn more about the real families who inspired this novel, or about my other books, please visit my website.

With love and blessings,

Roberta Kagan

www.robertakagan.com

 facebook.com/Rkagan4

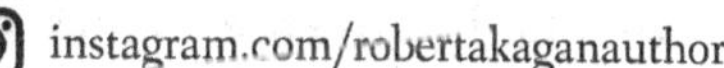 instagram.com/robertakaganauthor

ACKNOWLEDGMENTS

First, I want to take a moment to say how grateful I am for Claire, and Oliver, and the entire team at Storm Publishing for having faith in me and my work. Over the past year Claire has become more than just a colleague, she has become a dear friend. Thank you for believing in me, Claire. And to the entire staff at Storm, thank you for your patience, hard work, and all of the effort that you've put into this book. It truly means more to me than I can express.

I also want to recognize Cassandra, my occupational therapist. After my wrist injury I didn't know what my life would look like, but Cassandra stayed positive and worked me harder than I have ever worked before. She saved my wrist and my hand, and without her help I don't know if I would ever have been able to write again.

I also want to show my gratitude and appreciation for my family. My husband for his patience and his constant support, and most of all I want to thank my daughter. She is not only the most competent developmental editor on the planet, but she is also my best friend, my confidant, and when I lose confidence in myself, she is my cheerleader and often the reason I continue to write. I love you.